BUSH REDEMPTION

BUSH REDEMPTION

SEQUEL TO BLOOD GOLD REVENGE

Dave Wright

A copy of this publication can be found in the National Library of Australia.

ISBN: 9780646968872 (paperback)
       9780646968889 (ebook)

Published by Blood Gold Publications and Productions Pty Ltd

This is a work of fiction. All characters, names and places are fictitious, or fictionalized, dramatized or adapted from fact for the purpose of entertainment, (including the QLD Police Force). Accordingly, any similarities between characters contained within this story and any living or dead person should not be considered to be true and accurate reflection of that person.

Written by Dave Wright / /2016. Email: bloodgold@bigpond.com

Printed & Channel Distribution
Publishing Consultants/Interior Design—Pickawoowoo Publishing Group
Lightning Source | Ingram (USA/UK/EUROPE/AUS).

This Novel is dedicated to May and Wal Randal,
RIP 2014.

You both have a special place in my heart that will
never be forgotten.

Dave Wright resides in sunny North Queensland, and urges any budding writer to put doubt behind them and just give it a shot like he has done. Bush Redemption is the sequel to his first novel Blood Gold Revenge, it was only after receiving great reviews from readers that inspired him to continue on with the second edition. "I hope people enjoy this Australiana fiction story as much as the first, I am always nervous when the first person reads the original draft. Thanks to the many family and friends that helped me work through this story, (you all know who you are). After all the hours spent hopefully I have done it justice in the end result. Lastly I would like to thank my wife for putting up with me through this process."

Contents

Chapter 1

TOUGH AS BOOT LEATHER

Three troop carriers of police arrive at Hatchet River Station after an anonymous tip-off by a male caller, claiming repeated gunfire and billowing smoke from the remote area. Grace, the detective who had taken Tim's original formal statement in Bankston, sat in the passenger side of the lead vehicle as it crossed the Hatchet River. The second 4x4 wagon's two-way radio came in loud and clear to the rest of the convoy. "Car one, we spotted some movement to your right in the downstream direction." All four officers turned their attention towards the location relayed over the radio. Breaking the intense silence that spanned a few seconds, a burly male officer in a gruff voice stated, "I can't bloody see anything" as he drove slowly, tightly gripping the steering wheel of the lead vehicle. "There," stated Grace pointing, "looks like something purple moving our way, pull up on the river bank." Applying the brake a little too eagerly, they all exit the police 4x4 with handguns at the ready as they watch a young woman break through the final maze of lantana vines and into the clearing. Two of the policemen re-holstered their weapons and moved forward to assist the limping survivor towards the dirt road, her bare feet swollen from the razor sharp rocks she negotiated in her desperate effort to get rescued before the convoy of vehicles passed her by. Sinking down onto both knees in the soft river sand beside the stationary vehicle, she let the purple sleeping bag slide off her shoulders and began sobbing uncontrollably in sheer relief. Her face and body were covered extensively in fresh bruises, cuts and abrasions from her brutal captor who she and her fellow captive named the Beast.

The other two police vehicles remained stationary with motors idling while its occupants waited impatiently halfway across the slow flowing crystal clear river crossing. The two-way came to life. "Is someone going to move that bloody truck blocking the road so we can all get out of this water"? Finally, both police vehicles moved forward onto dry land. Grace, being senior in rank spoke. "We need blankets, also grab a set of our overalls from out of the back." Fixing her gaze on a young constable standing idly close by, she continued. "Call it in to headquarters." Crouching down on her haunches Grace softly rested her hand on the distraught backpacker's shoulder. Suzie jumped at the touch. Grace instantly removed her hand and asked in a soothing but clear voice: "Who did this to you? Do you know where they are now? Are you alone?"

The beaten and abused backpacker shook her head in an abrupt and frantic manner at the last question, pointing her slim bruised arm that shook erratically in the downstream direction. "Terri," she managed to get out of her split and swollen lips. Officers who stood in near proximity to Suzie heard the weak response then looked to where she was pointing. Grace stood erect while changing her tone to one of authority and gave the command. "Find out who is down there." Four uniforms responded instantly and moved off swiftly along the river bank fighting against the multitude of lantana vines with their service revolvers in hand. They emerged half an hour later with Terri barely clothed being heavily supported by two of the officers. She was in a visibly worse state than her friend who was now dressed in police overalls and tenderly sipping hot coffee out of a Thermos lid. Suzie gave Grace and another officer a brief recap of their ordeal in broken sentences. Some of the heavy English dialect was hard for them to interpret, especially when she spoke rapidly and emotionally between gulps of hot sweet coffee. After listening carefully, Grace had comprehended enough of recent events to act. She raised her voice loud enough for all to hear. "Right, let's get to the homestead and find out exactly what we are dealing with here. Get some clothing on that girl and make some room for them both in the troopies."

The police vehicles' engines start in unison and they lurch forward, their rear tyres biting deep into the loose river sand as they climb the steep bank exiting the river course. Rounding the last corner of the heavily corrugated track, the extent of the damage to the homestead laid before them, instantly recognisable to those officers who had worked out here previously on a very recent unsolved case. "Holy hell," Grace mutters aloud to herself. The station guard dogs, now out of water, could only manage a spiritless snarl at the police 4x4s as they entered the busted homestead gates. Grace reached for the two-way mic to update headquarters. "We now have two survivors, from what I can see we are going to need a chopper, paramedics and the full outfit to go over this crime scene again…hang on, looks like a deceased person in that old Toyota."

Grace drops the hand-piece of the radio with it bouncing on the floor as she swings open the door while the vehicle is still in motion. Her government issued boots skid in the bulldust before her legs gather enough momentum to hit the ground running. Reaching the beat-up old station truck, she immediately feels for a pulse shaking her head with the result. The detective returns to the radio. "First body has been confirmed, send everything you can our way, including some body bags."

Both backpackers exited separate vehicles led by officers to identify if this was the man that had put them through a living hell. Laying their eyes on John's blood caked body, both girls break down, shaking their heads in despair. "No that's not him," Suzie managed to say as the coffee rose in her throat and tears streamed down her face. Terri, still in a state of shock, walked closer to the body touching its arm with a trembling hand. "Thank you," she whispered. Grace, standing closest, instantly picked up on the remorse and asks: "How do you know this man?" Neither backpacker answers, holding true to their vow with the prospectors.

Grace quickly sums up the silence and steps back towards the body in the vehicle with more interest, casting her well-trained eye over the cab of the ancient 4x4. The rear panel of glass along with the front windscreen had recently been smashed judging from the fresh broken glass covering the seat and the floor. Noticing the tip of a blood stained folded sheet of paper barely visible out of his top shirt pocket, Grace removes the item without even giving it a second glance at this point. She could tell it was handwritten in ballpoint pen from the impressions. Not exactly sure why, but out of instinct she quickly places the letter into her shorts' pocket to scrutinise it thoroughly later in private when she has more time.

It was a careless mistake made by John in the rush to get back out bush. After reading the letter's contents in the home office, his mind was elsewhere trying to rescue his best friend and he hastily shoved the damming letter implicating the others into his pocket.

The rest of the officers spread out to start searching through the burnt buildings for further remains. Two officers who had not been out to the station previously, made their way towards the homestead that still stood intact, oblivious to the pending danger. The two dogs, which had taken up position near the steps, let out a low, barely audible growl, and even though they were not in great condition they knew their job on the station well. Letting both officers get to within their range, the dog's launch simultaneously. The pair of rookies, not having the time to turn and run, start backpedalling in an awkward fashion and they both fall heavily on their arses in the bulldust.

The dogs hit the end of their chains hard, choking the wind out of their throats. Scrambling to their feet just out of range the young men started dusting themselves off looking around to see if anyone else had witnessed their embarrassing encounter. The officers working close by turned at hearing the commotion. They all sniggered at the predicament of the young constables, who now stood red faced and self-conscious. Some of the bystanders could sympathise with the young men from their own previous experience but could not pass up the opportunity of a good old Aussie ribbing.

"Hey Sharky, looks like you ripped the arse clean out of them strides mate…while you are at it you better check them jocks are still clean," one yelled out. They all broke into laughter as the young man walked past them towards the vehicles for a change of pants. Once out of verbal range the rest of the officers returned their attention back to the task at hand, trying to piece together what had happened out here in their absence.

The chopper did an overhead sweep before turning to land, throwing clouds of dust and ash not far from the remains of where Price's quarters once stood. The captain from the last Hatchet River search stepped out as the turbines of the chopper wound down behind him. The surrounds of the station were still very fresh in his mind from the unsolved case, and it frustrated him to this day at not being able to locate Ray's remains. This case occupied his thoughts regularly since leaving the station, trying to think of anything, regardless of how small, that he may have overlooked.

As the dust settles he walks towards the group of officers followed by two paramedics, taking in the destruction. "Looks like they have pissed off the wrong people since I was here last," he says to himself with a slight smirk of satisfaction.

The captain was met and briefed by Grace. "Right", he orders, "I want the paramedics to check over the survivors then fly them back to headquarters for interviewing, get a body bag and send that corpse in for an autopsy and identification. I want to know who the hell this bloke is and how he fits into this mess. That truck needs to be checked for fingerprints." Annoyed by constantly having to speak over the top of the incessant barking, he fired another order. "And while you're at it get someone to contact the nearest town that has a dog catcher for Christ sake. Get them out here to take these bloody mutts away pronto."

One of the young officers slowly opened the stiff car door of the old 4x4, the hinges protesting any movement after years of built-up bulldust and ageing grease. John's body, leaning on the door, falls heavily onto the ground and a large lump of congealed lung protruded out of his mouth from the impact. "What the bloody hell," said the officer taking closer inspection of the chunk of lung that lay in the dirt at his feet while another rolled out a body bag close by. "His eyelid just bloody moved, I'm sure of it." Stunned, the young man immediately felt for a pulse as his partner interjected, "what a load of horse shit, the bloke is dead as a door nail."

"Pigs arse he is, there's a pulse," was the reply as he stood abruptly yelling, "he's alive." Grace and the captain who were engaged in deep discussion on operational plans both spun around. "That's not possible, I checked him myself," said Grace. The captain once more barked out orders. "Get that chopper started, one of you paramedics go as well, we need him kept alive at all costs. Get them two troopies up to the airstrip, I want all those logs winched off the bloody strip in case we need the flying doctor out here to take out any further survivors." Once again, Hatchet River Station became a hive of activity.

The chopper laboured on take-off as the heat of the day climbed quickly, carrying its full load to Cairns. Five minutes after getting airborne the pilot notices a mass of birds congregated on the barren landscape in front of him. Thinking it unusual, the pilot changes his radio channel and relays his suspicions back to the ground crew at the station on the police channel. "There's something out here you need to check out. It's about 7km from the homestead in a south-east direction…hang on I will give you the coordinates." The pilot quickly relayed the digital numerals displayed on the dash of his chopper while it was buffeted by the thermal pockets of heat exuding from the vast wasteland below. "Roger, we will check it out," came the reply. "Right," said the captain turning to address Grace, "let's go for a drive. Grab that medic and a driver for this 4x4."

The rescue chopper landed in Cairns to a waiting ambulance, police and medics waiting patiently for the chopper's rotating blades to slow before leaping into action. By the time they wheeled him into the intensive care unit John's life was hanging by a thread. The chief surgeon removed the field dressings and inspected his torso. "We have two gunshot wounds, one has passed straight through but looks like the other one has collected a lung…let's get moving on this." After eight hours of emergency surgery John was left with one lung and heavily dependent on a life-support system.

The neurologist and surgeon confer on John's condition and decide to put their patient into an induced coma to try to reduce the swelling on his brain. The surgical team were not overly optimistic of a successful outcome considering the lack of fluids and the extreme temperatures John had endured since he was shot. Two burly officers were instructed to stand guard outside the ICU unit. Headquarters had backed up this precaution by issuing extra staff on an around-the-clock security watch over the patient who could be the only person left alive to assist in solving the bizarre turn of events in this unsolved case.

Both female backpackers had been escorted to emergency for a general check over and consented to a DNA swab for rape before accompanying police back to headquarters to give their formal statements. Both claimed that John had single-handedly freed them from their captors and placed them safely beside the river to await rescue. The detectives gained a detailed description of the station owners and the man they appropriately named the Beast which easily described the man police knew as Price. Confirming Scrubber and Max by their mug shots, the backpackers also stated that to the best of their knowledge John had been working alone. The victims tried honouring their vow to the prospectors who had saved their lives but unintentionally giving up John's involvement by assuming him dead in the old station vehicle.

Following hours of extensive interviewing the girls were free to leave. As the doors swung shut behind them one of the detectives conducting the interview commented to his counterpart: "They seemed fidgety to me on occasions. I reckon they know more than they are letting on." The other detective nodded as they watched them walk through the car park towards the taxi rank. "By the sounds they have been through a living hell, but I reckon you could be right, we better contact our people in the field to arrest them station owners and her brother Price, they're going away this time."

The girls wasted no time in contacting their families in the UK to let them know they were now safe. With no possessions left to their name other than the police issue overalls they still wore, the families organised enough money to be sent over until they could receive new passports. Both had decided to cancel the rest of their around Australian tour after their ordeal, opting to catch a flight home as soon as possible. Vivid flashbacks of the abuse inflicted in that outback shed returned every time they closed their eyes.

At the station the captain gave directions as the troopy bounced along a small track not marked on the dash-mounted GPS, passing two sets of smashed down gates that lay partially on the dirt track. "They weren't like that when we left," he commented, his memory of the station layout still sharp in his mind. Wanting to continue following his curiosity, the officer driving had to speak up. "Captain, from this point we need to head nearly due east for a distance of 3.6km to the spot given by the chopper." He grumbled acknowledgement while reaching for the two-way. "Car two and three, how much longer before you get all those logs off that airstrip?"

"Cap should be done in about half an hour I reckon," was the reply from the officer as he skull-dragging the larger ones off with the 4x4 in the comfort of the air-conditioning while one of his colleagues sweating profusely in the glaring sun rolling the smaller logs off by hand. "Good, when you're done there is a track at the eastern end of the strip. Follow it past some busted gates and find out where it leads…looks like some vehicle tracks that are just a couple of days old. I want all men fully armed and ready for anything."

"Yes sir," came the reply, a twinge of excitement in the officer's voice hoping for any sort of physical confrontation that might involve discharging his firearm other than at a stationary cardboard target on the shooting range.

The captain's vehicle swung sharply off the track entering the arid treeless landscape that lay before them, what the locals aptly call the desert. The heat increased rapidly over this flat wasteland as the morning cool abruptly changed into an instant furnace. Spasmodic whirlwinds appeared out of nowhere whipping up dust and sand, swirling like miniature tornados before dissipating as quickly as they formed. They weaved around dead trunks of sandalwood before Grace lent forward, looking at the screen. "How much farther to go?" The young officer glanced over at the GPS. "Bit over a kilometre". The captain spoke up. "Over there," pointing towards a black dot on what seemed to be the horizon in the heat haze. Troopy one picked up speed towards the dark object as it started to fragment. The birds took flight well before the encroaching threat, with a rapid flutter of wings as the vehicle approached. "What the bloody hell?" the captain uttered as they crossed the last fifty metres, skidding the vehicle to an abrupt halt in the soft sand.

The four occupants exit the air-conditioned cab and were smacked in the face by the extreme heat. All of them mouthed displeasure over the conditions. The captain was the first to the body and rolled it slowly onto its back. He winced at the sight of the man's face that was completely devoid of flesh on one side, including an empty eye socket. Sharp beaks from the scavengers of the sky had made short work of C's face while he lapsed in and out of consciousness. Having no strength left to fight, C finally submitted to the relentless attacks from hell's feathered fiends.

The medic gasped at the man's visual appearance. "His pulse is very weak, he will be lucky to survive the trip back to town." The captain turned his head towards the young officer who had been driving the police 4x4 wagon. "Get some water. Bugger me dead, how this man is still breathing has got me beat. Grace, get on the radio and call it in…we need that flying doctor out here now. We don't have time to wait for the rescue chopper to return. While you're at it, make sure that other crew have finished on the airstrip, tell them we have a plane on the way. Bloody tough as boot leather these blokes, that's two in the same day." After trying their best to trickle some water down C's throat all four carried him the short distance towards the back of the wagon, with Grace talking as they went. "The flying doctor is being dispatched immediately and the other vehicles are on their way to that other track like you ordered." Grace, carrying part of the lightest end of the man's torso, noticed the cuts to the tendons on his legs as they loaded him into the vehicle. "Hang on, this man has been purposely hamstrung. Look, both legs have been cut with a knife in the same spot…hell, whoever did it wanted this man to suffer before he died." The medic briefly examined the leg wounds that already contained hundreds of fly larvae. "I would have to agree officer, this man was not meant to live."

The group hastily retreated the way they had come with their patient barely breathing. The captain, after all his years in the force, had prided himself on never forgetting a face. Even though disfigured, he was positive he had met this man before. Putting his memory to task it was not long before it dawned on the captain it was the freelance chopper pilot from the previous search, and he stated as much to Grace. "Well, how does that work out? Who in their right mind would have gone to all this trouble, driving way the hell out into the middle of nowhere to hamstring him then leave the man to slowly die, why not just shoot him?" The captain shrugged his shoulders replying, "Don't know yet, at a guess I would say some kind of payback. It could be a good idea to keep the pair of survivors separate from each other in hospital until we can try and work this out." "Hmmm," agreed Grace as her detective mind went into overdrive, making a mental note to check up on this bloke when she got back near a computer. Reaching for the mic the captain radioed in to headquarters. "We have located another survivor in critical condition, make sure when he is admitted to keep each of them apart and unknown to each other, and I want all this strictly kept out of the media. Hopefully we will get to interview at least one of them."

The captain's 4x4 swerved back onto the original track, with clearly visible fresh tyre tracks leading further south, confirming some of his men had recently passed. The vehicle reached the eastern end of the airstrip and the driver cut the engine to listen for the drone of the twin-engine Beechcraft King Air that should not be too far away, going by the captain's rough calculations. "Right, I reckon we park on the side of the strip half way up. I cannot be sure which way he will come in to land." The wait was not long before the twin-engine aircraft did a low flyover with its flaps set on maximum to get a good inspection of the condition of the airstrip before circling for a final approach to land from the western end into a slight breeze. The pilot landed skilfully, applying the brakes hard and pulling up well short of the airstrip's length before cutting both motors. The paramedics were out to meet the oncoming wagon as soon as the props came to a halt, quickly inserting an IV drip into his veins to replace fluids while they loaded C onto the plane. The radio silence broke as they stood watching their precious find getting loaded into the plane five meters away. "Cap, best you get down here and bring every spare body bag you have."

Hearing his name over the vehicle's radio he quickly turned facing the 4x4. Grace, standing close by, could hear his neck muscles crack and sinews grind on her ageing boss. She sympathised with the man after hearing rumours around the station that this was the only case in his whole career that he had not successfully solved. Though still holding his intellect and perception in the highest regard, she could see that this case had taken a toll on him both physically and mentally. In her mind, he seemed to age further as she observed him reply to the call exasperated, "we are on our way."

Grace realised she could learn a lot from this man and took to bouncing her ideas off him about the myriad twists and turns in this case as they travelled along. The captain gave his opinion quickly by either dismissing or giving more thought to various scenarios she presented – they both clearly enjoyed the mental stimulus. Back-up finally arrived at the Hatchet River Station. Consisting of a dog catcher in his council ute, followed by another two police vehicles, one with forensics the other with three more officers to assist in the search and recovery. The back of both vehicles was loaded with sufficient supplies and equipment to accommodate the extra manpower that had now swelled to a total of fifteen personnel. The dog catcher made short work of muzzling the weakened station guardians, loading them into the steel mesh crates on the council ute. Leaving in a cloud of bulldust back towards town, the young council worker calculated the extra overtime he would pick up to add to this week's meagre pay packet while bouncing along the dirt road.

The lead troopy followed the winding dust track until it came across their colleagues' vehicles parked beside each other. Two officers were lounging over the bull bar in conversation while waiting to lead the new arrivals towards the meth lab cave. "It's a pretty gruesome sight up there," stated one of the men as he nodded towards the incline while trying to swat numerous flies that buzzed relentlessly around his face. "How many?" asked the captain as he slung a water pack over his shoulder and reached for his hat on the front seat. "The count is now up to nine," the other officer chimed in. "We have covered a fair area, the dingoes have got stuck into a few of them, there are some limbs missing. One is a female, while others are burnt beyond recognition." The captain turns his head to look at Grace after the female body was mentioned, both thinking along the same lines. "Lead the way, take us to the female first."

Walking around the troopy, Grace picked up the tracks where the old station truck had careered off the dirt track leading into the bush in the opposite direction. "Has anyone followed this set of tracks?" Both officers gave each other a quizzical look, "what tracks?" "These," pointed Grace. "No" answered the men. "We have had enough on our plate up the hill." All five set off single file towards the deceased that littered the landscape. The captain surveying ground zero had never seen so many bodies in one area. "What a fucking mess," he stated as he bent down to get a good look at the half-burnt features of the female corpse. "Yep, that's her alright." He rose off his haunches and walked around the area talking to other officers while inspecting the other victims before finally pulling up at Scrubber's headless body. "At an educated guess, I would say this is the male station owner," aiming the statement directly at Grace. "Yes, I would agree sir, he and the female are wearing different attire to the rest of the deceased and no visible tattoos…aren't there three of them though?" "Smart girl. Yes, there were three on the station, we will widen the search tomorrow to see if we can pick him up… I can tell you right now it was a hell of a lot more than one man that has caused this devastation."

They both briefly inspected inside the burnt-out drug lab

before he instructed the men, "I want each 4x4 to return to the station and gather camping gear and food…we will be setting up camp on site down here, at least until forensics try to get on top of this mess and all the bodies are removed for autopsy and hopefully identification. Tonight, I also want these corpses protected from further mutilation by feral animals."

Grace and the captain made their way back down the slope to relay the grim find to headquarters and try to confirm how far away their back-up crew was. While he was on the radio Grace started following the tracks she had pointed out earlier. On closer observation she realised there were two sets of tracks though now partly obscured after days of dust moving on the breeze and settling. Grace's two-way erupted to life. "We have to get moving, where are you?"

"I have picked up some tracks over here, do you need me back at the homestead or can I continue on?"

"Come on Grace, you know better than to wander off by yourself, we will look further into it tomorrow when we have more daylight and more manpower, them tyre tracks could run for kilometres." Grace, sighing at her boss's reasoning and knowing he was right on all counts, replied, "on my way back now cap." The three vehicles turned towards the homestead in haste as shadows cast by the sheer sandstone cliff faces raced them along the ground before leaving only a slight glow on the horizon in the west.

A rriving at the station's front yard under headlights as a swirl of bulldust from behind the lead vehicle cut across the bright spotlight beam, momentarily obscuring the officer's vision, the captain murmured something under his breath as he only picked up the outline of two additional police vehicles. The door swung opened while the tail end of the dust still lingered thick in the air. "Where is everyone?" asked the captain shaking hands while doing a quick head count of his new back-up crew. The officer in charge of forensics freed his hand from the firm grip. "We have been split three ways at the moment, there is a party of four missing bush walkers lost in the rainforest for what we believe is at least two days now, no personal locator beacon between them and minimal supplies to last a day. There is also a riot in one of the remote missions with reports of fatalities that were yet to be confirmed when I left."

"Fair enough," replied the captain cutting him short. "Let's get going, we still have men on the ground at the massacre site."

The five vehicles arrive back at the burnt-out drug lab with officers now sitting around several fires scattered over the incline. Various packs of dingoes had been attracted from all directions with many covering considerable distances seeking the inviting smell of decaying flesh high on the four winds. Increasing howls of protest echoed off the cliff faces, amplifying their presence in the darkness, at the human intrusion that was robbing them of a fresh feed on the ripe and bloated corpses that were still left exposed along the hillslope.

The senior officers gathered to discuss sleeping arrangements. "There is no way I am sleeping in a tent tonight, the locals are not happy we are here," Grace said above the howling dogs. The front seat of that Troopy will do me just fine." The other officers nodded in agreement, an issue the captain had not contemplated. Exhausted after the day's events he wearily gave out orders; "OK, all that gear in the back of the vehicles must be taken out to make sleeping room, a rotating shift will have to be organised to protect the bodies. We will all fit if we utilise the seats as well. There is a shotgun issued for every 4x4 located behind the driver's seat, break them out and pass them around to the men on shift with the order shoot to kill."

The packs of dogs clashed constantly throughout the night as each tried to lay claim over the area, at times just outside the flickering light of the fires. The sounds of shotgun blasts echoed out randomly in the darkness until it all fell eerily quiet as the dogs moved away from the cave in the pre-dawn light.

Chapter 2

HOSPITIAL HELL

Tim weaved his way through the bush in the darkness on the now partially obscured quad tracks from Mac's place making good time back towards John's truck and trailer. Before loading the quad, he lifted off a heavy potato sack that was tied securely at the neck with some rope, placing it on the passenger-side floor. The brief conversation he had before leaving the mine site with Mac played continuously through his mind. The old timer had asked where John was, and if their elaborate plan had been executed successfully. Tim went through the details as precisely as he could remember, leaving old Mac's first question till last as it was the hardest for Tim to answer. "Mate, John was shot twice in the heat of things at the lab site, he died before we could get him out of there." The old prospector fell quiet while shaking his head looking towards the ground reflecting on the night he had spent with both young men at his camp, the friendship, comradery and trust they had for each other was unmistakable. He shuffled over towards the fire feeling the need to take the weight off his legs. Sitting down on his chair he asked: "Did John have a wife or kids?"

"Yeah, he did Mac, an honest and loving wife but no kids involved."

He just nodded taking in the information while patting his new pup, pondering on this for a few minutes. Without warning the old timer sprung out of his chair and walked towards his hut. "I want you to give his young widow something from me. That young man was worth his salt in my eyes, it won't bring him back but it will certainly help with the bills. I will also throw in a bit extra for the tools and other stuff we will need to open up the reef as it goes deeper." Mac opened his old chest pointing towards a used hessian potato bag in the corner of the hut. "Bring that over here lad." He began stuffing it full of large chunks of specimen gold.

Tim snapped back to the job at hand as he finished hooking up the trailer and loading the quad. He was still undecided whether to go straight over to John and Meg's place to drop off the gold and the vehicle. It was still very raw in his mind and the emotion on Meg's face would tear him up once again, that he knew for certain. Before hitting the bitumen hours down the track, he had decided to drive directly towards Jack and Sue's place to get either Rob or Rick to help him retrieve his own vehicle that had been left abandoned out bush since the chopper had picked him up. That now felt like a distant memory.

Driving through numerous towns that appeared abandoned in these early hours of the morning, Tim eventually arrived at Jack and Sue's home town. Not wanting to wake her at this early hour he opted to park on an obscure road away from traffic with no street lights and grab some shut eye. Having the time to take everything into account while driving in from the bush Tim realised the full depth of the situation; he was missing, presumed dead, to everybody including the cops. Only very few that were classed as close family knew the truth. The need to tread very lightly in everything he did while in town became paramount. The reunion with Sue and her sons was a very special moment for all concerned and tears were shed for her late husband Jack. Tim spoke to Sue while she was in the kitchen making them all a cuppa. "Both your sons made me very proud the other day, they have heart and did not take a backward step under very trying circumstances…you should be, and I'm sure Jack would have been, very proud of them." Rick entered the kitchen. "I will run you back out to get your 4x4." "Thanks mate, just got to drop off John's bush rig on the way past, how's the foot going?" The young man looked down at his bandaged foot. "Bit tender to walk on, but it could have been worse, a lot worse."

Both men's vehicles pulled up behind each other out the front of Meg's place. Tim slipped out of the 4x4. Jumping the fence he took a deep breath before knocking on the door several times. He felt guilty and hoped no one was home as it would be another awkward moment where he would have trouble expressing his thoughts into words. With no answer, he opened the side gate and drove up the back to unload the quad before parking the vehicle in the back shed. Tim found a used fertiliser bag and placed a few of the large gold nuggets in before stashing the keys. He jumped the fence and opened the passenger door of Rick's truck. The bag clunked heavily as he put it on the floor. "You got a pen and some paper?" He quickly scribbled a note sliding it under the front door.

While on the trip back out bush both men, now in the same vehicle, had many hours to catch up on all the events at Hatchet River Station. "Have you heard the funeral date for John yet?" Rick started. "No mate," was Tim's short reply. Not wanting to expand on that particular conversation, he changed the subject. "Not too far up here we turn off the track into the scrub. I will walk the last hour to my truck bro…the country is rough as guts through there and it will be quicker than you trying to drive."

O utside the Cairns hospital, an ambulance pulled into the front parking bay flicking off its sirens as a waiting group of medics rushed to the rear of the vehicle to unload C who was lying on his back unconscious on a stretcher. Getting the vitals on his condition, the surgeon in charge took one look at the patient's face. "Get this man straight up to ICU, we must try to stabilise his condition. We will need to pump the patient full of fluids before preparing him for multiple skin grafts, call in the plastic surgeon on duty. He is going to have his work cut out for him on this one." The group moved off in a quick but orderly manner, wheeling C along a corridor and into a curtain-partitioned room two down from where John lay already hooked up to an extensive array of life-support machines.

A week to the day after both men had been admitted to hospital, authorities located John's wife, Meg, who had left town for a short period to be with family in Brownsville after receiving the shattering news from Tim that her husband was killed out at Hatchet River Station. Hospital staff had moved John from ICU to a private room that was still guarded 24 hours a day. They had brought him out of the drug induced coma earlier that morning. Though he was still heavily medicated with painkillers, his eyes slowly opened trying to focus on his surrounds. John groaned and tried to reach for his head that was pounding before lapsing back into unconsciousness once more. Re-opening his eyes after what felt like minutes though in real time six hours had lapsed, his wife Meg was now sitting in a chair at the bedside holding his hand as he slightly moved a finger to touch her hand. Meg looked up at the contact with a fresh wave of tears forming quickly in relief and happiness, not hope and despair. "He's awake," Meg stated loudly as a nurse paused at the door. "I will go get someone," she hurried off to the nurses station to page John's doctors.

John was put through a variety of brain scans and tests over the coming days with not a word spoken to anybody, including his wife who had hardly left his side since she walked in days ago. His bullet wounds were changed daily without any emotion present on his face. Both the neurosurgeon and operating surgeon had conferred over their results meticulously before entering the room to discuss their findings with Meg. "Excuse me Meg, do you have a minute?" one said as they moved to the end of the bed. "Yes," she replied as she turned to face them. "Your husband was admitted into this hospital with horrific injuries and was, in one instance, reported as deceased. On the bright side, it appears that the removal of one lung and the projectile has been successful, the other gunshot wound is starting to heal nicely."

"Now, the extent of the brain injuries is another matter," chimed in the neurosurgeon. "We know for certain that he has suffered some percentage of brain damage due to the extreme heat without fluids, but to what extent we are unsure. What we have observed is that he has no discomfort or displayed any facial expressions or speech to date, though we are confident that he can understand what is going on around him by his eye movements along with eye contact." Meg's chin started to quiver slightly while she tried her best to fight back the tears as she stared back at her husband with the doctors' voices now becoming a distant drone. Realising Meg's lack of attention, both doctors left quietly as there were still many patients to see before the end of their shift. Standing close by his side she spoke in a dull monotone voice. "John, I have to go home and get more clothes and will see if I can get a hold of Tim and Danni to let them know you are in here." Meg bent to kiss him lightly on the forehead. As she left the room a single tear rolled down John's face that he wiped away with the back of his hand.

Just down the hallway was C, on the mend with the majority of his face still heavily bandaged, totally oblivious to the fact that one of the men who had just successfully dismantled his multi-million dollar operation was just a few doors down. C had also been placed in a private room making a few key phone calls to people left in his organisation that was now in total disarray, not only from the entire destruction of the lab out bush, but also the supply chain into the city and surrounding towns which was now in chaos. Propped up with pillows behind his back he was now well enough to give the hospital staff a hard time, more out of frustration with his own imminent business demise than anything else. The drug lord waited impatiently for his corrupt cop informant Marko to arrive as he tried to save what was left of his empire. The police guard outside C's door knocked and entered.

"You have a visitor." "About bloody time," murmured C. Raising his voice he said, "Let him in." His jaw dropped as the captain from the Hatchet River investigation entered the room with a clipboard and a clear steely stare that spoke a thousand words. This man wanted answers.

C recovered his facial expressions quickly – even behind bandages – and affected a slim smile. "Hi captain, what are you doing here?" The police officer returned the slim smile. "I was going to ask you the same thing mate. Let's cut to the chase…why was your burnt-out chopper found not far from a sophisticated drug lab while we found you hamstrung in the middle of a barren lifeless landscape that would have been impossible for any man to crawl to considering the distance from your chopper?" C was put instantly on the back foot with the surprise visit. He knew someone would eventually interview him over the events but he did not expect it would be this man and so soon. He was smart, and gave the captain enough credit that he could eventually piece things together. I need another hitman pronto, C thought briefly. Nobody had accounted for or even heard from Ox judging from recent calls.

"Well it is quite simple, I was travelling in between jobs when I heard a distress call on my radio with billowing smoke and people on fire. It stood out from the air very distinctly from where I was so I decided to fly over and land to see if there was anything I could do to help…thought somebody might need an emergency lift to town with injuries. That's what us bushies do, try and help each other out especially where bushfires are concerned. I just happened to be in the wrong place at the wrong time, if you could call it that."

"Righto," said the captain flicking through the pages on his clipboard while drawing a pen from his pocket. "I will need the name of your last employer and the station you last mustered on with its location – and a date would help the investigation. Surely you will have a copy of invoices and payments that would coincide with your bank records I assume? And while you are at it the station you were traveling to, so we can confirm that you were going to be engaged by them for work. We also need to collaborate your story that Hatchet River was in fact near the direct flight path you had taken to respond to any distress call."

C readjusted his pillows and reached for a glass of water, sipping it slowly while taking precious time to assess the line of questioning before re-engaging in the game of intellect. "Look captain, I am the victim here, my chopper is destroyed, burnt to a cinder along with the invoice book you are now requesting. I was hamstrung and left for dead by a bloody madman. What the hell are you doing about that? Have you got this bloke in custody yet? Or are you too incompetent and fishing for a scapegoat to take the rap for all of this? Seriously, think about what you are trying to imply here, that I have done this to myself? My lawyers will have a field day with you mob."

The captain remained calm over the accusations, replying: "I don't believe in multiple coincidences and now you have been in a few over this case. Did you get a good look at this man?" C spat back the reply, raising his voice. "I will never forget the face of the man that fucking did this to me," pointing to his bandages. "Now officer I am tired, we will have to finish this discussion another day." On that note C rolled onto his side and closed his eyes. The captain shrugged parting with, "you can bet on that. I will be back tomorrow and I want answers."

Down in the car park Meg and Danni fussed over Tim standing in a bright floral summer dress before entering the building to take the short elevator ride to level four. The prospector did a last-minute adjustment on his makeshift boobs as the elevator door slid open. The group walked towards Marko who was partially blocking the corridor as he stood talking to the police guard out the front of C's room. Marko gave Tim a long stare then briefly looked at the other girls before focusing his gaze back on Tim. What an ugly bitch Marko thought to himself. I pity the poor bastard that has to sleep with her. The prospector, realising the extra attention, dropped his head so the long blond hair of the wig covered the majority of his face while trying to inconspicuously increase his step to get past this nosey cop. Tim exhaled a long slow breath now that his back was the only view Marko could get. He stepped in front of Danni to position himself in the middle of the girls as they continued down the hallway in single file. Meg approached the officer out the front of John's room as Tim adjusted his dress.

"Got some visitors today," Meg announced happily as she opened the door, adding "this will be a very private and emotional visit, could you please make sure we are not disturbed?" The guard just nodded and let them proceed. Once inside Tim immediately pulled off the wig and slung the handbag off his shoulder onto the small table beside the bed with a thud. "Hey bud, how you feeling mate?" John's stare and facial expression did not change as he looked back at his prospecting partner. "John, I could have sworn you were dead buddy. What a miracle. Look at the extent a bloke needs to go too just to see his best mate." Tim did a swirl in the dress he wore with a smile on his face trying to get some sort of reaction from John, without success. Turning his attention to the handbag he continued. "Mac was devastated when I told him what happened to you out bush and he has sent in some gold to cover any expenses that Meg might run across in the future. Now we can use this," holding a large nugget up to show John, "to get you into the best facility in the country…we need you better mate. I'm not going to be able to dig all this gold up without you buddy." John grabbed two handfuls of the sheet tightly under the hospital blanket before closing his eyes.

Meg was talking in the corner with Danni. Noticing the sudden silence she broke her conversation and began walking over to inspect her husband. "You must have worn him out Tim. Thanks for coming in, I was hoping that maybe seeing you might flick something in his brain. Looks like I watch too many movies," Meg said in a disappointed voice. Tim placed the wig back on, also looking disheartened. "There is a heap of gold left inside a sack on the passenger-side floor of the truck when I dropped over to your place. I want the best people looking after my buddy regardless of cost, I'm heading back out bush tomorrow…just need to organise a few more things before I leave. There is a new gold buyer in town by the name of Million Bullion Buyers. Ask for a bloke called Fu, it's at the end of Kimbo Avenue, a small red brick building, he seemed OK and paid the right money per ounce. I would like to get any progress reports on John's condition while I'm out bush…just get a hold of Danni."

Meg thanked them both once again and walked them past the two guards. When far enough away Tim said, "did you notice the way that first cop was looking at me, could have sworn he had lust in his eyes." The girls looked at each other and giggled. "What's so funny?" he said with a smile, adding "I wonder who he is guarding?" They continued down to the car park before parting ways with Meg who was also going home – with a mountain of bills.

Marko entered C's room a little sheepish. "About bloody time, where the hell have you been?"

"I took some annual leave," Marko answered. "I was down the coast visiting with some of the family in the motorhome. None of this has been in the media, they must be keeping it quiet for some reason and my wife refused to come away with me unless my phone was turned off." C nodded, "yeah, the fucking motorhome that I would have paid for no doubt after all the cash I have been stuffing in your pockets over the years. The time I need you most and what do you know, you are on fucking holidays for fuck sake. Bet you have to give notice for annual leave, well where is my fucking notice? I pay you five times your piss-weak measly wage." Marko coloured slightly as the truth struck home about the purchase of his brand new 40-foot state of the art motorhome, and all the other luxury items he was now able to afford. "What do you want me to do boss?" C simmered down a bit. "Well, first of all nobody I have talked to has heard from Ox so we need another hitman, none of these local backyard idiots. We need somebody with class. I want that prospector Tim located and taken out along with all his family and friends, he must suffer the most. He has no idea who the hell he has just tried to fuck over, but he will soon find out."

He continued after taking a short breath. "As for the business, get the rostered-off cooks and the remaining crew to set up eight portable labs, I will give them house rental locations within a few days." "OK boss," Marko replied as he wrote down on a note pad what needed to be done. "When I turned on my phone at the beach I got a voice message from my city mate relaying info he had received, the two station owners were confirmed dead, they were still looking for the brother who was missing and another three survivors were found. Two of them were female backpackers who have been released and left the country but the other one, a male, is still in hospital. After having a brief talk out the front with your guard, apparently he is just down the corridor also under police guard."

"Hmmm," C said aloud. "The plot thickens, I will be paying him a visit very soon. I have not got time on my side to wait for a new hitman to get this cop sorted. That captain from the Hatchet River is right up my arse and getting closer to working things out and you need to take care of him now."

"Me?" Marko stammered, scrambling for a solution. "Come to think of it C there is a bloke I was talking to a while back who has had dealings with Ox's younger brother who operates out of Western Australia. The story goes that he is as good as Ox though he does not work in the Eastern States, likes to keep his distance from his brother."

"Yeah right," replied C, "well, looks like he won't have to worry about that anymore. Try and make contact and tell him his brother has been taken out by the same people I will pay him to kill. Tell him I have plenty of work over here at a good pay rate.

You got 24 hours for a positive response otherwise it is you that will have to take down the cop." Marko nodded and left the room in a hurry, already talking on his mobile to try to source a contact number for the hitman. Admitting to himself he might have done a lot of grey things in the past and had mixed with some bad people that paid ridiculous amounts of money for his inside knowledge, but one thing he knew for sure, he was no killer. To do over a cop, that sort of job was best left for the pro, provided he could find him in time.

The captain passed Marko near the front doors of the hospital, neither giving much more than a brief glance at each other. He had been advised of John's condition before returning, though like most things these days he liked to check on information personally and not rely on hearsay from others. The senior police officer was positive that John held the answers to solve this case and maybe even expose the players that were left hiding in the shadows. The captain walked up the corridor and nodded to the first guard, "any visitors"? "Only one of our own captain," the young burly officer replied. The response raised his eyebrows. "Is that so? I will be back for a chat with you shortly," he said as he continued along to the second guard speaking briefly with him before entering. "Hello John, good to see you are awake," he said as he shut the door behind him.

On leaving the room he once again talked briefly to the guard at the door entrance while turning on his mobile phone. Missed calls and messages sounded and vibrated on the phone as he walked down the corridor. Looking at the screen he redialled one of the numbers placing the phone to his ear at the same time pointing towards the second guard. "I will be back to talk with you about that uniformed visitor tomorrow."

Meg was up early leaving Bankston for the city with two large gold nuggets sitting on the passenger side seat. She had been up half the night working out the bills that were well overdue, sorting them out by priority. With no income from John's business for quite some time now, it left her with no other option than to sell some of Mac's gold. The generous gift was a totally unexpected windfall from a man she had never met before, warm in the thought that her husband had such a positive impact on the old miner. While driving along Meg occasionally glanced over at the nuggets, not having any idea of what they were worth but confident they would cover the bills and possibly the cost of the private room at the hospital and the doctors' bills. Health cover was one of the first big bills that arrived well over a month ago and which Meg deemed not essential. The cash she had put away for a ship cruise was also gone and the credit cards had been maxed out by John before he went bush. There was some gold John had found that was still left in the safe along with more in the sack from Tim that she had hidden well after arriving home yesterday and reading the contents of the note inside the front door that described where he had hidden the truck keys and the generous donation left on the vehicle's floor.

It took Meg some time to fight through the morning traffic and to locate the gold buyer's address. Pulling up out the front below the newly painted sign displaying Million Bullion Buyers, she wound down the passenger's window to read the trading hours sign on the door. "Ten minutes early," she muttered to herself reaching for her handbag to make room for the nuggets. While emptying out the larger items Meg realised she had left her mobile phone on charge on the bedside table. She swore under her breath as small things like that annoyed the shit out of her.

The lights flicked on in the building and a slim Asian man opened the door, flicking over the closed sign to open while inquisitively looking at Meg's car parked right out the front.

Meg entered the shop with the straps of her handbag straining under the weight of the gold. Placing it on the counter she stated: "Hi, I am here to see a Mr Fu." The Asian finished off his opening ritual of turning everything on and replied, "good morning, yes that would be me. What can I do for you, would you like to buy or sell?" Fu flashed a smile revealing three shining gold teeth, sharp piercing eyes and an immaculate suit that fitted perfectly to his slim frame indicating to her that this man was all business. "I would like to sell some gold, and I have heard you give a fair price." Fu's smile increased. "That would be correct. What have you got to sell, some old jewellery perhaps?" Fu took pride in being able to read people quickly. "No, something bigger," replied Meg as she unzipped her handbag and placed the large nuggets on the counter with a solid clunk and a slight smirk.

The proprietor's eyes bulged but he managed to keep his composure at the sight of the large nuggets. Breaking his stare away from the gold, he now reassessed the lady that stood in front of him closer, with her manicured finger nails, soft looking hands and no suntan. He was positive this lady was no prospector and would bet his left nut that she had never dug a gold nugget in her life. "So, may I ask how you came to acquire such lovely specimens of gold? Sorry, I missed your name."

"The name is Meg, and the rest is none of your business. I would like a price for a cash deal or do I need to look elsewhere?"

"Fair enough, like you say it is not my business," replied Fu shrugging his shoulders not wanting to agitate the lady. Playing his hunch that this female had only a vague comprehension of gold at best, the gold buyer cunningly put it to the test. "Because they are not completely pure gold nuggets and contain some rock we must give them a specific gravity test to work out the exact gold content, and to be frank I would not have enough money on the premises to pay for them right at this moment. Can you come back in a couple of hours?"

Meg, realising their worth was substantial, replied: "OK, but I need to go shopping. What have you got in the safe?"

"Only thirty thousand at this current time." Meg's face lit up. "That will do…a couple of hours you say?"

"Yes," replied Fu, "we will have the final payment all sorted out before your return." Meg turned to leave after counting the neat small piles of hundred dollar bills done into ten thousand dollar parcels. "Oh, I nearly forgot, could you please weigh them and give me a signed invoice that you have received the nuggets. Less the thirty thousand in advance of course, can't be too careful when it comes to money these days." Mr Fu flashed another golden smile. "But of course, they are worth a considerable amount of money, I do not hesitate with such a fair request." Placing them one at a time on the digital scales, he pronounced, "the total comes to ninety-two ounces less the rock attached, and then less fifteen per cent for a no-questions asked cash deal and my three per cent standard dealers fee still applies."

Meg smiled inwardly as she exited the building. Things were finally starting to look up after months without an income and the sudden life-changing circumstances she now had to endure that were helplessly and completely out of her control. She put that negative thought aside and began planning the rest of her day which would include some shopping for home necessities from various stores then returning for the final transaction before spending the rest of the day with John in hospital. The car had barely left the parking space before Mr Wong appeared out of the back room after watching the whole transaction on closed circuit TV. Both the Asian men had bought the Bullion shop three months earlier, adding to their portfolio of other well established bullion stores in Brisbane, Sydney and Melbourne. Having very strong ties with the Chinese underworld they had done their homework thoroughly before deciding to invest in the Far North. The Chinese businessmen did not recognise any well-organised crime syndicates in the area, and in their view it was more of a free-for-all with many they classed as small-time players who would get sorted out in the very near future.

Wong walked over to the counter beside his business partner exchanging glances before examining the nuggets closely. "She has no idea at all, they are not far off nearly being solid gold. This to me looks like it's come from the same reef source that we bought a few days ago off that other prospector. I want both sellers' gold tested for purity and other mineral composition to make sure. Get a hold of Chang, we need him down here before she returns."

Chang had been picked up by Fu's crew midway through his teenage years in China, struggling since the age of eight to survive on the streets of Chongquin with a population of more than twenty million. The boy had mastered the art of street fighting from an early age, gaining respect from his peers as he grew into a hardened battle-scarred teenager. Rising to a position of leadership, the young man soon had a swelling network of juvenile thieves under his command at the age of fourteen. Fu could see potential and took him away from that life after Chang killed two of his best men without even raising a sweat over a territorial issue. The art of becoming an assassin was taught to the adolescent over a short period as the young man was a natural, no matter what they threw at him. The time-consuming part of his training was learning the English language even with a tutor aiding him full-time. The paperwork to deploy Chang into their new operations in Australia was easily obtainable from connections within the network and he soon became Fu's personal bodyguard and right-hand man for any issues that needed physical persuasion anywhere around Oz. Chang was naturally their first choice to accompany them interstate into new territory, having successfully injected himself into their other business interests in Brisbane, Sydney and Melbourne, just in case there were any teething issues in the Far North that needed sorting out while they settled in.

"I want her followed, we need to know where this very rich gold reef is located or where she is getting it from," Fu stipulated in no uncertain terms. Wong agreed making the arrangements over the phone. Meg, feeling more upbeat about things overall, bought her husband a gold prospecting magazine before leaving the shopping complex and returning to the Bullion buyers to finish business. Entering the store void of customers other than a single large Asian man wearing black leather gloves who was perusing a glass cabinet full of second-hand rings in all shapes and sizes with prices that varied from a couple of hundred to many thousands, Meg called out. Fu, with his back towards her, rolled his eyes before turning around to face this woman with a gleaming smile.

"Hello Meg, the gold had more rock attached to it than first thought, according to our tests. The result came in at eighty ounces, and since you will not give us an idea of a goldfield location you must understand we must take the gold purity of eighty per cent as an average to cover ourselves." Keeping a totally straight face he went on. "So that comes to sixty-four ounces less the gold purity comes to fifty-one point two ounces less the fifteen per cent cash deal and my three per cent commission comes to a total of forty-two ounces net, then we multiply that by the current gold price of fifteen hundred an ounce is sixty-three thousand, less the thirty already paid leaves thirty-three thousand owing." All this equation stuff went over Meg's head though she had a feeling of being shafted. With no previous experience of gold transactions let alone gold purities or weight tests for rock content she had to take them at their word. "Thanks for your business Meg, hope to see you again soon," said Fu flashing a smile as she finished counting the stack of hundred dollar bills and stuffing them into her handbag. Chang had left the shop via the front door after getting a good look at Meg then memorising her numberplate before walking down the side alley beside the store to where he had parked the car ready for his first assignment in the North.

Another to make their debut in the North very shortly was Ox's brother, Hugh, who had responded to the challenge of taking up the offer to hunt down those who had killed his brother while planning to pick up a handsome sum at the same time. Stepping onto the national bus service in Perth, the lanky West Australian carried his only luggage on board. He preferred this method of transport since, even though it was slow, it was more about being able to blend in and avoid luggage detection or inspection throughout the different states. Hugh had booked two seats for the entire trip – to be as comfortable as possible and to have his tools of trade beside him. Reaching into his jeans' pocket with the tight fitting black leather gloves he handed the ticket to the ageing driver. The only thing that gave Hugh away was his eyes – men who had been around trouble long enough could read it easily, breaking direct eye contact and avoiding him. Most females picked up on an aura of power and strength from the young man but also a vibe of danger that excited some, but scared away the majority. This gave Hugh a slight complex with women in general.

Meg swung into the undercover car park in the hospital complex. Looking at the time on her wrist watch she realised time had gotten away from her. Grabbing the handbag bulging in cash and John's magazine under one arm she hurried for the entrance. Arriving on level four, Meg made her way down the corridor to see only one guard standing out the front. Her mood quickly changed from contentment to concern as she passed the guard and continued increasing her pace towards John's room. Pushing open the door Meg was met by a young nurse making up the empty bed. "Where is my husband?" she demanded.

The nurse spun around from her chore of replacing the bed linen startled. "I am not sure, I just clocked on thirty minutes ago. The nurses at the station towards the end of the wing should know where your husband has been moved to." Meg burst through the door with a sinking feeling in her stomach fighting back the tears. She grabbed the police guard's sleeve stationed at the front of C's door in desperation. "Have you seen my husband from a few doors up?" "No ma'am, I was not on night shift. The only movement from up that way today was a handful of cleaners." Meg broke into a deep sob as she made her way towards the nurses station on unsteady legs. Rounding the right-angle corridor with the station in sight, Meg's emotions changed from despair to anger – she wanted answers, her face set in stone. "Where has my husband been moved to?" The head of nursing walked around the counter. "We have been trying to reach you all morning on the contact mobile you supplied and the home phone. Your husband passed away from a blood clot to the brain in the early hours of this morning." Meg let go of her handbag with the magazine under her arm falling to the floor as she blacked out.

Meg came to on a waiting room couch with the captain by her side on his phone. "Yes, we want it released to the media now with a back-up article once the funeral date has been established. Yes sir it will be interesting to see who turns up." Realising Meg's eyes were open he cut the conversation short. The captain had come up to interview C again before his hospital release date set for tomorrow. "Hello Meg, I'm very sorry to hear of your husband's passing." Still slightly dazed but also confused at who this man was and how he even knew her name, she thanked the man. Her brain was clouded and she found it difficult to think rationally. The captain patted her leg softly in reassurance then rose to his feet. "We will get to the bottom of this, that I can promise you. There is no way you are in any condition to drive. Have you got friends you can stay with down here?" Meg just shook her head speaking softly. "Can I see him?" "No, I am afraid not, at the moment they are currently doing an autopsy. Look, I will get the nurses to book you into a motel across the road for the night, do you have money?" "My bag," said Meg frantically looking around. "The nurses have it behind the counter at the station just around the corner when you are ready. I will be back at 9am tomorrow." Slipping one of his cards into her hand, he added, "we can go see John then if you feel up to it." Confirmation from Meg was just a slight nod before the captain made his way towards C's room.

He had done some homework since his last visit. On paper this man was a saint – no arrests, no warrants, not even a driving infringement on record. The man was as cunning as a shithouse rat. But on closer investigation he stumbled across some things that did not quite add up. Armed with this information and many other leads that had come to light in the past twenty-four hours, the captain now had no doubt in his mind that this was the man he was after, but he had to convert this assumption into rock-solid evidence. He was under no illusion that to catch this mastermind was not going to be a walk in the park by any means. He would have to be shrewd and cast a wide net to catch this one. With his folder under one arm the captain opened the door, confident this interview would make the self-proclaimed humanitarian freelance chopper owner squirm.

A young nurse entered the room an hour earlier to change C's wound dressings. "Sorry Chris, I am running a bit behind today, how you feeling? Heading home tomorrow I hear. Now let's have a look at these wounds." The young nurse made idle conversation while she unwound the bandages. "We lost a patient two doors up from you yesterday, I felt so sorry for the poor wife, the lady was a mess when she arrived at the nurses station having no idea that her husband had passed." C didn't mind this young nurse, always bubbly and friendly but she had one shortcoming – she never shut up. The nurse continually told him stories of other patients throughout the hospital as she tended to his wounds. He normally paid little heed to the gossip but this topic caught his attention.

"Just up from me you say, what was his condition?" The nurse accustomed to only receiving one word replies for weeks on end from this patient responded with vigour. "Well, he was admitted with gunshot wounds about the same time you arrived I think, but a blood clot got him in the end…as I was saying, poor lady." The conversation was interrupted just as the nurse who loved the sound of her own voice was starting to get into top gear. Opening the door, the captain entered the room just before the nurse had finished her work. "I won't be too much longer officer." The nurse cut short the hospital gossip and wished C all the best for the future. "No, thank you," smiled C, "you have just made my day." Eyes narrowing, he now turned his full attention towards the cop. Making a deep sigh he visually engaged with this man that was becoming a bigger pain in the arse by the day. Aware he was about to partake in a contest of the minds with a dead man walking made things more annoying, a complete waste of his time and effort.

C had a lot more pressing issues to deal with…he was losing

market share on a daily basis, with other players reportedly now entering what was originally his domain. "What do you want now pig?" asked C irritably, having enough of playing this game of cat and mouse. The captain smiled. With the new information that had come to light and C's response cementing his recent thoughts, he knew this was the man he was after. Relishing the idea he was now getting under his opponent's skin, even moderately, the police officer ignored the derogatory comment and cut to the chase.

"You have a very considerable sum in your bank accounts for the small property you own in relation to the volume of cattle you have sold…it is just not feasible. The cattle you have spread out state-wide to various livestock auctions would be to avoid attention at an educated guess." Injecting more pressure to the conversation he added, "think I'll get the stock squad and our forensic accountants to look more closely into this." C responded as the captain flicked open his folder with pen in hand to jot down anything forthcoming of relevance. "I don't charge per hour to my customers on mustering time, I charge per head of cattle not on hours of flight time. If that's the best you have on me pig, get the fuck out of here, and you can take it up with my lawyers from now on. I have had a gutful of these accusations, be glad to get out of this fucking hole tomorrow. A smart cop would take all their long-service leave starting tomorrow. Now get the fuck out of my face and stop grasping at straws, you got nothing. And I have fuck-all further to add." In a test of wills, they locked each other's stare squarely and silently for a period, each trying to gauge a reaction of weakness. The captain broke the silence. "Don't stray too far from your property. Retirement you reckon, not a chance I am just starting to sink my teeth into this now, we will see each other again very soon."

"I don't think so," was the response from C as the captain opened the door to leave.

Chapter 3

KILLERS FOR HIRE

Hugh arrived into town early. Taking the final step out of the coach onto a concrete platform the hitman stretched to his full height. Slinging the bag over his shoulder he made the short walk from the bus terminal towards the city centre. His first impression from passing pedestrians told him to alter his dress sense if he wanted to blend into tropical North Queensland lifestyle. Selecting a small motel and paying cash, he made brief contact with Marko. The first hit sounded an easy one he thought, asking the elderly desk clerk for directions to the nearest car hire business. Hugh sifted through his wallet selecting a Queensland driver's licence. He had high quality fake driver's licences for every state even though this was his first trip out of WA for business purposes.

He was still waiting for more information on the locations for the other targets. Unsure of what vehicle would be required, he settled for a plain white 4x4 wagon. Hugh figured it would easily blend in with the thousands he noticed from the bus window on the roads since entering the state while also covering all bases that might need to be explored. The owner of the car rental yard started the paperwork. "Great choice of vehicle sir, brand spanker, it only came in last week. Can I have your driver's licence and I will need an imprint of your credit card. The hitman shook his head. "Don't believe in credit cards, anything I want I pay for in cash, do you have a problem with that?"

"Well, this is very unorthodox way of payment in this day and age, I'm not sure how this will work if any damage is evident on the vehicle's return," the owner replied. "Do I look like a hoon to you?" Hugh smiled. "Listen, I will pay for two weeks hire and a thousand in cash as a deposit up front. Cash is every business owner's friend these days, wouldn't you say?" The owner, desperate for the business and trying to compete with the big end of town in the car hire sector, finally agreed thinking of ten different ways to spend the cash. "Can you take care of it please?" asked the car hire owner as he passed over the keys. Hugh gave him a wink. "Don't worry mate, it won't even have a squished bug on the windscreen when I return it." Before leaving the car yard the hitman retrieved his black leather gloves from his pocket and activated Google maps on his mobile phone searching for the location of the city's hospital.

The captain walked out of the hospital complex into the tropical night of the North making his way along the well-lit car park towards his vehicle, still smarting at the manner he was treated by C. "That slick prick is going down if it's the last thing I do," he promised to himself on leaving the car park. Deep in thought as he travelled homewards the policeman started braking for another set of stop lights where the city's arterial road connected with the main highway. The captain still found the need to vent. Selecting Grace's number he pressed loud speaker. The call rung out and went to message bank. "Grace its Cap, just want to give you an update on the case as it stands to me now. What the fuck?" exclaimed the police officer as Hugh in the 4x4 behind him had turned off his headlights, engaged low four-wheel drive for maximum traction, then nudged the rear bumper before planting the accelerator to the floor. The 4x4 lurched forward forcing the captain's vehicle onto the highway with heavy oncoming traffic travelling at speed.

The hitman had been following his target patiently, arriving at the sixth set of lights before the timing he needed all fell into place. A fully loaded semi travelling at 80kmh had no chance of pulling up in the short time it took Hugh to push the cop's vehicle into its oncoming path. The captain let out a mouth full of obscenities riding his foot hard on the brake pedal. Caught by surprise, he dropped the phone on the floor and fumbled for the handbrake as a last-ditch effort.

The semi driver, also realising the impending collision, applied the brakes with black smoke billowing from the tyres as they howled and locked up on the bitumen. Being an experienced truckie who had encountered many close calls with reckless motorist over the years, he glanced in the side mirror of the semi for any other possible options left open to him. The lane beside him was jammed packed with traffic. With nowhere else to go, the semi smashed into the driver's side of the captain's car. The impact was severe, crushing it like an aluminium can as they both skidded down the highway with the captain's car now a twisted lump of metal, wedged half underneath the front of the truck. The exposed metal scouring along the bitumen showered sparks from the bare wheel rims of the sedan, void of tyres from the initial impact. Fuel leaked from the ruptured fuel tank before igniting. The captain's car burst into flames moments before the semi finally ground to a halt.

Hugh surveyed the carnage as other vehicles behind reduced speed immediately, managing to swerve into adjacent lanes. With just some panel damage, the West Australian smiled at his handy work. Spinning the 4x4 around he quickly selected two-wheel drive before careening over the top of a traffic island and returning the way he had come. Hugh flicked back on the rental car's headlights when he considered the distance was far enough away from the accident site for anyone to view his number plate. The hitman had programed in Marko's number and made the call. "The bank account is now open. I will text you through my details now and expect payment before I proceed any further." Marko on the other end of the line was still scrambling to organise C's other priorities. "Don't worry the money is good trust me…very quick work by the way. We are having a few issues locating the other targets, though they should come out of the woodwork with their mate's pending funeral."

Hugh did not respond to the pat on the back for his efficiency. "Just get my money or you will be next," he said, hanging up before the cop had time to reply. Marko felt a chill run up his spine. Trust had been a major issue for Hugh in the past, to the point of having to take out a couple of previous employers who conveniently changed their minds on payment terms after the job was completed. Thinking their wealth and connections made them out of his reach, they soon found out the hard way that they were gravely mistaken.

Weaving through traffic back into the city, he texts through the account numbers before swinging into the rear car park of his motel. Hugh made a quick inspection of the bull bar for damage or revealing paint marks from the cop's rear bumper. Satisfied, he walked towards the room relishing the thought of sleeping in a bed for the first time since leaving WA.

Overnight, Meg had chopped and changed her mind numerous times over viewing her husband, finally deciding to give it a miss, preferring her last favourable thoughts of him instead of a cold corpse that she knew would then be etched into her memory forever. Meg located the card the helpful police officer had given her and made the call to let him know of her intentions. An automated voice answered saying, "this number is currently unavailable". Meg decided there was not much use staying in the city so she paid for the room then crossed the road to her vehicle still in the hospital car park and headed home to contact Tim and Danni along with other family members, and then start making funeral arrangements.

Grace had also been trying to return her captain's strange call. She had listened to the message three times now and had no success trying to contact him. Concerned, she made the call to headquarters to see if he had arrived for work. Grace was put through to the superintendent's line. "Hello Grace, we need you to come into the station for an immediate briefing. It has just been confirmed that his vehicle was involved in a horrific traffic accident last night. It was fatal I am sorry to say, we are not ruling out foul play. In light of this tragic event, I have just gotten off the phone with the commissioner after considerable discussion about the current investigation. You have been involved in this case from the start; we would consider it a huge backward step in the time frame we have to work with to try and bring in someone new and then get them up to speed on all aspects surrounding this perplexing case. The captain spoke very highly of your quick intellect and solid judgement over the time you have worked together; we need you to take over as lead investigator. This case is now yours if you want."

"Yes sir, I am on my way into work now," replied the detective in a dull monotone voice unable to savour the fact that she had just been offered one of the largest ongoing investigations in the state that hundreds above her rank would envy. Still shaking her head in disbelief at the topic of the conversation, her boss and to a further extent, the possibility her new friend had just been murdered, Grace pondered the situation. "What were you going to tell me, Cap?" Grace said quietly to herself as she pulled into a car park in police headquarters. She shoved a few handwritten notes of research into the front Velcro compartment of her laptop computer case before entering the building. With an expression declaring 'don't fuck with me today' written all over her demeanour, Grace made a direct path to the superintendent's office, avoiding all eye contact with any fellow officers along the way.

The female detective knocked and entered the room with a large framed man behind the desk beckoning her in with a wave of his hand and prematurely ending his conversation on the phone. "Hello Grace, grab a seat, we have a lot to catch up on in a short period." She sat as instructed. "We've lost one of our best men over this investigation. It's been confirmed by witness statements that his vehicle was intentionally pushed into oncoming traffic." The emotional female detective interrupted. "To me sir this has now become very personal, are there any updates on a suspect? Listen to the call I got from the captain." She replayed the phone message. The superintendent's cheeks flushed red with anger as he listened to the sound of tyres screeching and the captain swearing on the recording.

"This is where we were up to Grace," he continued, recounting recent intel from the week leading up to the captain's murder. After a solid hour of information, the now new lead investigator, Grace, was up to date shaking her head in disbelief at how quickly the case had advanced over the last couple of days. Uploading all the files from her captain's recent reports her resolve became stronger with every page she read. The superintendent gave Grace a short time to absorb this latest information before firing questions at how they would approach the current situation. He scrutinised every word she spoke, observing body language, her responses, including some very relevant questions that Grace introduced that had not been previously addressed. The superintendent was pleasantly surprised at the result, now realising why the captain had held this officer in such high regard. This female detective was switched on and would be their best shot to get a positive result. The department had spent millions on this case, and they needed a conviction soon.

Tim had spent most of the day scouting through second-hand machinery dealers, top of his list was a second-hand front-end loader that was in good nick along with anything else that caught his eye to make extracting the gold-bearing ore easier. The third place he pulled up had a lot more to choose from and the old bloke wearing grease covered overalls who met him at the gate seemed friendly and keen to make a deal. "Everything is for sale young fella, make a decent offer and we will talk turkey. Do you have anything in mind?" Tim smiled. He liked these old timers who were set in their ways and didn't muck around with small talk or bullshit. "Yeah mate, a loader and a rock crusher to process gold ore. The machinery dealer's bushy grey eyebrows shot up. "A gold mine hey, not too many small shows left around these parts since they brought in that native title…yep, got exactly what you need over here." They haggled over the price with the old bloke sweetening the sale by throwing in a quad bike sitting in the corner of the shed collecting dust after Tim also queried about its price. Shaking hands on the deal the owner offered to sort out transport. "If you haven't organised anyone on the freight side of things my young bloke has a semi and can have you on the road with your gear today if you want."

"Sounds good to me," replied Tim. "I will have to go and cash in some gold nuggets first, unless you don't mind some gold as payment?" The old bloke chuckles, a gold miner himself formerly. "Show me what you got first son and we will take it from there I reckon." The prospector smiles. "No worries old mate, you got any scales?"

The semi driver that followed Tim along the winding dirt track into the bush carrying the long machinery load was as experienced at outback deliveries as he had seen, expertly weaving through and around obstacles in his path, including negotiating creeks and gullies that Tim didn't give him a chance of getting out of. He was impressed at how far along the track they got before the driver called it quits over the two-way. Both men unloaded the gear, chaining the rock crusher to the bucket of the loader and slowly lowering it into the back of his four-wheel drive along with the quad. It took Tim three full days of toil to blaze a rough track into the mine site, parking the loader up roughly every two kilometres to walk back and retrieve his truck following the freshly turned earth of the machine before repeating the procedure. He managed to make a few shortcuts from the original quad track that he and John had initially followed with the powerful bright yellow loader moving rocks and tree stumps with ease.

Though old Mac was happy to see his young mining partner

arrive at camp just before dark, he was not overly impressed with the idea of an access track at all. In his mind roads brought trouble. They had now lost their anonymity, feeling somewhat apprehensive at who would be the first outsider to enter his world. Mac was not one to hold back with his thoughts and would bring his concerns to the table after his partner had time to settle in. Tim lowered the loader bucket to the ground before scampering down the side steps of the machine with a broad smile plastered on his face. "How's it going, old fella?" Mac shuffled towards the parked-up machine with the smell of hot hydraulic fluid getting stronger as he moved closer. His pup ran around him excitedly, also happy to have another's company in the camp. Breaking into a grin, the old prospector offered out his calloused wrinkled hand, warmly shaking his partner's. "I am good my young friend." The pup intervened, jumping up with its front paws on Tim's lower thighs appealing for some attention. "Hey, little fella," said Tim giving his head a brisk rub. "Have you given him a name yet?" Mac smirked, "Yep, called him Nugget." Tim laughed out loud. "Now that's a fitting name. What's for dinner, old mate? I could eat the crutch out of a set of jocks that have been worn for a week."

The old prospector smiled at Tim's dry humour, appreciating someone else to talk to other than Nugget. "Heard the machine coming for the last day and a half. Figured it was you so went for a walk this morning with the shotgun and snagged a couple of black ducks for dinner…should only be half hour away in the camp oven," Mac replied proudly. "Sounds bloody good to me mate. Stuff the truck for tonight, I've had a gutful for one day…I'll walk back and grab it at sparrows fart." The men devoured the exotic bush meal in virtual silence, savouring every mouthful, before retiring beside the fire for a yarn. Tim rubbed his stomach. "Mate I am full as a bull before mating season."

"It was a good feed," Mac chuckled. "On another subject, I don't 'think much of the road right to our doorstep. Roads bring trouble in my view, especially when gold is involved…from previous experiences in many goldfields here and abroad it turns many good people to greed. I have seen men change first-hand, even some of my friends in the past; I was younger and a lot more naive back then. That's why I have been a loner until now." Tim nodded slowly taking in what old Mac had to say, pushing a half-burnt timber log with the toe of his boot into the red-hot coals. It smouldered momentarily before bursting into flames throwing enough light for Tim to see the concern on Mac's wrinkled face from the flickering fire.

"Mac, we needed the road to get the machinery in to go forward with the mine mate, you have already picked up the easy gold. The shovel and pick have their place for sure, but now we need to open her up and go deeper, what other options did we have? Bring the loader in by chopper in bits? That would cost a fortune buddy; then we have nothing here to lift the parts and put one back together even if I knew how. I'm no mechanic or diesel fitter, bush mechanic at best to get me out of trouble." Old Mac just shook his head. "I know what you are saying Tim, and the reasoning for it but this road will bring trouble for us, mark my words." Tim stood, stretching out, he placed his arm across the old timer's stooped shoulders in an act of friendship. "I'm knackered mate and need a camp, at worst we might have to turn away some weekend warriors swinging a metal detector or a wayward adventurous tourist…that other bush scum upstream are all dead. Chill bro, it's all good, don't stress."

"Hmmm, we will see," replied Mac still not convinced. Tim reached the front of the tin shed before turning and saying: "Hey mate, talking about improvements around this joint I have a present for you on the truck that will save you wearing out them spindly old legs quicker than what they need to." Mac looked up from the mesmerising flames of the fire deep in thought, the wood smoke now blowing in his direction with a slight breeze change. Wiping his eyes from the irritating smoke he replied: "It better not be a wheelchair or a walking cane or look the hell out." Tim laughed. "Good night old mate, you will have to wait and see."

Both men were up early eager to get their day under way; the morning air was cold and crisp with the steam rolling off the top of their coffee cups. Tim slipped on his work boots before taking another sip of his cuppa. "Shouldn't be too long getting the truck Mac, it's only a couple kilometres back. Shit, I left the sat phone in the truck, should have checked in with Danni last night." Mac dropped a cupful of dry dog biscuits into Nugget's food bowl as he replied, "righto then, well I will be down at the mine starting to place the explosives. They are bloody old, been carrying them around for the last thirty odd years but reckon they should still work OK. Take Nugget with you; he will enjoy the extra exercise."

"No worries then, I'll see you down there, you just select the spots and I will drill them when I get back. We still have to unload this other gear off the truck and set up a position for the crusher. This will be the last time you will have to hoof it to the mine ever again," smiled Tim. Old Mac returned the smile. "I like the sound of that young fella."

It took Tim two hours to arrive back at camp. Swapping over to the loader, he opted to push a rough track down to the mine site initially. The main reason behind his reasoning was to get the 4x4 easily onsite and reduce the chances of staking a tyre with the extra weight of the machinery still on the back. Mac, hearing a motor in between drilling, popped his head out of the mine entrance. His entire body ached and he was caked head to toe in dirt from the fine dust in the confined space after placing a sequence of well-executed holes for a clean shot that he hoped contained the richest part of the gold vein.

Welcoming the break, Mac walked gingerly towards the loader. "You look stuffed old mate, what the hell are you trying to do, kill yourself?" Tim said. The old miner looked at the ground without giving an instant reply, admitting to himself that his young partner's words rang true, he had pushed himself way too hard. "Just trying to pull my weight," he replied, conveniently changing the subject before his young partner could answer. "So, where do you want to put this crusher plant?"

"Ha, nice try Mac, seriously old mate, that's what I am here for is the hard physical work. If you are too stubborn to accept that best we part ways now." He looked up at his young partner with a moistening in his eyes conceding the fact this was the first man ever on any goldfield he had been on who was more concerned about his welfare before the gold. "I accept your terms, stay with me mate," he said humbly. Tim felt a pang of regret for having to put his foot down on the situation. Lightening the mood he replied, "damn old age, hey pard, I need to put a bridle in your mouth and pull back on the reins to slow you down some. Just give me ten to get a level bench done for the crusher then after placing it in position we will head on home to unload your new chariot off the truck." Mac smiled at his analogy. "Yeah I got the message, whoa up to a walking pace."

"Now you got the idea," Tim smiled. "How about you drive my truck home and I will spruce up this track up some more with the loader on the way back." Mac broke into a grin. "Haven't touched a steering wheel in near on fifteen years, I could be a bit rusty." The old miner had problems coordinating the clutch while changing gears crunching through nearly every gear shift on the way home swearing aloud to himself every time. Arriving at the camp behind the machine Mac bunny hopped the truck to a stop. Tim was in fits of laughter watching from the seat of the loader. He climbed off the machine, hooking up the quad to unload. After going through how to operate the quad with his old partner he let him go on his maiden ride after a few words of caution. "Don't break any bones for Christ sake." As dark started to approach old Mac had a full hour of riding under his belt, increasing speed every time he passed the hut with a priceless smile from ear to ear.

The mid-morning breeze was picking up, effortlessly bending the ghost gum branches that waved aimlessly, forever dictated by the winds that whistled through their leaves. The miners crouched for protection behind a huge boulder before letting their first denotation go. The rumble from the explosion rolled out through the valley basin shutting down all the bird chatter in the nearby trees as they took flight for a new sanctuary. Clouds of billowing dust spread out across the steep incline that contained the incredibly rich reef of gold that old Mac had found many years earlier. Tim dusted himself off as a fine film continued to descend towards the ground. "That should do the trick old mate, what do you reckon?" Mac let go of Nugget's ears before rising to look at the front of the mine shaft. "Yeah, should be some nice gold in that lot; you may as well start loading the ore into the crusher."

Mac and Nugget begun to make their way to the piles of rocks strewn around the entrance while Tim jogged back towards camp to get the loader. The old prospector started to shuffle around the ore scanning with his expert eye for any colour of free gold. His eyesight was going purely due to his age and the continuous dusty conditions he had worked in all his life, but one thing he did not miss was the glint of gold even if it was only a speck in a gold dish. Disappointment and doubt started to enter Mac's mind as he made way around the blast area searching for the elusive colour. He could hear Tim getting closer with the loader scraping metal on rock as he further improved the track towards the mine's entrance. Nugget, walking faithfully beside his owner, paused and half-cocked his leg up against a large rock the size of a house rubbish bin. The yellow stream of urine trickled down the face of the rock washing away the heavy coating of fine dust from the blast exposing the speckled glint of gold. Old Mac's mood had turned slightly sour as he twisted at the hip to beckon his dog in an annoyed voice. "Come on boy, we haven't got all day." Mac's eyes rested on the wet patch partially covering the rock. "What the hell," he yelled, as he hastily made his way to where Nugget now lay with both ears laid back thinking he was in trouble for something.

"Well stone the crows' boy, you found the bloody thing. I knew there had to be more gold down there." Old Mac excitedly knelt to reassure the pup giving him a good rub around the neck. "Good boy. To celebrate you can have a pork chop for dinner tonight." Nugget's tail started to wag realising he was not in trouble, giving Mac a big lick across his cheek as the old prospector carefully inspected the large gold specimen. Tim broke into the clearing to see his partner waving frantically with both arms in the air. His heart skipped a beat as he drew nearer on the loader to see the excitement on his partner's face. "Have you got any drinking water on board?" Mac yelled. "Yeah mate, it's nearly full, what have you found Mac?" The old timer lifted off his hat with a wide smile as he attempted to jump in the air and click his heels together nearly falling flat on his face in the process. "The mother lode son, the fucking mother lode."

Tim laughed loudly at Mac's antics as he rarely swore. The excitement was infectious as he clambered down the ladder of the loader with the blue water bottle containing four litres of water in one hand. "Slow up old mate, you will have a heart attack at this rate."

"Here I will show you my boy." Mac reached for the handle of the water container, flicking open the lid. The water glugged out of the spout splashing away more dust and dirt revealing spider-like veins of gold virtually covering the whole side of the boulder. Tim's jaw dropped in awe as Mac kept rubbing other smaller rocks nearby with the aid of the water. More veins of gold, some thicker than a man's thumb, appeared.

Fu opened the door of the Bullion shop promptly at 9am as usual; one customer was waiting out the front who he recognised instantly. "Morning Brad." "Morning Fu," replied the prospector accompanied with a cheeky grin. "Am I going to get a good gold price today?" Brad was a regular to the shop and had covered most of Australia in the last twenty-five years with various metal detectors. He knew his stuff but struggled with the bottle, drinking away all the profits he had found over the years. Brad was a friendly and harmless enough bloke and was always in the mood to give out some gold gossip to whoever would listen, though sometimes Fu took the stories with a grain of salt. "You hear about any prospectors running across big reef finds lately in the area?" According to Brad he had contacts in most of the goldfields around Australia that he befriended in his travels over the years. The ageing detector operator thought for a minute before answering. "All depends on what you mean by big. There is the odd reef that has produced one to two kilos of gold locally, and the best I have heard of was four kilos last year."

"No, it's bigger than that," replied Fu a touch disappointed, but he realised it was a long shot at best. Brad's interest increased. "Yeah is that right, how long ago?" Fu filled in the main details about the prospector, then the woman entering the store to sell the gold. He had only received the assay reports in yesterday confirming his suspicions that it was an extremely high probability it was from the same source. The gold purity was the same and the silver content and other trace elements were identical. Brad rubbed the grey stubble on his chin while in thought.

"A woman you say, well now that is interesting…come to think of it I ran across this chopper pilot at the pub a few years ago; he was drunk as a skunk having to use the bar to prop himself up. His fiancée had recently shot through with another bloke. He just had their wedding rings done with some gold that was gifted from an old prospector up Hatchet River way that he choppers in supplies for."

"And the point is?" asked Fu feeling they were getting off topic. Brad smiled. "Now here is the thing, the daughter used to get the supplies together to send out, and on occasion the backload was that heavy the pilot had to help the prospector lift the locked tin box into the chopper. He reckoned the chances of him lifting it himself into her car would be like pushing shit uphill with a forked stick and had to get one of the ground crew from the aircraft hangar to help him move it. Never knew if it was just the piss talking but then two years ago, I was out prospecting that remote Hatchet River area and blow me down a chopper flew overhead with a pallet in a cargo net underneath. I can tell you right now that the years I have been out that way it is not a typical flight path for any aircraft, other than the smaller odd mustering chopper flying past to the next job."

Fu gave Brad a beaming smile. "I will give you ten dollars a gram above today's gold price with no fees deducted if you can point out on a map where you were and what direction the chopper was heading." The prospector shrugged his shoulders. "Deal, found jack shit up there anyway and that area is vast, remote, and unforgiving. You will have more chance of finding the Pope in a brothel in Cairns than finding that gold mine. No disrespect to you Fu and your friends, but honestly bloke that is tough country, you are way out of your league on this one. Reckon you lot would not last more than a day walking that terrain in the heat." It was Fu's time to shrug his shoulders. "We will see. Now where is your gold to weigh in?"

Soon as the happy prospector walked out the door with his pocket full of cash Fu walked into the back office to discuss this new information with his partner Wong. Being the more proactive in the partnership Fu asked, "Did you hear that? I think we should call Chang back in, forget the woman and try to pick up the prospector. Rewind the camera to when he sold us the gold, I want a picture of this man for Chang. Then bring up the outside camera footage for the same time period to see what he was driving and hopefully we have a rego number." Wong brought up the outside cameras, "Looks like he walked, there is no car in the film at that time and date." Fu threw his hands up in the air in frustration. "Impossible, rewind the tape further." He leant over his partner's shoulder viewing the TV monitor. "Look there, that man driving a four-wheel drive in a khaki shirt the same colour as what the prospector was wearing. "He is smart this one…look, he drives past slowly twice then five minutes later walks to the front of the building and looks directly at the hidden camera. Fast forward to when he leaves…that's him for sure – look, five minutes later the same vehicle drives past again. Slow that down to see if we can get the rego."

Wong jotted down the number and looked at his partner. "I don't think we have anyone in the Queensland Department of Transport yet to give us an address." Fu shook his head at how dumb his business associate could be at times. "No, but we do in other states, they can contact them for the information. I want that address today, before Chang gets back here."

The front door buzzer sounded as a young couple entered hand in hand moving towards the jewellery cabinets. Fu hurried out the front while Wong made the call to their contact in Melbourne.

The assassin returned to the shop by mid-afternoon walking straight into the backroom nodding to his boss Fu who always preferred to talk in English to strengthen both their skills in this department. Chang had improved very well in this field over the last couple of years and could comprehend most things other than some Aussie slang that still had him slightly confused. "Tell me Chang, what have you discovered about the girl?" Shrugging his broad, well-muscled shoulders, Chang replied. "Not that much boss. She had someone in hospital that has died as I also followed her to a funeral home. I guess it might have been her husband as no male has been or visited her house. We are not the only one watching this woman – last night a man was lurking in the shadows around the house, I'm sure he also picked up on my presence. He was good, and moved as silent as the fog." Fu waved his hand shutting down the remainder of the reply to his question. "Forget that for now; we have the address of the prospector who sold us the gold, that is your new job. I want the location of that reef no matter what action you might have to take to get it." Chang left the building happy with his new orders. The assassin had been missing the action and conflict of his job since moving to the North of the country.

C finally arrived back at the front gate of his seaside property, tired after wasted hours of mundane road travel with his brain having to work overtime to compensate for the vision left in only one eye. He was not overly surprised as the surgeon had already pointed out this fact after the operation. The doctors also expressed doubts about him passing a pilot medical exam anytime soon, if ever, due to the injury. The kingpin of the North was far from fit after many operations to get him walking again, with considerably more cosmetic surgery to follow in the future. C looked countless times into the rear vision mirror with his one good eye during the five-hour trip home. The skin grafts from both bum cheeks to his face had been successful though still not completely healed; it reminded him of a handmade patchwork quilt cover made by a ten-year-old novice with a severe case of conjunctivitis.

His appearance angered him every time he looked at his distorted facial features. The prospector responsible for this along with all family members, associates and friends would pay for his condition with their lives. C was smart enough to put the passion of revenge forcefully to one side as it could easily distort his judgement on more pressing issues surrounding his drug empire. The Chinese had quietly moved into town months before and set up in a professional manner with small groups of southern bikers trickling into town over a period of the last week, keeping a low profile until they had the green light from Fu and Wong to start business. While all this was occurring right under his nose, C was consumed with other problems including his near-death experience in the desert. Intel from various sources had started to report that large volumes of high-quality ice had become readily available to his significant client base and was being distributed by a rival gang at a heavily discounted price compared to his product.

C entered the house and made straight for the landline to see what new information Marko had for him. The phone rung twice before his newly appointed right-hand man recognised the number. "You made it home alright then?" "Yeah, now what the fuck is going on with these fucking slope heads trying to take over my customers?" Marko paced with his mobile phone as he tried to answer the boss's demands. "Well, from what I have found out so far they are well organised and well-funded though we don't know yet exactly by who. They are getting a foothold pretty quickly by the sound of things. Several clashes have also occurred with the rival gang...from all reports we got hammered in every encounter. Apparently, they can knuckle quite well. Have some good news though, Ox's brother has taken care of the captain, and has already contacted me demanding payment." C was livid on the other end of the line with one cheek flushed bright red in anger while the reconstructed side of his face was splotchy in colour. C started to twist the ring on his finger subconsciously.

"Demands payment does he; the job has only just friggin' started. Who the fuck does he think he is? I will pay him when I am good and fucking ready. Now, how are you going to locate that prospector's family and friends?" Marko quickly reflected on how the hitman had threatened his life over the payment before replying nervously into the phone, "I don't know C, this bloke is different to his brother. Not telling you what to do, but if you want any more work done by the West Australian I would pay him for the first job. Yes, I have also just received some addresses and licence photos for him to start work with. That funeral for that other bloke who got shot at the Hatchet River Station is on tomorrow." C simmered down with his accomplice's wise words. "OK, whatever, give me his details it will be in his account within the next 24 hours. Tell him to be at that other prick's funeral. Also, tell him when I say I want their heads I mean literally, there will be another five thousand per person in it for him. Now get off your fat arse and find out who is running this rice burner outfit, and drop our price to match theirs."

Old Mac trod wearily towards Tim's truck after a hard day's work for a man of his age, grunting as he swung the door shut with his aching arm muscles. Tim was not too far behind, lifting Nugget into the back of the 4x4 tray. The smiles on both men's faces were priceless as Tim opened the door and slipped into the driver's seat. On arrival back at camp, Tim was busting to tell Danni of their gold find. When the phone finally locked onto the satellites and powered up Tim noticed three missed calls from his home number. He swore under his breath, now concerned at the multiple missed calls, and kicked himself for leaving the phone in his vehicle overnight on the new track.

Tim rang his home number before even exiting his vehicle leaving Mac to retrieve Nugget from the back. "Hi babe, I stuffed up and didn't have my phone on me last night, we hit it big today on the gold," the other end of the line was silent. "What's up?"

Danni, still somewhat cranky about her husband not answering the phone when scheduled, and more so after recent events, replied: "What's up is, John is dead, and his funeral is tomorrow." Tim tried to comprehend what his wife had just told him, as the smile quickly dissipated from his face on their triumph for the day. "I will leave camp now, what has happened?" he asked, the euphoria of the gold find with his old partner now at the back of his mind.

"It was a blood clot," Danni replied. "I don't know the full details as Meg was very upset when she called. I don't think it will be safe for you at the funeral as the place will be crawling with cops. There was even a newspaper article on John's death. I talked to Rick and Rob about this matter yesterday after not being able to contact you, and both agree, they will not be attending John's funeral for the same reason. I will, however be there to pay our respects." A blank expression covered his face. "So, he is dead?" Danni's voice started to break down at her husband's response. "Yes, he is dead." Trying to change the conversation after hearing the hurt in her husband's voice to a better topic. "So, you had a good day, what did you find?"

"It does not matter too much now," Tim replied in a soft voice.

The morning was overcast in the northern part of the Sunshine State, a periodic sprinkle of rain passed with the odd burst of brilliant sunshine breaking through the low, menacing cloud cover. The coffin rolled out smoothly from the hearse beside John's plot. The small congregation of mourners consisted mainly of family members with a light scattering of former friends from an earlier era in his life. Grace was in attendance along with a handful of plainclothes officers spread out trying to look inconspicuous at a distance while the funeral proceeded. Danni, fractionally late, pulled into a parallel car park in front of the cemetery trying to withhold her frustration after being stuck in a long line of morning traffic following multiple-vehicle accidents on the slippery rain affected Kuranda Range. Hastily adjusting her dress after exiting the car, Danni made her way down the grassy slope to Meg's side, embracing her in a very emotional hug.

Chang, after sleeping in his car for a brief period overnight, had been observing his new assignment before following Danni from her house that morning. He always remained a few cars behind while keeping her vehicle in visual sight throughout the busy morning city traffic. On entering the cemetery gates, Chang pulled his car to the side of the road for several minutes before locating one spare park a short distance from the main congregation of vehicles. The late arrival of Chang went mainly unnoticed other than by Hugh, who had parked outside the grounds at the very end of a cul-de-sac an hour before any vehicle had arrived for the funeral. The West Australian hitman had walked the length of the entire cemetery twice before the first car arrived that morning.

Hugh flicked through the intel provided by Marko the night before on his phone after being assured of payment for services within the next 24 hours. Once again he scrutinised the licence photos. It was not too difficult to pick out some of the targets on his employer's hit list in the small gathering. He was disappointed it was completely devoid of the males that needed to be dealt with, including the man who had reportedly killed his brother.

As the mourners made their way slowly to the funeral plot, Hugh could easily make out several plain clothes cops positioned at various distances from the activity trying their best to look inconspicuous. They stood out like dog's balls to the trained eye as he quickly did a head count of four plain clothes and one female officer who was not hiding the fact as she mingled with family members, embracing the mourning wife and the female that had just turned up. The hairs on the hitman's body stood to attention as he concentrated on the last vehicle to enter the cemetery gates. Its occupant made no attempt to leave the vehicle and join the congregation of mourners. Hugh raised his binoculars to focus on a single large Asian male sitting in the car with leather gloves clearly visible holding the steering wheel while he intently looked down upon the funeral gathering.

The hitman made the decision to confront the car's occupant as he certainly was not a cop. Hugh had no fear of any man on this earth, entirely confident in his abilities to fulfil every aspect of this unique field of work without detection. At the same time, it excited him to test his skill against another in his specific job description. It was extremely rare that two paid killers clashed on the same job. The only time he had ever encountered this before was in the initial stages of learning the trade – being young and cocky with only two successful contracts under his belt had nearly cost Hugh his life. It was his brother Ox who saved his arse on that day, and the young hitman took away a valuable lesson – never, ever underestimate anyone in this line of work.

Hugh emerged from his hiding spot behind a slight cluster of trees that held a high vantage point for the perfect shot. Placing the rifle on the ground he ambled casually down the gentle slope towards Chang's vehicle. Hugh worked the angle so the Asian could not see him coming from any direction and would have to turn his neck at an unusual angle to pick up on his advance towards the car. Hugh tapped on the heavily tinted side window and gestured a wind-down movement with his free hand while resting the other on the butt of his handgun fully cocked. Chang had been periodically checking all car mirrors, but his primary attention was focused on the funeral. The Asian was completely startled at how this man suddenly appeared at his window undetected. Instinctively resting his left hand on the knife handle positioned in between the car's handbrake and the edge of the driver's seat out of sight, Chang started to wind down the window and was met with a large smile from Hugh.

"Nice day for a funeral wouldn't you say?" Chang nodded

without reply as he took in the West Australian's body language, noticing his right hand was resting at rib height against his torso, concluding the man standing at the driver's door was armed. He also calculated from his sitting position the percentages of a successful kill using his left hand with an across the body throw with the knife. Chang continued to wind the window down to its full extent to increase the size of his target. Hugh unsure at how well the Asian could comprehend what he was saying pointed towards the small group: "See them people down there they are my meal ticket, you get it, mine," he added pointing towards his own chest in an amplified gesture. Chang locked stares with him before shaking his head, replying in his best English, "like fuck they are."

An old light blue 4x4 dual cab with heavy tint on the windows drove slowly past the men at walking pace momentarily diverting both men's attention away from their own situation that was getting uglier by the second. It came to a complete stop thirty meters farther on in the middle of the road with the engine still running. This had now also gained Grace's and the other plain clothes officers' attention, and her line of sight also took in Chang's car that she noticed was occupied and had not been there previously. The West Australian looked up and swore under his breath realising they were now both receiving unwanted stares. Hugh spoke quickly knowing he did not have much time up his sleeve. "Listen, you bag of fucking fried rice, get on the next flight home, and change your profession to something safer like making chopsticks. If we ever cross paths again, there will be blood spilt, and it won't be mine." Grace and the other officers were starting to make their way up the rise; the old blue 4x4 left towards the gates at the opposite end of the cemetery. "You have no idea, Chang sneered." "Now back off from my job or you will find yourself in takeaway containers getting served around town as sweet and sour pork."

Hugh was infuriated, and with no time left to resolve this matter permanently, sprinted in a half crouch from Chang's vehicle back towards his original position behind the tree cover to retrieve his rifle, trying to keep the car between himself and the advancing police officers. Chang slammed his car into second gear and tromped the accelerator to the floor; his vehicle took off, wheels spinning causing the remainder of the mourners to turn towards the road to witnesses the commotion in disgust. Grace was unsure if the man she had seen standing beside the driver's door entered the car before it took off or not. Reaching the road puffing slightly, Grace asked two of the male officers who marginally beat her up the slope, "did you get the plate?"

"No, they had the bloody things covered," they responded. Grace sighed. "Well, call in the make, model and colour even though it's one of the most popular vehicles on the road today. I think we will have more chance of finding the light blue dual cab. Also, do a scout of the grounds just in case that other male was on foot." John's funeral was finished by the time Grace made it back. Meg and Danni were sobbing on each other's shoulders. Grace moved forward and gave Meg a brief hug before embracing Danni and whispering into her ear: "Good to see your husband was not silly enough to turn up. Tell him to leave it alone. This has now become very personal for me as well, we are on top of this one. There have been way too many unwarranted deaths in this case already." Danni did not respond vocally but gave a slight nod of her head.

R ick and Rob had recovered well from their injuries after the ordeal at the Hatchet River Station. Both had taken accrued sick leave but now had been back at work full-time for well over a week. The young men were passionate about racing their dirt bikes in ironman events, they both oozed natural talent as bike riders in the bush and were always in the top group of riders from across the state. On overall points in the North Queensland competition they stood fourth and fifth on the ladder. Music cranked out of the stereo speakers positioned on the tiled rear porch of Rob's house while the smell of recently cooked steak from the barbie still lingered in the air. The fresh cut lawn covered a good half acre at the rear of the house before backing on to semi-rainforest thickening quickly into a full-blown jungle not too much further in. Both young men had worked hard spending countless hours over the years carving out a motorbike track through the rainforest to hone their bike skills and fitness.

The brothers had not long finished lunch on the back lawn with their girlfriends before the 450cc four stroke racing bikes emerged from the shed to start their circuits. The girls both had office jobs during the week but now it was time to spread out their beach towels on the lawn and peel off their clothes to their bikinis. It was time to enjoy some rays on parts of the body that rarely saw sunlight. Rick and Rob strapped on their boots and body armour. The bikes roared to life and after briefly warming up the engines they shot off out of sight into the rainforest, both young men vying fiercely for the lead to start their training laps. The times tumbled quickly as the riders completed each circuit with the girls following their progress via the stop watch on their mobile phones.

Rob locks up the brakes hard after entering the clearing near the house, riding slowly over towards the audience to check on his lap times with Rick following suit. Pressing the kill switch on the bikes, they ask, "how we looking girls? It felt pretty fast to me." "Not too bad," came the reply. "Rob, you are currently a good second ahead of Rick, but a full one and a half seconds behind your personal best." Rick turned at the hip while still sitting on the bike. "Hey bro, have a break for half an hour. I'm feeling in the groove on the bike, sit back and watch me smash your record." Rob smiled as he pulled off the helmet. "The track is all yours brother, can I have one of them phones girls?" Rick adjusted his dirt bike goggles before taking off along the track. After ten minutes he came back into sight riding hard. Rob glanced at the stop watch. "Shit he is hammering hard, only 15 seconds behind my personal best!"

Halfway around the next lap Rick was feeling as one with the powerful machine. Leaning low towards the ground with his leg stuck out directing the front wheel he powered out of the corner causing the wheel to lift slightly off the ground. Ahead was a small crystal clear creek. He straightened the bike at speed. Wire cable had been strung at neck height across the track and fastened tight to trees on opposite sides after his previous lap. Rick squeezed more out of the throttle as the light gauge wire cable bit deep into flesh. Rick briefly felt a sharp burning sensation before being decapitated. The bike and Rick's torso continued forward with the motor revving erratically before crashing heavily into trees off to one side of the track pinning Rick's body underneath the bike. Lying on its side, the motor spluttered before stopping completely. Rick's head and helmet bounced several times before rolling to a stop up against a small sapling, well behind where the bike lay. Wearing a pair of black leather gloves, the killer emerged from the thick foliage picking up the bloodied helmet before shoving it unceremoniously into a large black plastic garbage bag then dropping it onto the ground. The killer swiftly made his way to untie and roll up the wire slipping it over his shoulder before returning to retrieve the garbage bag. Entering the small shallow rainforest stream to erase any tracks, he followed it a good distance downstream before carefully selecting an exit point where the ground was covered thickly in fallen leaves. Leaving no visible trace of his arrival or departure, the man instantly disappeared into the heavy rainforest canopy.

Rob, with timer in hand, heard the bike rev unnaturally high before the engine stopped. "Ha, thought the pressure would get to him, now his gone leg up, bloody goose knew he was pushing too hard," he said slapping his hip. A few minutes passed before Rick's girlfriend lifted her head off the towel. "I hope he hasn't hurt himself again." Rob looked doubtful himself before answering, "probably just having trouble starting the bike, they can be a real bitch to get going when their hot after a crash." Another couple of minutes passed before Rob, now concerned, slipped his helmet on. "I will go see if he needs a hand," he said casually not wanting to worry the girls.

Rob slowed his bike part way around the circuit where he

thought his brother might have come unstuck, watching the edges of the track where they had cleared all the vegetation previously for any tell-tale skid marks. Continuing on, Rob rounded a corner to spot Rick's bike on its side with only part of his brother visible, lying motionless under the motorbike. Giving the accelerator a quick squirt to close the gap between them, Rob's face drained of colour as he noticed a large amount of blood covering the seat and rear mudguard. "What the fuck? Rick!" Dropping the bike to the ground, he ran to the crash site. With adrenaline now exploding into his bloodstream, he lifted the bike with ease shoving it in the opposite direction exposing his brother's headless body. Accumulated beside him was a large pool of blood. He sunk to his knees in disbelief and horror.

Anxiety soared, he fumbled with the release strap on his own bike helmet. Today's barbie lunch soon found its way from the pit of Rob's stomach to his throat, and beyond. "What the hell happened bro?" Rob was extremely distraught as the beat of his own heart was the only sound he heard pulsating loudly in his ears while surrounded by the silence of the rainforest. The young man rose off his knees wiping the tears out of his eyes to focus on finding the remainder of his best friend and brother. Rob was still having problems trying to comprehend how this could possibly happen over a spot they had now ridden for years. Thoughts of foul play started to enter his head as he continued to walk very slowly back along the track with his bush instincts now rising to the fore.

Spending the best part of half an hour without success he extended the search further towards the tree line. With a keen eye for detail he closely scrutinised a small unnatural clean cut into the soft bark of a juvenile rainforest tree. Glancing back to where Rick had exited the corner under power, he also noticed where the bike tracks started to waver before coasting to its existing position. Walking to the opposite side of the track from the fresh scar on the tree, he found the identical marks. It instantly fell into place for Rob with the hairs rising on his back in a tingling sensation.

"Fuck, we are being hunted!" he uttered as he spun around in a complete circle looking further afield for the person responsible.

Rob's mind started to race. He had formed a habit over the years of talking aloud to himself when in highly stressful situations. "The prick had to stand here to string the wire up, it had to be wire, the marks are too thin for rope…there should be prints here somewhere," he said, casting his attention to the ground around him. He continued a slow grid pattern searching for any sign – a cigarette butt, anything, muttering to himself as he went. "What sort of sick fuck would take Rick's head? Is it a statement, warning or maybe even a trophy? That's what's happened for sure or I would have found it by now. All sign of the killer, or killers, presence has been totally erased…this must have been a professional hit. But by who?" He thought aloud, racking his brain as he walked. "Fuck knows, all the Hatchet River mob were dead. None of the bikies knew they had any involvement in what had transpired up bush. They were not seen by anyone out there who was still breathing, he was positive of that. The young man straightened instantly as realisation dawned on him, the girls were alone!

Exasperated, Rob raced for his motorbike. Leaving the helmet on the ground, he reached for the handlebars reefing the bike upright onto two wheels. Flooded from being laid on its side, it took Rob four attempts to start the machine. Eventually it spluttered to life after turning off the supply of fuel to the carburettor. Rob with his pulse racing took off back along the circuit towards the house at a speed that easily smashed the fastest time on this track to date. The girls had also become very apprehensive with neither of the men returning to the house for what they considered had now become an overly long period of time. Worried for both their boyfriends' safety, they embarked on foot following the track from the start line. The girls could hear a bike coming at speed and smiled at each other relaxing their tense composure.

Rob spotted both girls as he rounded the last corner, applying both brakes hard. "Have either of you got a phone?" he screamed. The women's smile quickly disappeared as they could see Rob's distraught face. Rick's girlfriend was nearest to the bike and hastily handed over the phone. "Is Rick badly hurt or something?" she asked crying. Rob shook his head emphatically as he called triple zero, replying in a broken voice, "worse, he is dead." He immediately regretted being so blunt to his brother's girlfriend, but at this point he could not keep his own emotions in check with his mind on overload, bordering on unstable. The emergency operator answered the call as Rob pulled himself together giving the police all the details. The girls stood to one side clutching each other, tears streaming down their faces as they listened to the description being given over the phone. When the call had finished, he looked up at the girls, tear ducts starting to moisten in his own eyes. He fought back the sensation. "I need to get you pair over to the house, there is still a killer lurking out here, there's a good chance the sicko could still be somewhere close, maybe even watching us now," he uttered scanning their surroundings.

It did not take much encouragement from Rob for the girls to climb on his bike after his last statement. Sitting high up on the fuel tank – not wanting to risk leaving either of them behind and alone for two separate trips back to the house. With the rear suspension now overloaded because of the extra weight on board, Rob slowly rode back towards his place. The girls under Rob's direction locked themselves in the house immediately on arrival. "Do not open the doors for anyone unless it is the police or me." He tried to ring Tim's home number but that went to the answering machine. Frustrated, he decided to not leave a message. Not thinking rationally he then rang his mother's house, feeling the urgency to tell somebody other than the police of what had happened.

Rob dialled his mother's number walking towards to driveway to look for any unusual cars along the cul-de-sac. The street was empty with not one car parked along the kerb what so ever, he paced up and down the bitumen still in shock that his brother was dead not exactly sure what to do from here, feeling useless. The police sirens could be heard in the background while he tried to make contact with Tim before being swamped with police officers, the call went to message bank on their home phone, he didn't bother leaving a reply and hung up.

Sue arrived at her son's a nervous wreck, finding it difficult to get a park amid all the police cars and detectives' unmarked vehicles. Rob had walked into the rainforest with a handful of senior officers to show them where his brothers body lay and the marking on both trees, leaving them to piece together their assumptions on what had transpired. Emerging into the clearing as he neared the house, Rob passed two officers with police dogs straining on their leads, pulling their handlers along as they barked and yelped excitedly with their noses to the ground making their way to the scene. Sue was now running towards her son, clutching him in a tight embrace, her body shaking from despair and loss. With her head leaning on his chest, Sue broke down further whispering, "it's them, I know it, God help us." Rob tried his best to hold himself together to console his mother replying in a soothing tone as he could muster at this point. "No mum, that's impossible, everyone from Hatchet River Station is dead."

Rob supported his mother as they slowly walked back towards the house, not wanting her to witness the bloody condition of Rick's remains, as he tried to recall what the strongest sedative he had inside the house. Police had called for an ambulance on their arrival. The medics checked Sue's rapid heart rate and suggested she stay in hospital overnight under heavy sedation.

Rob watched on as they led his mother to the ambulance giving her comfort as best they could under the circumstances. He returned inside to check on both girls who were now sitting on the three-seater lounge in the entertainment room still in shock. Rick's girlfriend looked up as he entered asking in a quiet voice, "could you please grab our clothes from the back lawn. We have been told some officers will be interviewing us very shortly. I feel uncomfortable wearing bikinis with all these people about, and where is the toilet, I feel sick!" Rob nodded, and pointing to his bedroom door said, "use my ensuite in the bedroom, it will be more private."

Bending down to pick up the girls discarded clothing from the backyard he froze, as a blood curdling female scream came from within the house. All police personnel in or near the house congregated inside before Rob had the chance to sprint back. The piercing hysterical screaming multiplied as he also recognised his girlfriend's voice. Rob pushed through the uniforms as he fought to get near his bedroom door. Both girls were physically being carried out by officers who were also going pale after their discovery inside. They struggled to contain the thrashing arms and legs as the girls lashed out vigorously against being restrained over what they had just witnessed. Rob shouldered open the door with force that was being shut seconds after the girls were carried away from his bedroom doorway, the officers inside surprised by the forced entry as they tried to contain Rob. This was all the time he needed to see his brother's bloody head still in the helmet lying on his pillow with crude large letters written in black marker pen across the cream coloured face of the helmet. YOU WILL BE NEXT! Rob went ballistic taking three officers to subdue and restrain him before escorting him out of the room. Resuming their job, the police began to work thoroughly over the extraordinary new crime scene.

M eg was part-way through preparing her dinner. From this point in time until she fell asleep every night was the most difficult as she constantly struggled with her loss, heartache and loneliness that had been unexpectedly cast upon her. With the kitchen darkening as night started to fall, Meg flicked on a few lights totally unaware her house was being watched from a distance. The phone rang with one of John's old mates on the end of the line. "Hi Meg, its Rex, sorry about the late call but I have just been snowed under with work. Listen, I have John's superannuation and life insurance policies that I need you to sign off on, I take it you now have the death certificate?" Meg, a bit taken back by the late blunt call replied, "Yes, I received it over a week ago. Can I come down to the office tomorrow during working hours to get this done?"

"Look Meg, I am booked on a flight at 5am in the morning for an insurance broker's conference in Brisbane. I have the paperwork in the car and can drop by to get it all finalised for you now if you like?" Meg pondered on this briefly before replying, "OK, see you soon then."

A dark blue two-door sports car pulls up on the opposite side of the road twenty minutes later. Rex looks into his rear vision mirror to check on his hair and adjust his tie before getting out of the vehicle, briefcase in hand. Meg hearing the car pull up flicks on the exterior house lights. Recognising him she walks down the driveway to open the gate for Rex. He opens his arms wide offering his condolences. "Sorry to hear about John, was out of town when the funeral was on." Meg broke out of the extra-long tight embrace, colouring slightly in the cheeks. "Will this take long?" Rex flashes a perfect set of teeth as he smiles, "well that's up to you Meg." Confused with his reply, she opens the door to let the insurance broker inside.

Meg was slightly uneasy about having a male in her house at this hour. She dismissed the feeling as a personal issue that she needed to deal with after the recent loss of her husband. Rex made himself at home as he opened the briefcase on the kitchen table sorting out paperwork. Meg speaks up. "I will get the death certificate and other relevant information out of the safe, I won't be long." Rex, seizing on the opportunity of being alone in the room, jumps out of his chair and silently closes all the timber blinds along the front windows of the house blocking all vision from outside. Meg reappears down the hallway, not paying any attention to the fact they had been shut. "This is what I have," she said as she handed the file over to Rex. He gives a wide smile and a wink that went unnoticed as Meg bent to turn off the oven. He started flicking through the file until finding what was needed. "Great stuff, would love a coffee."

Meg, apologising for her lack of hospitality, turned to fill the jug over the sink asking, "how do you like it?" Seconds later Meg felt the hot breath on her neck as Rex whispers into her ear while at the same time pressing the rising package between his legs hard up against her buttocks, "whichever position you like sweetheart, I'm easy. You must be so horny by now without anyone around to service your needs." Rex slid his hand around to fondle her breasts breathing heavily. Meg stiffened, horrified. Reaching for the knife drawer directly in front of her as she shrugged off his advances, she spun around with an extremely sharp butcher's knife in hand. "Get the fuck out of my house before I gut you like a fish." Rex backs away with hands in the air. "You crazy bitch, I was giving you a no-strings attached offer of a bit of meat." Meg now displaying her total disgust in this man that used to be her husband's friend, moves forward with the knife held inches away from his chest as he backs away. "If I wanted meat I would buy a steak," Meg retorted.

Rex collected his paperwork shoving it all roughly back in the case under knife point, Meg's resolve unwavering. "Now, like I said before get the fuck out of my house you disgusting piece of filth, and don't come back." Fuming at his advances being shut down, the insurance salesman muttered to himself on the way to the gate: "Easier pickings than you around town ya stupid bitch." He hit the key remote unlocking the sports car, throwing the briefcase carelessly towards the passenger's side seat as his heart rate started to settle down. Reaching for his mobile phone with his sexual needs heightened after the confrontation, Rex sat in the car and scrolled down for the most appealing female from memory on his list who lived nearby.

The observer, wearing tight black leather gloves, had scouted around the house trying to gain entry after the interior lights had been cut by the shades. Finding it locked tight, he positioned himself closer to the sports car. Not sure if he was wasting his time he waited patiently. Suddenly the outdoor lights get turned off leaving Rex fumbling in the dark with the gate latch, then enter his car. He quickly moved out of the dark shadows and thrust the crowbar with strength, driving it through the front windscreen with such force that it speared the occupant though the chest continuing straight into the plush leather seat impaling the man like a shish kebab. The killer watched his victim thrash and squirm for a brief period before he went limp. Walking back to the front door of the house he tried to turn the knob. Finding it locked, he turned and left the yard leaving the gates wide open. On the way past he kicked the sport cars door closed cutting off the interior light.

Early morning joggers alerted police to their grizzly find, alarmed that such violence had occurred in their quiet neighbourhood. A doorknock was conducted throughout the street. Meg awoke to a series of loud knocks on the front door – she hadn't had much sleep and was still upset over the attempted unprovoked sexual attack from Rex. Opening the timber blinds near the door she glanced through the window to see a pair of police officers standing on her front porch. "Good morning Miss, we are conducting a doorknock in the vicinity to see if anyone recognises this man," the officer produces Rex's driver's licence. Meg stunned, took time to answer aware that it would not take long for them to check Rex's phone for recent calls, and he had also shoved John's file hastily into his briefcase.

Having nothing to hide Meg answers, "yes, he was at my place earlier last night to finalise documents for my late husband's insurance policy. Is there something wrong?"

"Yes, I'm afraid there is Miss, he was found murdered in his car across the street from your place." "Really," Meg responded without emotion, craning her neck around the burly officer's shoulders to get a look at the crime scene that was now gathering a small crowd of spectators as other police ran crime scene tape at a distance around the vehicle. "You are going to have to accompany us down to the station for fingerprinting and questioning in relation to this matter."

"Of course officer, I will just grab my handbag and I will be with you."

Grace entered the police station in a hurry, walking past the interview rooms. She halted abruptly as she recognised Meg from the funeral the other day. Another officer was about to enter the room when Grace asked, "what is she in here for?"

"We had another murder overnight…nearly as bizarre as the headless rider from yesterday. The victim was speared with a crowbar while sitting in his car. This lady was the last to see him alive, that we know of." Grace nods, quickly processing the information. "Any connection between the two murders?"

"We basically only have brief preliminary reports on yesterday's grizzly finds, nothing has come back yet from the lab on fingerprints or DNA." The detective passed over the slim file to Grace who quickly flicked through the contents. "That surname is the same as the man who went missing at the Hatchet River with his car turning up in Western Australia." She looked at Meg. "And that lady's husband has just died after the Hatchet River massacre. I was at his funeral – connected, you bet they are. I would suggest you are looking at professional hits although completed in a very unorthodox manner. That woman in there probably doesn't realise it yet but her life and others who have any connection with Hatchet River could also be in extreme danger. If I was you, interview the brother again who reported yesterday's murder and good luck with the case." Impressed, the male detective ventured, "OK then, so tell me how an insurance broker is involved in all this?" Grace shrugged her shoulders. "Wrong place at the wrong time." She passed back the file and continued towards her own office as the Hatchet River case was moving quickly and it needed her undivided attention to keep abreast of matters. Grace also made a mental note to ring Danni later to warn her of the assumptions she had just made.

Tim and Mac had been doing extremely well processing the rich gold reef ore. Mac, still apprehensive about the road, had decided to process all the contents of his old steel chest into gold bars while they were at it, as they deliberated on a more secure spot to hide their bullion. It took the men till after lunchtime to finish crushing and smelting the raw product into ten-ounce gold bars accruing a handsome pile of gleaming gold. The miners had finally settled on stashing the bars in the bottom of the fresh water dam positioned on a small hill that gravity fed water down to the old hut. They loaded the finished product into a timber crate that Tim had secured to the rear rack of the quad for Mac to carry items to and from the mine site. The suspension sunk lower as both men counted the bars as they went. "Eighty-one old fella, is that what you got?" Beaming Mac replied, "yep, that's the number alright." They both stood in awe of their achievement. "I will run them up to the dam if you want to keep going down at the mine mate." Tim put his arm over Mac's shoulder. "You sure bud, I will walk up and give you a hand if you like." "No, it's OK I can handle it, I don't need my hand held for everything that needs doing around here…there is still a pile of rock down at the mine that needs to go through to clean up the first blast. If you make a start on that I will drop this off, and I still need to organise some tucker for dinner. How about I ride down and see how things are going around knock-off time." Tim, not wanting to show that his partner had suddenly become useless responded, "no worries bro, just asking if you wanted a hand that's all. I will see you down at the mine site then." Over the last couple of nights the old timer had also taken the time to amend his will to involve his new business partner, including the outright ownership of the mine as well as other mining tenements that he knew his daughter held no interest in. He felt the need to advise Tim before he next left for town.

Mac took off slowly with the heavy golden load towards the dam after mastering his new wheels in a short time. No longer walking anywhere, the quad was his new set of legs and gave him a fresh breath of life. His emphysema filled lungs had somewhat restricted his movement, slowly creeping up on him over many years, pulling him up continuously short of breath. This occurrence was becoming more apparent to him as the years passed. Even though he had given up smoking many years ago, the damage had already been done. Tim, realising Mac's condition, knew his old mate's number could only be years away which deeply saddened him, after losing so many friends close to him recently. His body was starting to break down with age, while a hard life of mining was now taking its toll but his mind remained sharp as a tack. The work load did not worry Tim in the least as he encouraged the old fella to take it easy while he did the work of two men. As a surprise, Mac had organised a feast of roast suckling pig on the spit to celebrate their first pouring of gold bars. He rode down to the mine site in the late afternoon after taking a nap that now seemed to be becoming more frequent in occurrence and longer in duration. Nugget happily bounded behind the quad in the dust after his owner.

Tim sat in the loader after dumping in a dusty load of dirt and rock and pulled the machine to a halt as he supervised the crusher slowly consuming the material. Suddenly, he could hear steel grating on steel. Lowering the bucket, he let the machine idle while he ran over to immediately shut down the crusher plant to avoid any further damage, before starting to define the problem. Touching each bearing housing with the back of his hand to feel for abnormal heat as he tried to locate which one had failed. Old Mac rode into sight on the quad as Tim identified the problem. "Mate, going to have to head to town to get some new bearings. Anyway, I need to catch up with Danni before I get divorced," he laughs out loud. Mac being a loner had to take his young partner's personal needs into account. "Of course mate, I understand. Why don't you take a couple of weeks' break, the gold will still be here when you get back. I'm feeling tired myself mate, you're a hard man to keep pace with." Tim laughed. "Righto mate, pass me them spanners and I will rip this bearing off, might even hit the track tonight to give Danni a surprise. That's if you haven't already cooked up something special for dinner?" Mac could see

Tim was biting at the bit to hit the track, and told his partner a white lie. "No mate, just leftovers, bet Danni would love to see you tonight."

Handing Tim the spanners, Mac continued. "I have changed my will to incorporate our deal, Tim, over the gold mine and its leases." Tim stopped pulling off the bearing, and turning to Mac said, "what's going on old fella? Come clean is there something you are not telling me about? Are you OK?"

Mac smiled. "I'm not hanging up my boots anytime soon mate, just letting you know where things are up to. This will be a very important document for you in the future. It will be put under one of the large slate rocks to the right-hand side of the dam in a sealed waterproof container, do not ever forget that son. I don't want anything of importance left in the hut anymore." Tim rested his hand on his old mate's shoulder, "and that's where it is going to stay for hopefully a bloody hell of a long time my friend." Finishing off the job at hand, Tim threw the buggered bearing into the back of his truck. "Right, well I'm going to hit the track bud, are you sure everything is OK?"

"Yeah mate, have fun in town." As an afterthought, Tim reached into the glove box before starting his vehicle. "Here mate, it's easy to use, just lift this and turn it on…when it beeps it's ready to go. My home number is programed in if you run into any problems."

Tim left along the rough track as darkness descended over the serenity of the North Queensland Outback, the anticipation of seeing Danni surpassed any tiredness he was feeling after a very productive month-long stint on the mine site. Things were finally starting to look up after a horrific period in his life. While driving into town he contemplated making it known to the police and media that he had survived for all this time lost in the bush. Sick of hiding from that fact, he reasoned it was only a matter of time travelling back and forth along the highway before he was pulled over for a random breath test or licence check. The Hatchet

River mob were all dead. His prospecting partner, now deceased, had copped the brunt of the blame and nobody other than the backpackers, who were sworn to secrecy after being saved along with Jack's sons, could prove any different. Tim was exhausted as he struggled to keep his eyes open finishing off the last ten kilometres to home.

Chapter 4

THE GLOVED STRANGER

The afternoon breeze stiffened along the ridge tops of the Hatchet River as the hunter lay in the long grass, downwind from a series of mud puddles where he had picked up on fresh wild pig spore and tracks earlier that morning. With water now a scarcity other than the main river system, the hunter was confident of the pigs' return. He grasped the butt of the rifle wearing a set of tight-fitting black gloves and sighted in the distance to the wallows, while also considering the increasing wind speed. He had to be sure of a successful kill as it was now the main source of food on the station after all the cattle had been mustered and sold off. He knew there was no way the muster would have cleaned out all the cattle, some of the wily and stubborn stock would have no doubt escaped into very inaccessible areas of the station's terrain. But to locate and try to carry out a kill on foot from these areas would be near on impossible, especially with the old light blue dual cab 4x4 he had acquired not long ago that wouldn't pull the skin off a rice pudding let alone climb many of the steep gullies and ranges that the station mainly consisted of.

On the wind, he could hear the mob returning, squealing and grunting while the young boars in the mob contested each other over the fertile young sows. He took aim as they came into sight picking out a nice sized young sow as his. Without any meat for days this was an important shot. Squeezing the trigger slowly the hunter missed the clean kill shot, having to quickly add another two shots leaving only the rear two hind legs without bullet damage. Grunting in displeasure over his marksmanship, the hunter walked down the boulder strewn slope. The rest of the mob had scattered after the first shot. Drawing a sharp hunting knife from his hip he made quick work of separating both rear hind quarters, carrying one over each shoulder as the late afternoon shadows spelt that darkness was soon to follow. He made his way back to what remained of the Hatchet River homestead.

A group of local pig hunters out of Cairns pull into the Hugo Servo to top up their tanks. With only one diesel pump, the three vehicles line up behind each other. Gus, now the appointed new manager, ambles out to engage in idle chatter. "Hi fellas, where are you off to?"

"Just up the road a bit," replies the young man leading the trip as he reaches for the bowser nozzle. Gus casts his eyes over the load in the back. "Looks like you're well set up, going out for a while are you?"

"Yeah maybe, all depends how many hogs are running around."

"Yeah right," answers Gus. "What station did you say you were heading to?" The young bloke hangs up the fuel hose replying, "I didn't." The servo owner knew when to back off, picking them as locals as they did not ask for directions.

Leaving the young men to top up their fuel tanks he eyed off the three teenage girls who had left the air-conditioned comfort of the 4x4s making their way towards the building's entrance to grab some last minute treats before continuing their outback adventure. It only now jogged his memory that he had not seen or heard from Scrubber or his cousin Price since sending out those other two young beauties some time ago. Ringing up their purchases he listened in as they talked between themselves enjoying the excitement of the unknown. It was their first trip out bush with their boyfriends who disappeared pig hunting at every opportunity. After being left in the dark on their destination outside by the young man Gus thought to himself, more than one way to skin a cat, and injected himself into the conversation. "You sound excited girls, any idea of where you are heading?" The girls laugh at a personal joke between themselves before one answered, "I don't know, a place called Hatchet River Station I think." Gus gave a partial smile. "Reckon you girls will have some fun out that way for sure," he said handing back their change. As the pig hunters left the service station Gus reached for the phone to inform Scrubber they had visitors heading their way, oblivious to any information they were all dead, the line disconnected.

The three vehicles pull up at the only gate to enter the property, the Hatchet River sign half hanging off the fence at an awkward angle covered in bullet holes. The teenage girl threw a glance towards her boyfriend as he went to open his car door. "You sure it's OK to camp in here?" "Yeah babe, it's all sweet, the place has been abandoned since all the murders…they have even stripped all the stock off the property to pay their legal team. Trust me babe, we won't have any dramas, the place is ours." His girlfriend went to respond when the driver of the 4x4 behind them sounded his horn impatiently with the third vehicle also chiming in. "Smartarse pricks," he voiced. Hopping out to open the gate, the young man turned to give both his mates the single finger under the illumination of their blinding spotlights. Once on their way again she returned to the conversation inquisitively asking, "what murders?" He chuckled reaching over to pat her leg. "Nothing to worry your pretty little head about. I even put in the Ouija board to spice up the trip a bit for you girls, reckon we should play it at the old homestead one night see if we can contact the spirits." He turned up the stereo gently shaking her shoulder. "Chill dude, it's going to be fun."

The group of hunters run across a couple of lone boars and one good sized mob of over twenty on their trek towards the homestead, putting them behind schedule to set up camp on the river bank before nightfall. Passing the only timber building left standing in the dark, he pointed at her window saying, "that's it over your side." She followed his index finger and wound the window down to get a better look. Staring into the darkness the young girl could see a soft illumination of light through one of the broken windows. Blinking a couple of times to reassure herself, she intently focused back on the window before her vision was obscured by passing trees as the vehicle continued into the night denying her of another opportunity to confirm that what she had seen was candle light. Not wanting to be the brunt of jokes, the teenager decided to not mention it to the others as she still had some doubt herself.

Tim parked the truck behind the house. Reaching for his house keys from the glove box, the dash clock read 2am. Yawning loudly he open the rear door and flicked on the hallway light to make his way to the bedroom. Danni jumped from the doorway into the hallway wearing a nightie and brandishing a baseball bat. Tim smiled. "You don't look very menacing to me," he said as he looked his wife up and down. Danni dropped the bat and rushed into her husband's arms. After a long passionate embrace she looked at him. "Why didn't you tell me you were coming home? You scared the living shit out of me, you must be buggered, what's the time?"

"Bit after two, sleep will come later, first things first," as Tim led her back into their bedroom.

Tim woke up late catching up on some much needed sleep. Rolling out of bed he picked up the baseball bat from where it fell last night placing it back in its home behind their bedroom door.

The smell of bacon and eggs wafted down the hallway as he could hear Danni rattling around in the kitchen drawers. He walked up behind her gently kissing her neck, Danni giggled and shrugged her shoulder in reaction while trying to serve up the eggs onto their plates. Pushing him to one side, she half protested, "at least let me get breakfast finished." Tim bent down and turned on the oven. Shoving both plates inside he led Danni back into the bedroom. Time got away from them both. Danni called in sick for work before they shared a shower followed by sitting down to eat crispy burnt bacon and hard fried eggs.

The phone rang, Danni looked at the caller ID. "It's Rob, I missed a call from him yesterday but he didn't leave a message." Tim got up from the table swallowing his last mouthful. "It will be for me. Hey bud, what's going on?" Tim fell silent as he listened to what Rob had to say. Danni had finished clearing the table and looked over at Tim puzzled as he still had not said a word while listening intently to what was being said. Reading her husband's facial expressions she knew the news was not good. He started to pace with phone in hand. "Hunted by who? No mate, that's impossible, they are all dead. You're sure that big prick, you know the one I mean, the brother of hers, was positively dead before you followed the other pair to the lab? Yeah right, so that was Rick's kill, you didn't see the body for yourself? That's a worry bro.

"His helmet said what? You're fucking kidding me. Bloody hell mate I don't know what to say, it has got me absolutely buggered, who else it could be? The bikies wouldn't have a clue who you are, I will come over now and we will try to work out what the fuck is going on. Ah righto, your place is still crawling with cops and you have another interview at the station later today. OK, well let's catch up tomorrow, it will give me more time to think things through. Give you a ring in the morning." Tim hung up the phone in silence, before saying in a quiet tone that Danni was barely able to hear, "When is all this going to ever end?" Her husband looked gutted, shaking his head in disbelief. She had never seen him look so defeated since the beginning of this spiralling nightmare that had entered their lives and appeared to have no end. "What's wrong?" asked Danni moving to his side. "Rick's dead, and some low-life scum has taken his head as a trophy placing it on Rob's bed as a statement."

Danni gasped, moving towards her man and hugging Tim as he continued. "Police dogs have been deployed for the second day now without any sign, there is no visible tracks and the prick had the gall to walk inside and place that on his bed while people were just outside." Tim started talking through things aloud, trying to figure out what the hell was going on. "It has all the signs of a professional hit, but by who? The hitman was croc tucker...actually they are all dead, the only survivors taken out of that place was John and the two backpacker girls." Danni stiffened, correcting Tim. "No, Grace told me there were four survivors in total...don't forget the man who was found in the middle of nowhere with both tendon's cut and left for dead."

It took Tim a brief second to comprehend what his wife had just said. "What do you mean a frigging fourth? Why didn't you tell me?"

"I thought I did pass that information on to you," Danni stammered. "I must have just got caught up in the excitement that your best mate was found alive at the time." Tim's mind started to race. "No babe, you didn't tell me that, is there anything else you have forgotten to mention to me?" Danni's mind flicked back to the numerous conversations she had held with the female detective over the past months. Blushing slightly she answered, "Well, I haven't seen you much since then, and when I do there is so much going on, but the detective gave me a blood soaked letter from you to John." Tim swore under his breath as that now directly implicated him in the Hatchet River bloodshed. "I have to go." Danni followed her husband out the back door to his 4x4 with tears in her eyes. "I'm sorry if I have done something wrong. Where are you going?" "This bloke is slipperier than a tadpole in a bucket of snot," he replied tersely.

Tim swung into a servo at Bankstown to top up both tanks

before heading out of town towards C's place. He knew exactly where it was situated on the coast after talking to John extensively at the mine site along with the time spent together catching up on all relevant matters driving into Hatchet River to set the well thought out trap. Driving the long periods of straight bitumen that ran for miles, Tim tried to work out what the hell he was going to do when he got there. He knew the location and that was about it.

C was still at home mending, he had waded through the pile of insurance papers regarding the written-off chopper while also searching the internet for another to purchase. He felt disabled being grounded, after using flight as his primary source of transport over the last fifteen years. The land line rang and Marko's number appeared. "Things have been quiet from your end, was expecting more updates by now on that list you gave the West Australian."

"Yeah C, haven't heard a word since he got the list and his phone has been turned off," Marko replied. "You paid him for that first job, didn't you?" C had completely forgotten the payment, having other major issues to contend with at that time. C lied, turning on his computer to transfer the funds as he spoke. "Yes, that's all taken care off." Marko breathed a sigh of relief. "Good. Looks like you will be coughing up some more very soon, just got confirmation from a mate that a headless body has been found and the name is on the list." C smiled. "It's about bloody time."

The conversation continued for a brief period on other business-related matters with the tide of lost customers now slowing to a standstill since the price drop to match their new competition. C started to flick through the paperwork laying it all over the desk trying to locate the sports betting accounts that Marko had passed on to him to pay the WA hitman. Eventually finding the bit of paper that he had hurriedly scribbled them down on some time ago, C proceeded to enter the amount he wanted to transfer pressing send. Getting up to make a coffee he returned to the computer to see if he had received any return emails from the various enquiries made regarding online aircraft brokers. "What the fuck, insufficient funds my arse," C bellowed as he repeated the procedure. Looking at the figures he could plainly see there was a very healthy balance. The same message flicked up on the screen. "Piece of fucking shit computers," he growled, reaching for the phone to contact his local bank branch to get this matter sorted out.

After being transferred numerous times then being put on hold he finally got to speak to the bank manager. By this time C's patience was running low. "Has your internet banking system shit itself? I am trying to complete a bloody simple money transfer but your poxy bank is rejecting the transfer." The bank manager was offended by the language and tone used. In a slight French accent the manager replied: "Listen sir, I suggest you calm down and speak to me in a more civilised manner or I will terminate this call." C's blood started to boil, and doing his best not to retaliate, shut his mouth. "Now that's better sir," the bank manager added with a touch of sarcasm. "Can you provide me with your bank account details so we can investigate what has happened."

C, barely able to contain his temper, spat out the password and the account. There was a pause before the manager replied clearing his throat. "Ah yes, I see the problem now," smiling smugly to himself. "As of yesterday, all your accounts have been frozen pending an investigation by the crime commission." C let rip. "I will give you a more civilised manner, you fat, short pimply turd, how about I come in there and beat you round the head with a fucking lump of timber you four-eyed fucking frog." The line went dead before C could finish his rant. Slamming the phone down C started to pace, twirling the ring on his finger. Snatching up the phone again he called Marko. "The pigs have just shut down all my goddam bank accounts, let the rest of the crew know to hold my share in cash at their end." "OK C, but what am I going to tell this WA bloke when he rings for another payment?"

"Fuck the hitman he will have to wait till I get to town…look I have half a million buried up the back that will easily take care of that."

Grace finally got the nod from her superiors that the intel they had accumulated over the period of time since C had returned home was enough evidence for a favourable conviction to put him and some of his crew away for a long time. The house had been extensively bugged before his return from hospital and all phone communications recorded. This had been put in place by her captain before his tragic death. They now had the evidence to prove it was cold-blooded murder of the officer, orchestrated by the man she was now rushing towards in her car to arrest personally. Grace had also just given the order to locate and arrest the corrupt cop – he was in her top three right behind C and the hitman. It left a dirty taste in her mouth…that one of their own, a man in his position with countless years in the force could participate in the murder of another police officer. A significant group of local police all wearing vests, were assembled as back up to a large tactical response team sent from Brisbane a week earlier. They were to be briefed and wait for the word to commence raids on the bikie headquarters along with numerous residential addresses. The hitman, she realised, would be far more elusive to locate as they had scant information to work with, not even a physical description or any ID. Today was the day Grace had been tirelessly working towards since taking over from her captain. She was sure he would have been proud.

Following the tedious long periods of straight road Tim knew the turn-off was only about five kilometres up the highway according to his GPS. He casually glanced in the rear vision mirror with not one vehicle passing him since leaving Bankstown. Tim looked a second time, quickly checking the speedo to make sure he was not over the speed limit. Well behind he could see red and blue flashing lights closing the distance between them fast. Four police vehicles and one unmarked police car went screaming past him like he was standing still. Tim breathed a sigh of relief as they started to pull away quickly. He started to press his own accelerator down trying to at least keep the last car in sight. Not too far up the road he could see the flashing lights cease as the last vehicle turned off the main highway. Tim looked down at the GPS lying on the seat – it read one kilometre to the turn-off on the right. He swore under his breath. Judging the distance, he knew they were going to beat him to the punch.

But the prospector still needed answers and wanted to finish this off once and for all – turning back now was not an option he would even remotely consider. Tim swung onto the dirt road coasting the truck along in a high gear with lower revs till the GPS told him he was 500m from his destination. Driving off the dirt track into the bush, he ran the remaining distance crouching behind a thick line of trees before it opened onto a large sprawling lawn. Two officers escorted a handcuffed C towards one of the patrol cars citing his rights. He struggled against being restrained while protesting profusely. "You got fuck all on me you dumb pricks." Both officers laugh as they roughly shove him into the backseat. "We know who the dumb prick is, your house and phone has been bugged for weeks." They handcuffed C to the steel mesh partitioning the front from the rear slamming the back door shut. The last comment quietened C down considerably, now in damage control. "Just shut the hell up and sit tight till we finish searching the premises."

With the prisoner now securely contained, the officers walked back towards the house to join the others conducting the search. The beachfront homestead and adjacent sheds made up a significant area to cover thoroughly which would take the squad considerable time to complete. Tim seized the moment, sprinting from the bush line to the patrol car containing C. Crouching out of view from the house, he opened the driver's door to spot the keys still in the ignition. Smiling, Tim slowly lifted his head to look back towards the house. The coast was clear as he jumped into the driver's seat. Turning to look at C, he stated, "Always wanted to drive one of these things." C just looked at Tim incredulously. "I fucking don't believe this!" Tim with a slight smirk of satisfaction from the reaction replied, "You will be believing it very soon." He slipped the cop car into gear leaving slowly and quietly until out of sight of the house, then gunned the vehicle down the dirt track at speed. Reaching the bitumen, Tim dropped the patrol car down two gears before dropping the clutch, burning rubber in a Northerly direction up the highway. "Got a bit more grunt under the bonnet than my old girl," he commented aloud.

C, with their last encounter still vivid in his mind, knew that what was about to transpire with this prospector was not going to be a healthy outcome for him. "I have got money, lots of it, you can have it all," C started. Tim turned to look at C. "And what figure would you put on Ray's, Sam's, my uncle's, my prospecting partner, and my young cousin Rick's life?" Tim's eyes hardened with the thought of all the people he had just mentioned who were very close to him and who were now dead. C went quiet thinking of another angle that might save his bacon. The prospector was well aware time was not on his side and it would not be long before there would be a swarm of cop cars hitting the highway in pursuit. He swerved to the side of the highway a kilometre up the road pulling on the handbrake hard as the car abruptly skidded to a halt.

With C handcuffed securely to the steel mesh and without the keys to release him Tim knew escape with his fugitive was futile considering the brief time frame he had to work with. He turned to face C. "I'm not letting you off so lightly this time around if you don't answer my questions. Who killed Rick, where are they, and how many of them are there?" C could not help himself. His anger rose instantly pointing to the side of his face. "So you call this getting off fucking lightly? Go root your boot." Tim slipped the small and still blunt pocket knife from his belt producing it high enough for his captor to view as he flicked out the tiny blade. C scoffed. "What the hell you going to do with that? Give me a shave." Tim now getting annoyed at the waste of precious time got out and opened the rear door. "No. If you don't tell me right now what I want to know I will pop that other eye out with this blade and stomp the fucking thing into the bitumen." C swallowed hard as the blade was held by a steady hand extremely close to his eye. "OK, OK, so we got a hitman in from the west…"

Grace walked down the steps with an armful of files and paper-work from the accused's office to process back at the station. She was hoping it contained further damming evidence to convict others involved in this elaborate crime syndicate. Grace dropped everything out of her arms when she realised the police vehicle including their prisoner was gone. "SHIT!" A tight knot formed in her stomach as she looked up the driveway, nothing, not even a slight trace of dust. Grace felt sick, running to her unmarked sedan she hit the horn, officers came running out from the house. "They couldn't have got too far he was only marched out here fifteen minutes ago. Who the hell left their keys in the car?" Grace started giving orders. "Two units go north the other two go south, call it in, we need back up. I want them to immediately set up road blocks in both directions, all side roads in between will need to be checked systematically."

They could both hear the sirens approaching fast. Tim listened to the chatter on the police radio organising the road blocks. C smiled like a rat with a gold tooth then broke into a laugh. "Fucking saved by the cops, who would of thought, what a turn-around of events." Having gained all the information he could in the short amount of time he had, the prospector flicked on the flashing lights that would easily be seen from the dirt turn off. "Killing you would be too easy, I want you to suffer. I happen to know a few people on the inside that will make your life hell. When your arse is getting a drilling every night of the week you will think of me." Tim's fist connected hard to C's jaw, his single eye rolled back in his head and he was out cold. The urge to continue further with his fists took all Tim's will power to break away from the situation. He could see the first cop car drifting sideways as it hit the highway at speed. With no time left he sprinted into the bush, evaporating out of sight.

The four police cars braked heavily around the stolen vehicle. With guns drawn they advance with caution, but apprehension soon turns to mystery as the officers realise the car has been abandoned. Grace re-holsters her weapon and opens the rear door to witness C slowly regaining consciousness. Searching both sides of the highway they come up with nothing. Once again Grace gives out orders, "Cancel them road blocks and call off the back-up, report that we have the prisoner back in our custody." A young officer questions the directions she had just given. "Shouldn't we keep the road blocks in place to apprehend the person who stole the vehicle?" Grace looks over at him. "Are you serious?" She walks towards her car to reach for the mic passing it in his direction. "OK, here you go… this should be interesting. What physical description and car make are you going to give the officers manning the road blocks of our car thief so he can be detained? He no longer has the police vehicle or the prisoner." Embarrassed, the young officer thought about it briefly before shrugging his shoulders as the other officers sniggered. "I will also have to put in a report on how our prisoner escaped in your vehicle with your keys," Grace added, before continuing. "All I can think of is this could be just a distraction to get us away from the house. We need to get back before anything goes missing and I want two men outside to stand guard over this bloke."

During the last couple of days Hugh had been doing some surveillance on the list Marko had given him. The West Australian had memorised the names and familiarised himself with their residential addresses including a series of drive-bys noting escape routes in case of the unexpected. One thing he had learnt over the years was to always have a back door if things went to shit. Placing them into a sequence of what order the marks would be completed, the hitman exited the hire vehicle to enter his third place of residence since arriving in the North. Another habit he strictly adhered to if staying for a period of time in one area, was not to reside in one place too long and always mix up the type of places he stayed. He entered the backpacker accommodation hostel and climbed the steps to the tiny single room. Occupants on both sides of him were up until the early hours every night, from partying to rooting with the odd argument thrown in. It gave the hitman little sound sleep, but was simply unavoidable through the paper-thin walls.

Once again Hugh checked his laptop on the balances of the sports betting accounts he had opened. No deposits had been made. The lanky killer had initially given his new customer some leeway because of the size of the contract but payment was now well and truly overdue. "This mob must think I wasn't serious about coming after them if I wasn't paid." He rang Marko's mobile phone for the second time today, the same automated message came through, out of service or switched off. He had mastered the art of patience, this was essential for one to stay successful in his profession, but patience on payment was a totally separate issue that the West Australian did not tolerate. "Right, change of plan by the looks," he stated aloud before lying down on the hard single bed. Flicking on the TV to take his mind off things, Hugh started to remove his boots. He paused as a name he had memorised on his list was announced on the afternoon bulletin of the local news. The hitman quickly reached for the TV remote to turn up the volume. The news reporter advised that the name had been released of a young man found headless and police were currently viewing the case as murder. "We will bring you further updates on this bizarre story as more information comes to hand," the reporter concluded. Hugh turned down the volume. "Might have to pay that cheeky Chinaman a visit after I sort out this Marko prick and his boss."

Marko, after receiving C's phone call about the bank accounts being frozen, broke into a nervous sweat – knowing the way the department worked, the cop was mystified how this valuable information could have eluded him. Quickly realising that the net was now tightening, and his phone could also be monitored, he had a gut feeling that deep shit would be heading his way soon. He wiped both clammy palms down the sides of his shirt at the thought of going to prison. Being cautious on not giving away any information that could be intercepted and acted on before his escape, Marko dialled his wife's mobile number speaking calmly. "Are you home? Good, stay put I will be there shortly."

Marko had been planning in detail an escape route just in case a hasty departure was ever needed, this was the main reason for his purchase of the motorhome, unbeknown to everybody including his wife. After months of reading reviews and magazines Marko knew exactly what size and model he wanted. He organised a deal allowing his brother to borrow the luxury penthouse on wheels one month out of the year to take his family on holidays provided he sign the ownership paperwork. They had both entered the RV showroom where, after haggling down the asking price, they purchased the expensive motorhome under his brother's name, including the registration, so nothing could be traced back to himself. It was always kept fully fuelled and packed other than a few personal items that would take no time to round up. All he needed to do now was remove the hundred and thirty thousand in cash that he had hidden in the shed and they would be on the road escaping this partnership with a clean set of heels before its imminent demise. Marko planned to drive all night putting what he considered a safe distance to his first scheduled stop. He had even gone to great lengths of selecting the more remote coastal locations for longer periods of occupancy without drawing attention to themselves…he was looking forward to the idea of escaping from the corruption and blending in with the grey nomads' laid-back lifestyle.

The pig hunting party had been out at the Hatchet River for two days now. The teenage hunters had been doing reasonably well on their tally, only keeping the jaws of the best boars as trophies. The girls had soaked up the sunshine taking advantage of their remote outback location. Stripping off, their skin had tanned noticeably from head to toe while their boyfriends were out burning gunpowder. Used to nightclubbing, computers, mobile phones and Facebook, the novelty of their outback experience started to wane considerably after their second day in camp, hundreds of kilometres away from the nearest internet service. Hitting the vodka cruisers from the Esky earlier than the previous day to prevent boredom from setting in, the girls were half smashed by the time they heard the 4x4 returning to camp. Bravado was increasing with every drink the girls took. It was not long before the subject of the Ouija board at the old homestead entered the conversation.

"Let's just do it tonight, it will be a spin out," slurs one as the alcohol started to take full effect in the heat as her girlfriend, virtually in the same state of intoxication, giggled. "Yeah bring it on, let's talk to the other side," she chimed in as she polished off the last of another cruiser. The teenage girl that thought she had seen candle light passing the old station homestead was initially reluctant to respond. Reaching for another drink she shook her head before saying: "Well, you two are on your own, I will stay here." They both looked at her laughing in unison. "What's wrong girlfriend? Toughen up, surely you are not scared of ghosts?" After considerable ribbing from her friends she confided in them on her boyfriend's comment on all the murders and the dull light she thought she had seen. They crack up laughing once again, bravado running high. "Well if that's the case we can say, 'just seen your light on so thought we would pop in to say g'day'." All three teenage girls break into a drunken giggle. Feeling less apprehensive with the idea now, as her friends continued to make light-hearted jokes at her expense, she finally buckles. "OK then, count me in."

The hunters returned just before dark, half intoxicated themselves from a full day of steady drinking. The two men standing in the back under the glaring sun for hours on end were heavily sunburnt with slight dehydration setting in from the lack of water. Armed with rifles they jumped off the back of the truck covered in dust, both with dry cracked lips caused from the hot wind while they travelled along the outback tracks. The girls embrace their boyfriends before declaring they want to go to the station homestead that night. The hunters smiled in the semi-darkness at the women's eagerness to participate. The young man who had organised and led this particular trip had inside knowledge of events after hearing the many stories from his uncle who happened to be in the first group of police officers on the cattle station after the massacre. In turn he passed on the stories to his mates which sowed the initial seed of thought for this location to be chosen to bring the girls out for their virgin bush trip mixed with some fun. He now spoke up. "No rush, let's get some more firewood together and sit down for a drink, I have a few stories to tell that will get you in the mood before we go up there."

The group huddled around their fire as the stories flowed. The young pig hunter could tell a good yarn using the right tone of voice to give maximum effect to his captive audience in the flickering light of the fire. A slight moon rose silently above the trees while the two girls now pissed as ticks subconsciously moved closer to their men for security. The girls' giggling had ceased some time earlier as they now tried to focus and listen intently. "From what my uncle told me the body of the station owner's brother was never located, they still have him on a nationwide most wanted list," the hunter said drawing the story to a close. His girlfriend shivered at the thought. "So he could still be out here then?" Standing, he swayed slightly putting an arm around his girl who jumped at the sudden contact. "Nah, the whole station was searched, he must have cut for it. Chill dude, let's see if we can contact any of the dead, it should be a fun night. I have my rifle in the front, don't stress kitten."

Collapsing their fold-up chairs he threw them into the back of his truck while addressing the rest of the group. "Right, let's repack one Esky to take up, we will all go in my rig, you pair can leave your rifles here before you start shooting at shadows, and bring your headlamps." The girls giggle as they fail numerous times to climb into the back of the truck in their intoxicated state. The young men roar in laughter at their girlfriends' antics, finally giving them a hand to scale the side of the vehicle before they hurt themselves in their drunken attempts. Waiting in the front patiently for the usual tap on the roof to signal that the rest were all safe in the back and ready to travel, the hunter steered the 4x4 back towards the Hatchet River Station homestead with spotlights beaming and the sound of music blaring from the cab of the vehicle.

The group bounced along the track towards the remains of the homestead surrounded in darkness. A slight fragrance wafted off the river gums, mixing with the bulldust that hung in the air as the wide tyres ploughed through numerous potholes along the way. Laughter from both genders in the back echoed out into the remote vastness of the outback. Driving along one of the river flats, the young hunter had time to quickly glance at his girlfriend who had been noticeably quiet since leaving camp, and turned down the music to speak. "You OK bub?" he asks placing his hand on her smooth suntanned thigh. She smiled thinly after not indulging in any more cruisers since the men had arrived back at camp, trying to straighten her thoughts. "Don't know about this one, we have done some crazy shit at times, but seriously I reckon someone is living there. What happens if the story you just told us has some truth to it, and what if the station owner's brother is still living here? What are you going to do then, is that gun of yours loaded?" The boyfriend laughed turning his concentration back to the track weaving around a few nasty washout gullies in the process. "It's all good kitten don't stress, just enjoy the night," he said, thumping his chest with a clenched fist. "Would I let anything happen to you?" Finally cracking a smile after being reassured by her man, she rubbed his leg warmly then slithered her hand up towards his crotch giving the area some extra attention before replying, "No, you better not."

The 4x4 passed through the open gate into the deserted inner yard of the homestead, parking close to the front steps and the crew in the back piled out. "Catch me honey," yells one of the girls as she randomly launches off the 4x4 tray into the dark towards the direction where her boyfriend's feet had just touched the ground. He staggered to one side in his drunken state after the impact, taken by surprise with his girlfriend's command as he tried to rectify his stance to brace for the impending forward momentum of his companion's intoxicated airborne body. They both hit the dirt heavily as his knees buckled like matchsticks under the extra weight. Oblivious of the initial bruising, including superficial grazes and cuts, they both laugh as they roll in the dust before finally coming to a stop. The teenage girl could feel something cold and sticky on her arm. "What the hell is that?" she uttered, demanding her boyfriend to turn on his head lamp.

The rest of the group had also left the safety of the truck, shedding some light from their own headlamps to view what this reckless loud drunken female was now carrying on about. The other pair of girls clutch at their boyfriends' shirts on seeing the pile of hundreds of tiny carcasses that were significantly fly blown, juvenile maggots crawling extensively over the decaying flesh. "Your shitting me, what type of animal is that?" questions one of the girls standing nearby. They all move in for closer inspection under the combined beam of their headlamps. The prone pair clamber to their feet, sobering quickly while turning to view what the girlfriend had just rolled into. Frantically she starts wiping the cool slime off her forearm asking in a shaky voice, "what is it?"

"Got to be bloody skinned toads or I will stand rooting," stated the trip leader. In the same breath, he asked the question, "what kind of animal would do that?" He turned to his mates for a reply. "Fuck knows, never seen anything like this before," declared another of the hunters. Spinning on his heel the leader immediately walked the short distance to the truck and grabbed his rifle.

"You girls get in the cab and lock it, we will go in and check the place out," he ordered as he fed a shell into the rifle's chamber.

The three young men climb the old timber steps in single file with the gun out in front, the floorboards creak under the weight as they try the front door. Unlocked, they enter nervously. Cobwebs hang from every corner, the beam of their lights cutting through the darkness. The old timber table had two candles, one on each end. Under closer scrutiny they did not look very old. The young men spread out now breathing a bit easier that nothing or nobody had confronted them since entering the building. "Come check this out," one of the men said after stepping into one of the rooms. They congregate at the doorway with the light concentrated on two legs of pork, heavily salted, suspended in the air from some eight-gauge wire strung at height from one side of the room to the other.

"Someone is living here that's for sure." Sweeping the light further around the room the young man with the rifle paused on some shelving containing numerous jars with a liquid of some description. Moving closer he asked, "what do you make of these?" As he picked one up for inspection he answered his own question. "They're the skins off them fucking toads out front. Could be some kind of ritual or voodoo shit going on in this joint, maybe even a cult." The young hunters pile out of the building, not sure exactly what they were dealing with, nervously looking behind them out of fear of anyone following. The girls unlock both doors of the 4x4 at the sight of their boyfriend's dark silhouettes running out of the old homestead. The interior light reveals their worried looks. "Some heavy shit is going down around here, let's get the fuck off this station," the trip leader says as he passes the rifle to his mate who had just heaved his girl into the back. "Here, there is a bullet in the breach, shoot anything that moves." The doors swing shut as the truck spins its tyres in the dust heading back to their camp at speed, disregarding the comfort of occupants in the back who were hanging on tight to the head rail as they bounced heavily over washouts without slowing down.

Their camp had a visitor while they were away. Picking up both the young men's rifles that were left behind with his tight fitting black gloves, he slung them over his shoulder then bent to retrieve a hessian sack, a third full with toads. He had spent the last two hours removing them from the steep sided holes that he had dug some time ago. Each trap contained a torch half buried in the bottom with the light facing up to attract the moths and other nocturnal insects, the toads could not resist the meal on offer as they jumped into the smooth sided holes unable to escape and ready for collection. He was fully aware of the visitors since their arrival days earlier, and now moved back into the darkness to observe proceedings as the vehicle approached.

The girls had been filled in on what the men found at the homestead on the way back. The instant the 4x4 came to a stop the group jumped out, each moving to their own part of the camp to frantically start loading the trucks. Fifteen minutes into breaking camp one of the young hunters yelled out, "Hey anyone seen my rifle?" His mate added, "Yeah, mine is friggin gone too. I put it on my swag sure as shit." The young men started to feel more uneasy about the whole situation by the minute. They quickly come to grips that the unknown intruder is now armed with their fire-power. Surrounded by darkness while not having a clue where their enemy was made the situation more intense. The chances of the stalker still watching them right at this moment with one of their own rifles was extremely high.

Now down to one firearm and knowing for a fact that someone had been in their camp in the time they had been away accelerated everybody's anxiousness to get going. "I will keep an eye out, but don't fuck around," declared the young leader squinting into the darkness with his loaded rifle at the ready. He was acutely aware that any of them would be an easy target from the shadows, him-self included. All three vehicles start up minutes later and waste no time leaving the area.

Giving it a couple of minutes the observer re-entered the area going through what they had left behind in the rush to leave the station. Finding four tins of baked beans that the girls had put out to include with steak for that night's dinner and an unopened packet of potato chips, he grunted in satisfaction. Opening the hessian sack of toads, he threw in the luxury food items before starting to make his way towards the homestead. Following along the crest of the river bank under minimal guidance from the moonlight he finally trudged past the broken gate into the yard an hour later. The fresh 4x4 tracks were visible near the front steps. He grunted once more before entering, dropping the sack beside the table. He lit the candles before entering another room to collect his last bottle of vodka and two of the jars containing the toxic skins. Returning to the table he produced the razor-sharp knife from his hip sheath then sat down to attend to the first. Holding it tight with his gloves by the leg, he poked the point of the knife at its head teasing the white poison out of the glands before scalping it, adding it to a jar and topping it up with some vodka then giving it a good shake.

Chapter 5

LOOK WHAT THE RAT DRAGGED IN

Tim worked his way through the bush parallel to the high-way. Staying out of sight from the road, he moved back in the direction of where he had just stolen the cop car. Hearing the four police vehicles pass him by at speed, Tim cut across the bitumen adjacent to the dirt turn-off with confidence, heading directly to his hidden truck. Not wanting to risk being detected, the pros-pector decided to check out how close the cops were now after their return to the property before starting his vehicle. Poking his head around a thick clump of bushes, he could clearly see the prisoner still sitting in the rear of the police vehicle that was now patrolled by two officer's standing guard, firearms at the ready. Backtracking to the 4x4, he decided to err on the side of caution. Releasing the electric winch from the bull bar, he pulled out the entire length of the cable before securing it to a tree. Tim silently moved the 4x4 from its original position, repeating the procedure over and over again. It was time consuming but undetectable.

Now three hundred metres closer to the road, he started the truck confident the sound would blend in with any traffic travelling along the highway. Tim idled quietly along the dirt till he hit the bitumen turn-off.

Grace phoned headquarters informing them that they were not too far away from winding up. "How did the rest of the operation go?" The officer coordinating all intel on the operation replied: "We got a few addresses with cooking paraphernalia and a small amount of ice on the premises but not in the commercial quantity we had hoped for. We are still processing the charges. They must have moved all the drugs before the sting. The senior officer who had been involved with the drug syndicate has not been located yet and the bikers' clubhouse raid ended up in a small riot with many officers receiving injuries, some significant. We have a cell full of them charged with assault. You will be briefed fully when you return." Grace swore under her breath with the revelation that the corrupt cop had not been arrested in the operation. She now felt the urgency to be back in town. After the countless hours of gathering information, planning and now executing these arrest warrants, Grace at this point did not feel a great sense of achievement. As far as she was concerned this was not over until that cop was behind bars charged with organising the murder of her captain, and of equal importance, they needed information out of him as to the whereabouts and description of the hitman. This was a vow she had made to herself after being given the position of leading this case and be buggered if she would settle for anything less.

Tim was now in a conundrum of what to do next. He had no location on the hitman but he did at least get the information out of the chopper pilot that there was a hit list with Meg, Danni and Rob on it. He pushed the accelerator towards the floor deciding the main priority now was to get the girls out of town and into a safe place until he tracked down this killer. The prospector realised he had no idea on who would be next on the list, or even work out how the hell he was going to lure this hitman to him. He concentrated more on the last thought as the kilometres passed by. Tim's mind was brought back to the present as the wail of a police siren behind him grew louder. He glanced in the rear-vison mirror for confirmation it was the same group of vehicles and not a highway pursuit car. He immediately took his foot off the accelerator while hitting the steering wheel with his open palm exclaiming in frustration, "For fuck sake, you wouldn't read about it!"

Tim reached for the hat beside him, tipping the brim low on his forehead to mask his face as best he could. The first car passed followed by another. Feeling the sweat run down the side of his neck he risked a glance as the third vehicle passed. C, staring out of the window locked stares, instantly recognising the hat and his adversary's partial features. Tim's face drained of colour as the prisoner started vigorously pointing at him. C began yelling at the young officers in the front seat, "That's him, that's the bloke you fuckin want!" The police slowed noticeably while still in the overtaking position. The young officer in the passenger side tried to get a good look at the driver. Tim swallowed hard, and gave a small wave towards the officer. Their prisoner continued his rant. "He stole your car you fuck heads, aren't you going to stop him?"

Both policeman started to anger at the prisoner's verbal assault on them. Grace driving in the last car, could clearly see both vehicles were side by side along the straight stretch of road that ran for kilometres. Annoyed, she grabbed the two-way mic. "What the hell is happening up there?" The young officer, already in enough trouble over leaving the keys in the ignition while also being embarrassed in front of others over his road block comments, sped up to get around the 4x4. He did not want to put himself into another humiliating position, especially over some murderer's say so. C went more berserk as the car he was in started to pull away. Turning his head to look out the rear window he could see Tim smiling with both hands briefly off the steering wheel, making a circle with two fingers then with the other hand thrusting his index finger in and out of the circle in a forward and backward movement. "You will be seeing a lot of this action where you're going, arsehole."

C spat on the rear window in reaction to the obvious intent of the hand signals. Turning back towards the front, he began to yell. "You have got to be fucking kidding me, are you just going to keep driving and let him get away? For fuck sake, give me strength. You pair are dumb as fucking dog shit, how the hell you mob caught me has got me totally fucked." The young officer, senior in rank, finally snapped over the rants and turned to his prisoner. "Shut the hell up or I will pull over and Taser you in the forehead." His partner looked at him. "Do you want me to get one of the other cars to pull the 4x4 over to check it out?" Still fired up he replied, "Nah, he's full of shit, wouldn't mind having five minutes alone with this prick." He reached for the radio handpiece responding, "Nothing boss, just having a few problems with the prisoner." The rest of the police vehicles whizzed by the 4x4 at speed without incident, it was not long before they all disappeared out of sight. Once again Tim pushed the throttle to the floor keeping a close eye on the temperature gauge. He decided the best course of action was to ring his wife at the first phone box he came across to let her know of the impending danger and for her to alert others on the list. Hopefully he was not too late.

Chang had started surveillance on the address supplied to him by his bosses from the prospector's rego plate. It was the same place he had followed the lone woman to from that funeral a week ago. Only a single female was evident from movement inside the house since he had arrived but the clothes line told him a different story as he watched Danni hang out male clothing earlier in the day. Sick of just sitting in his car watching and waiting for the male's return he decided to take things into his own hands to fast-track proceedings. Danni opened the rear door with an empty white plastic basket in hand to clear the clothes line. Chang seized the opportunity, locking the car door as he made his way towards the house. Danni had just re-entered the rear door holding the full basket and leaving the door ajar. Walking down the hallway, she emptied the basket onto her bed to tend to the chore before she went to bed. Turning to leave the room, Danni was met by a huge Asian man in the doorway. The method he always adhered to with females was hit first ask questions later. His open hand struck with lighting speed sending Danni sprawling over the bed. "Where is your man?"

Blood trickled from a split lip. "He is not here, I don't know where he is," Danni said as she wiped her mouth with the back of her hand. She could see her baseball bat lying up against the wall, but to get within reach she had to somehow get around this man who was built like a brick shithouse standing menacingly in her path. She frantically looked around the room searching for what was within reach to use as any sort of weapon, quickly weighing up what minimal options she had available. Danni now dismissed her original idea of even trying to reach the goal of grasping the bat to try to repel this mountain of a man, it would be a David and Goliath battle. Escape was her only option. The phone rang diverting Chang's attention for a brief second. Reefing her bedside lamp from the power point, she hurled it with force at his head while trying to make a run for the bedroom door. Chang easily ducked the flying projectile as it smashed harmlessly into the wall and grabbed Danni by the arm on her way past. Danni struggled trying to break out of his grip and with her free hand managed to claw his face with her long nails, drawing blood. The Asian did not flinch. He backhanded her harder this time while the phone rang for a second time. "Do not lie to me, tell me where he is." Danni was forced backwards by the blow landing partly on the bed before falling to the floor. Her ears were ringing and her vision was blurred as she replied in a sluggish voice, "He will find you and kill you for this."

Chang smiled before grabbing a handful of hair and throwing her back onto the bed like a rag doll. "Well, I better make it worth his while then." He flipped her onto her stomach, and with a knee in the middle of her back he reached for a clean pillow case lying on the bedspread that had just come off the clothes line. Pulling it taught he effectively gagged his victim then dragged her by the legs to the end of the bed. Danni tried to scream as she heard and felt her skirt being ripped off her body. The phone rang for a third time. Tim slammed down the receiver in the phone box out of frustration for the last time, before running back to the 4x4. Home was still a good 45 minutes away from his current position.

The assassin had learnt from an early age of living on the streets in China to take what he wanted with no regard to any laws – women were no different concerning this rule as he grew into a fertile teenager. With his full attention consumed by the victim he did not see or hear the man behind him pick up the baseball bat with his black leather gloves and viciously swing it at his head. The bat struck hard, splitting open the tight skin of his skull. The huge man dropped to one knee before the next blow knocked him out cold. Dropping the bat, he retreated to the doorway to recover a hessian sack and masking tape that he had brought with him. Inaudible muffles sounded from behind the tight mouth gag as the hessian sack was placed over the top end of Danni's torso before being taped around her waist. He kicked the unconscious assassin with the sole intent of causing serious injury to the rib cage, the sound of bones snapping on contact with his boot sounding through the house and moving the limp body significantly from its original position.

Lifting Danni's struggling light frame with ease from the bed, he threw her over his shoulder. On the way through the kitchen towards the rear door he grabbed her car keys lying on the table. Pressing the unlock button on the remote as they neared her vehicle, he reached into his jeans pocket to reveal an old silver coin and flicked it onto the driver's seat in clear view. Satisfied, he dropped the car keys on the seat before carrying Danni to the faded blue dual cab and lay her down on the rear seat. He turned onto the highway back towards Hatchet River Station.

Chang groaned as he rolled onto his side, taking a sharp deep breath when the broken ribs contacted the carpet. The assassin's vision started to clear as he felt the nasty gash on the rear of his skull. Gritting his teeth in discomfort, he rose to his feet and saw the female was no longer on the bed. Chang went through the house room by room with no sign of the woman or the person who had come to her aid. Re-entering the main bedroom he tied a pillow case tight around his head to stem the flow of blood. Swearing in his native language the assassin started to ponder on how he was still alive. The more thought he put into it the more confused he became. The Chinaman knew he would have been unconscious for at least fifteen minutes, he ruled out the Aussie hitman and the female's husband or he would certainly be dead. Even his victim would have had enough time to get a knife and slit his throat, yet he was left alive. Turning onto the highway, Chang backtracked towards Cairns still trying to piece the puzzle together as he passed Tim speeding in the opposite direction.

Tim swerved off the highway twenty minutes later. Parking at the rear of the house, his heart jumped a beat as the first thing he noticed was the back door had been left wide open. Bounding from his truck he sprinted into the house with Mac's Glock in hand. Going through the house room by room he found it was empty. Breathing heavily, Tim returned to their bedroom where it was clearly evident there had been a struggle. The smashed lamp, blood streaks on their bedspread, Danni's torn skirt on the floor and a significant pool of blood that had started to soak into the carpet at the end of the bed. He knew what had happened was definitely not long ago going off the blood that was still yet to congeal on the carpet's surface. The prospector's mind raced. He felt a wave of nausea with the thought his girl was hurt in any way. Leaning on the door frame briefly Tim got himself together and he started searching for a sign of what had transpired. Anger built to a level he had never experienced before, with every nerve in his body ready to explode.

The search inside the house was fruitless other than an odd blood splatter leading towards the rear steps. In despair and desperation he walked out of the house as the sun started to set. Scouring the yard for any blood spots or clues as to his wife's whereabouts was made more difficult as the sunlight started to diminish. Tim glanced up at Danni's car after circumnavigating the outside of the house. He ran towards the driver's door, reaching for the handle. It opened. Tim knew for a fact that Danni religiously locked her car after a spate of petty thefts last year, mainly coins taken from the console. Tim immediately spotted her keys and a strange coin lying on the driver's seat. Picking it up for closer inspection he started to shake. This coin struck home hard. His mind churned. "This can't be," he murmured quietly to himself, looking at the old silver half-dollar coin again and again.

Tim raced into the house, skidding on the smooth lino floor covering as he reached for the phone and rang Meg's number. Halfway through cooking her dinner she sighed at being interrupted and turned down the heat to answer the call, hoping it would be brief and not spoil her meal.

"Have you seen or heard from Danni today?" Tim asked anxiously. "No," replied Meg slightly confused. "Should I have?" Tim dismissed the question asking another. "What about John?" Becoming more bewildered by this line of questioning she replied, "Tim have you been on the rum or something?"

"Well, I just found a 1789 Spanish silver half-dollar on the seat of her car and she is missing, our bedroom also has blood in it along with her torn skirt on the floor," he replies. Meg gasped, knowing the coin he just described very well as her husband's good luck charm. "You sure Tim?" "Yep, bet my life on it. I have a pretty good idea of where Danni might be, but I could sure use some help with this one if you are up to it. I can be in town in about thirty minutes to pick you up."

"Count me in," Meg replied with resolve. "Anything I need to bring?" Tim thought briefly before saying, "Come to think of it, if you have some mosquito coils and few boxes of matches with a couple of rubber bands I have a bloke on the way that I need to pay a visit to."

Tim arrives not long after his estimated arrival time. Meg shuts the front door and walks down the driveway carrying what was requested over the phone. He bounds out of the driver's side to open her door giving her a brief hug. "Thanks Meg, this means a lot. Have you got a mobile phone on you?" "Yes Tim, why?" "I ran out of time to ring somebody, can I borrow it?" The 4x4 takes off into the darkness as they head towards Hugo as the prospector rings Rob. "Mate, can't talk long, just get out of your place quick, there is another hitman in town and I know for a fact that you are on his hit list, and so was Rick."

Meg looks over at the bushie she had known now for many years. "What the hell have you got yourself into now Tim?"

"Nothing new, this is still the same mob that shot John...oh, I forgot to tell ya that you and Danni are on the list as well...actually come to think of it most people I know are on the list."

"So what are the mozzie coils and other stuff for?" Tim glanced at the clock on the dash announcing, "We have three hours before the Hugo servo shuts." He continues by telling Meg the conversation he and John had with the backpackers after they had saved them from the shed at the station that day, and the girls' own admission on how they were enticed in that direction to seek work.

"I wonder how many other women this low life animal has sent out there over the years? Meg asks. "Talking about low life's, had one in my house the other night, an old mate of John's called Rex." This was the first time Tim and Meg had actually caught up for any length of time. With Meg now hardened by nearly every turn her life had taken since that devastating day, she was now mentally strong enough to listen to what her husband's prospecting partner had to tell about their last few days together. Tim left nothing out as the kilometres rolled by.

The conversation finally came around to the coin. Tim pulled it out of his pocket, passing it to Meg. She flicked on the interior light to inspect it more thoroughly. "Yep, that's his for sure. How it ended up in Danni's car is a mystery in itself, and as much as I would like your hunch to be right I cannot see how it is even remotely possible." Tim thought hard on what his passenger said before replying. "I have no doubt that it was purposely left there for me to find as some sort of clue." Meg agreed. "After what you have told me just now, could it be possible that someone has taken it out of his pocket between when you left him in the front of the truck and the police turning up at the station to fly John out? To me this would be a lot easier to explain don't you think."

"Yes, it could be possible, but they were all dead," Tim conceded.

"But how could you be positive that one did not survive even if injured, or somebody could have just been in hiding the whole time," Meg replied. Tim's thoughts quickly went to the phone call he had recently with Rob over the station owner's brother, The Beast, as the backpackers called him. Doubt started to form in his mind as Rob could not visually confirm the kill other than what his brother had told him over the radio. "You could be right Meg, regardless, all fingers point back to Hatchet River Station, reckon we will find out soon enough."

Not being far from Hugo by this time, Tim changed the topic and started to give instructions. "Break down that mozzie coil into half-inch-long sections, empty a box of matches and bind them all in the rubber band nice and tight with the coil in the middle. It took Tim several attempts of instructing Meg as to exactly what he wanted, glancing over as they passed the 60km speed sign before entering town. They drove down the deserted main street, their destination on the other side of town.

Gus looked up at the clock hanging on the wall from his small office desk behind the counter of the Hugo servo. It read five minutes to nine. The manager had not had a single customer in the last hour and a half. Reaching for the padlocks to lock the fuel bowsers for the night he made his way outside. Padlocking both petrol nozzles he moved towards the diesel bowser. A set of headlights appeared, brightening his surroundings. Gus turned swearing under his breath as the vehicle swung into the servo. Annoyed, he yelled out as the 4x4 came to a stop with the motor still idling. "We are closed, you will have to come back in the morning." Tim, not even bothering to answer, flicked on the powerful spotlights mounted on the bull bar. Quietly opening the door, he walked around the back of the truck. The bright light blinded Gus as he put a hand to his eyebrows to try to make out what the hell was going on. With no reply and no apparent movement from the vehicle the servo owner became apprehensive, with robbery springing to mind. "Turn it off," yelled Gus signalling with a side to side hand motion across his throat into the bright light.

Undetected by the distraction of the spotlights, Tim appeared silently by his side grabbing Gus roughly by the shirt collar while giving him a good shake. "Been meaning to catch up with you for a while." Meg leant over to switch off the spotlights and turn the ignition, cutting the motor before getting out herself. "What the fuck is this all about? What do you want?" questioned Gus as he glanced back towards the vehicle to see a female walking towards him. "How many girls have you sent out to Hatchet River Station?" asked Tim, shoving him heavily up against the diesel bowser. A gush of air was forced from the servo manager's mouth as his back slammed hard into the digital fuel display. Gasping for a breath he shook his head. "I don't know what you are talking about." Tim reached for the unlocked diesel nozzle with his spare hand while the other still held Gus tightly pinned. Squeezing the trigger, fuel flowed all over the ground. "Wrong answer," stated the prospector.

Gus tried to struggle free from this man's vice-like grip as he held the fuel hose over his head soaking him in diesel. "OK ten, maybe twelve," he spluttered as fuel entered his nostrils and mouth. "Was just helping them all out with a bit of work so they could get some cash to keep travelling, what's wrong with that?" Tim leant forward so their faces were inches apart. "That's not what the English backpackers told me who I found chained in a shed out there not long ago. Arse wipes like you don't deserve to breathe." He turned to Meg. "The keys for those other bowsers are on the ground over there, can you unlock the nearest one and go grab the little things you made on the way out." Meg did as instructed while Tim looped the fuel hose around the owner's throat, pulling it tight as he walked backwards, holding the tension till he reached the unlocked bowser "pull that nozzle out will ya." Tim replaced the nozzle with the one in his hand and snapped the padlock closed. Gus fought to free himself but the tension was too tight around his neck, he realised that there was no means of escape. Meg walked up to the man, and looking him in the eye, swung a well-aimed kick at his groin. "This is for all the women you have crushed you germ."

Gus groaned loudly as the foot impacted solidly with his scrotum. Knees buckling, he started to dry reach. The fuel line held him suspended in an upright position tightening further around his throat cutting his oxygen supply. Gus fought to get both legs back under himself. "This won't stand up in court, nobody can prove I was aware or had any part in what happened out there." Tim passed Meg the lighter. "You can do the honours, my hands are covered in fuel." Turning his attention back to Gus, "Sadly you are probably right, that's why you are never going to see the inside of a court room." Meg lit the slow burning fuse of the mosquito coil placing them on the fuel soaked ground. The 4x4 was twenty minutes out of Hugo heading for Hatchet River Station when the sky lit up behind them erupting into a huge ball of flame.

Chang arrived at the Bullion Buyers store and parked his car down the side alley. He clutched at his broken ribs while stiffly getting out to enter the shop through a rear door. The store had been shut for hours now but the assassin knew Fu stayed back till after 9pm every night. Embarrassed about his own condition while still not exactly sure of how to explain this to his boss, Chang twisted the key to let himself in. Fu, initially not looking up from the mountain of paperwork that he was busily stacking into neat bundles, said, "So did you find the prospector?" His employee looked at the ground in shame as he answered "No boss." Fu with his back still to him waved his hand in the air cutting him short.

"No matter, we know where it is now after checking today on current gold leases in that remote area with the Mines Department and which was shown to us on a map the other day. There is not another lease for a hundred kilometres so it has to be them."

He spun the swivel office chair around smiling smugly until his eyes rested on his main henchman with four deep flesh wounds on one cheek and a blood-soaked cloth covering his head. "What the hell happened to you?" Chang briefly thought about how the truth would sound…getting caught with his pants down literally and then copping a serious flogging from behind. He dismissed that idea. "I was trying to get answers out of the prospector's wife when someone knocked me out with a baseball bat. When I woke up they were both gone." Fu reached for the phone speaking in rapid Chinese while scribbling onto a blank piece of paper before hanging up. "Go to this address, she will clean and stitch you up. We have a chopper booked to visit this gold mine. Make sure you are at the airport at 6am hanger 5 tomorrow morning." Chang nodded, relived that his boss did not ask any further questions over his failed attempt on gaining a location, knowing full well that would not be the same reaction if they did not already have some new information to work with.

Mac was embracing the solitude of his camp while Tim was in town. His young partner's pace of doing things was always so hectic that the old miner could not keep up. His mind was in the right place but physically it was tiring. Savouring the break, he looked down at Nugget playing doggo beside his chair. "Good to see the young bloke have a break and enjoy some time with his girl and the comforts of town…I remember them days myself. Stuff this getting old shit, it creeps up on ya while you're too busy, hey boy. No matter, we still have a lot to do before I pack it in, what do you reckon mate?" Mac rubbed his hand up and down Nugget's spine with his ears pricking up at every word spoken while his tail wagged with the extra affection. Adding some timber from the wood pile, old Mac placed the billy on the fresh flames to boil.

As the old miner moved around the old tin hut throughout the morning he could hear the distant noise of a chopper working around the area for a fair while. He thought it strange though not alarming, dismissing it at this stage as noise in the tranquillity of the bush carried for long distances. Mac put it down to what he thought was a grid pattern search, like they were looking for something in particular. After another thirty minutes the chopper flew straight overhead at speed before banking sharply to circle the tin shack. Mac looked up as the chopper prepared to land. He started to feel apprehensive and walked into his shack for the shotgun to greet the intruders. The dust started to settle as the blades wound down, and out stepped three Chinese men. Two with immaculate suits, the other a huge man heavily bandaged around his head with fresh facial wounds on one cheek that were still weeping fluid.

"Well, look what the rat dragged in," voiced Mac dryly to his dog as he walked forward pointing the shotgun squarely at the group of Asians. "What can I do for you men? Are you lost or something?" Fu flashed Mac a generous smile. "No quite the opposite, we have found exactly what we were looking for. You have been a very hard man to find." The old bushie cocked the shotgun. "Is that right, state your business then get the hell of my leases." Mac swung the barrel towards Chang as he went to move forward. Fu quickly spoke in Chinese stopping the assassin in his tracks. "So, this is the best you could find for muscle?" Looking the injured Chinaman up and down, he added, "He must like the taste of lead because I'm telling ya if he takes another step forward he will be getting a mouthful of it." The third Asian, who until now had stood motionless, glanced over his shoulder at the pilot watching from a distance beside the chopper. Fu noted his partner's gesture nodding slightly in agreement before continuing. "We are not here to cause any problems, actually we are here to make you a very wealthy man, we want to buy your mine."

Wong turned his back on the gun-wielding old bushie and walked back towards the chopper. Mac stood his ground. "The place is not for sale at any price, now piss off, looks like your mate is smart enough to already work that out. Is he the only one with some brains out of you lot?" Fu had to keep his temper in check while the assassin started to snarl closing both hands into tight fists. Reaching the pilot who was out of earshot from the whole conversation, the Chinese businessman spoke in clear English. "It could take some time to resolve this matter," he said looking down at his expensive wrist watch. "Can you come back at say four o'clock?" The pilot shrugged his shoulders. "He looks pretty hostile to me, are you sure that's what you want? It will also cost you blokes about another fifteen hundred for fuel and flight time." Wong nodded. "Yes we will be fine, the caretaker is a bit upset that we have just recently purchased the mine and we will be asking him to move on. The extra expense is not a problem for us." They both looked back towards the tin shack where Mac still had the others held at gun point, the chopper pilot climbed back into the cab of his machine. "No worries, see you at four then."

Fu continued to press the old miner. "Now come on, that's somewhat unreasonable…I haven't even given you a price yet. What about your young offsider, does he get a say? Is he down at the machinery that we flew over earlier?" The chopper fired to life with its blades starting to rotate. "Where the fuck does he think he's going?" yelled Mac as the chopper lifted off the ground. Since the old timer had first pulled the gun on them Chang had been slowly working his way towards the large wood pile to his left. In his mind he had selected a solid branch that was lying on top for the job and this distraction with the chopper was all that was needed. With lighting speed and precision, the thick lump of timber sailed through the air smashing into old Mac's temple. The impact made him momentarily drop a hand off the shotgun with both barrels pointing harmlessly at the ground. Before he could regain a grip of the gun Chang was on him kicking the firearm completely out of his grasp. With the safety button off both barrels discharged when hitting the ground, spraying lead harmlessly into the bush. Fu walked over as his hitman reefed Mac to his feet with one hand while backhanding him across the face with the other. "That's enough, we need him alive. Take him to the tin shed then go find that young prospector."

D anni was still gagged with the top end of her body tightly taped pinning her arms by her side in the used potato sack that still reeked of the rotten vegetable. They had been bouncing over a rough road for what seemed like hours. The vehicle stopped twice along the way, she was sure one was a gate as she could make out the rattle of a chain and a squeak as it opened and shut. The other stop took longer and she could hear something getting removed from the rear tray of the vehicle. Her mind was in turmoil. She had no idea who had saved her and for what reason but contemplated what lay ahead was not going to be her freedom. Danni started to quietly sob, she felt dirty and completely vulnerable. "Where are you Tim?" she mumbled through her gag. The vehicle came to a stop for a third time, the engine was turned off and the driver's door slammed shut. Moments later she was lifted off the seat with relative ease and carried up what she guessed were timber stairs and placed up against a wall on the floor. The distinct sound of footsteps moved around the room before a knife cleanly cut down the side of her restraints in one motion removing the sack and her pillow case gag. Her captor turned his back and walked towards a table and lit a candle before sitting down. In the poor light of the room Danni squinted as her eyes adjusted to the flickering candle light, trying to make out the facial features of this man. "Why are you doing this to me?"

Tim and Meg had been making good time along the dirt road. They had fallen silent the closer they got to the station, each deep in their own thoughts. Opening the gate, Tim got back in the 4x4 to move through. "There're fresh footprints, can only be a couple of hours old there is not even any night dew over them." Meg nodded in the darkness with anticipation starting to run high. "I will shut the gate." Re-entering the cab, he passed her the Glock handgun. "You could need this tonight. The mag holds eighteen bullets, all you have to do is point and squeeze the trigger, the gun will automatically reload so just keep pulling the trigger if you miss." "What about you?" asked Meg. "I still have my trusty old blunt pocket knife," he reassured her patting the tiny little leather pouch on his belt. "Anyway, they will be expecting me to have a weapon but maybe not you, well here's hoping that's the case...just don't shoot Danni or me. We are only a couple of kilometres away now." Tim swore when he heard the tyres gush out air and the steering suddenly become heavy, hitting the brakes, "Pass me my headlamp from the glovebox." The prospector walked back along the track and before long found the set of road spikes that had punctured three tyres. Slinging them well into the bush he walked back to the passenger side of his 4x4. "We only have two spares so we are on foot from here on in. Someone must be expecting our company."

The male captor got up without answering her question and walked into another room in the house returning with what looked like numerous glass jars containing some sort of fluid. Taking off his black leather gloves he unscrewed what looked like an empty jar and walked towards her holding one of the candles up high enough to expose his face to the light. "You are slow to work this one out Danni, hopefully your husband is more switched on. What's his name again? That's right, Tim the fucker that deserted his partner, leaving me for dead in the outback to fry my brains like scrambled eggs." Danni gasped as tears rolled down her face. "John, that's not what happened." John knelt in front of her, cable tying both wrists together with wild crazy eyes that chilled her to the bone. "That's exactly what happened, were you there? Now a few friends of mine have been waiting for you to turn up." He reached into the jar placing them on her neck and upper chest. "Five paralysis ticks should do the trick." Danni tried to squirm as she felt them start crawling over her skin before sinking into her soft flesh. "You are just the bait, sit tight…it might take him a day or so to find my good luck coin. Reckon he should work it out pretty quickly from there."

John had rehearsed this many times over in between periods of continuous high pitch ringing in his head and ears that sometimes led to a ruthless and violent dark side of his personality that had recently risen to the surface. Since initially lying in the hospital bed to now at the homestead table every night alone skinning toads, John savoured what he was going to say at this moment to the people who had bitterly let him down. "I cut a deal with the captain after he somehow worked out that I was able to communicate while in hospital, maybe he just guessed, very smart man that one. He offered an attractive package to give me a new identity and to relocate Meg and I until our house and other assets were sold provided I spilt my guts about what happened at Hatchet River Station and everything I knew about the drug king involved. I thought fuck it, what did I have to lose, my so-called mates had left me for dead along with a life sentence in jail hanging over my head if I survived. So I agreed, but he got killed halfway through upholding his side of the deal, that was the day he lent me the old blue dual cab from his hobby farm. Luckily, the mortician at the hospital had already been instructed to replace me with an old homeless drunk who had been run over a month earlier and had not been claimed. My funeral had already been organised…not many people attended to pay their respects did they Danni? Three mates were noticeably missing."

Danni gasped. "It might have looked that way but there were reasons behind it, the funeral was full of police officers." Her mind rewound back to that day. "So you were at your own funeral, and Meg knew you were alive?" John's expression changed from anger to one of hurt. "That fucking bitch had her legs spread nearly before my coffin got lowered into the ground, so much for mourning, I didn't see that one coming either." She shook her head in disbelief. "No way, that's not true, Meg loves you, we all do, it's your mind playing tricks on you."

He dropped to one knee in pain, hitting the side of his skull with an open palm as the loud ringing began and his eyes glazed over. "Playing tricks, are you kidding me? Think what you like, I saw what was going on when I snuck home to tell her about the deal with the cop. They even closed the blinds. Another so called fucking mate, didn't think a pen pushing insurance salesmen would be her type, just goes to show how wrong I have been with a few things lately." John cocked his head to one side breaking into a sinister smirk. "You could say when he left my house I pinned him down over fucking my wife. Enough talk for now, let's wait for your knight in shining armour to arrive and see what he has to say." John walked over to place his rifle on the table and stab the sharp hunting knife into the timber table before swirling the sediment at the bottom of one of the jars containing the skins, vodka and toxic toad poison, mixing it into a milky green substance. John took a significant swig, it always dulled the noises in his head.

Tim and Meg walked side by side, following the dirt road in the outback silence by the light of his headlamp. After what he roughly estimated was a kilometre the prospector slowed to a standstill, flicking off the light. "Just wait for your eyes to adjust. Been thinking more about when we get there, reckon it would be a good idea if I enter first unarmed and you wait out the front in the dark until we find out who we are dealing with. They will not be expecting you at all, so we should keep that up our sleeve to start off with." Meg nodded in the darkness. "OK, but when will I know you want me in there if things don't work out?" Tim put a hand on her shoulder. "Look Meg, the only reason I brought you was on a hunch, the last thing I want is to bring any harm your way. If things go to shit and I can see no other option I will yell for you."

Within twenty minutes they could pick up a very dull light inside the neglected old timber homestead.

He felt a tingle of adrenaline course through his body, unsure who or what he was about to encounter inside. Positioning Meg just to one side of the steps on the veranda, he whispers close to her ear, "Stay put unless I say." Resting his full weight on the first step instantly gave away his position as a loud creak broke the eerie silence, swearing softly to himself. John snapped out of his half comatose state immediately reaching for his rifle. "Looks like we have a visitor already Danni, no flies on your man he is quick off the mark." Tim recognised the voice, regretting that his initial presumptions were right. Meg, who gasped in the darkness after hearing his voice, tucked the Glock in the back of her jeans breaking Tim's stern instructions as she moved towards the open door with an overwhelming anxiety to greet her husband. Tim caught her movement in the dark and quickly back-pedalled grabbing Meg by the shoulders giving her a good shake. "I said stay put," he whispered urgently. John's voice sounded agitated. "Come on old friend, I know you are out there, let's not stuff around, Danni is in here waiting, so is the jury." Meg shivered at the sudden harsh change in her husband's voice, this was not the way she remembered her man.

Mac was roughly dragged to a chair inside the hut, bleeding from the temple and the mouth. Chang swiftly produced a thick grey tape wrapping it tightly around the rattled old timer. The Chinese businessmen sat down making themselves at home as the assassin walked outside heading towards the mine site in search of the other prospector. Fu produced a document from his top pocket placing it on the table as he addressed the old miner. "Do you know what this is?" Mac shrugged his shoulders answering dryly, "Leftover shit paper from wiping your boyfriends arse this morning." Wong stood, his face bright red with the insult raising his fist to punch their captive. Fu broke into a laugh revealing his gold teeth before instructing his partner, "Sit down before you get blood all over that new suit. Now old man what this document contains is a transfer of title for mining leases that I picked up at the Mines Department the other day." He got up and slid it in front of Mac then reached down to his left hand that was pinned by his side with the tape, sharply bending back one finger till it snapped, then another. The old miner yelled in pain. Still smiling Fu continued, "I hope you don't sign with your left hand because that could make things more awkward for you. Now I have already taken the liberty of nominating a price for our purchase, ten thousand sounds more than a reasonable sum to me." Mac replied while wincing in pain, "You pricks are getting jack shit out of me." Ignoring Mac's outburst, he turned to Wong. "Look through the place for any bank account details so we can deposit the money via internet as proof of payment while I persuade my old friend here to sign a bill of sale and the transfer papers."

Chang, who was lathered in sweat from walking in the heat of the day, returned from the mine site, disappointed at not being able to locate and confront this mysterious prospector in physical combat. He could hear the yells of pain while still a good distance away from the tin hut. Both his bosses were also dripping in sweat from the stifling heat of the small tin shack. Re-entering the shade, he looked over at the old man who had now passed out with his head on the table. "There is nobody down that way, no vehicles…did he sign?" Fu answered irritably as sweat continued to trickle into his eyes, "Only after breaking five fingers, ten toes and both ankles… even then I had to break a leg on the dog, that was the turning point. He certainly has a soft spot for the animal. That line of thinking just amazes me, bloody old fool who puts a dog's life ahead of their own? The wretched thing also bit me before taking off."

Wong wiped the sweat off his forehead with the already soaked handkerchief, turning his wrist when completing the task to look at his watch. "That chopper will be back for us in thirty-five minutes. There is not a speck of gold hidden in this shack." Fu nodded checking his own watch. Two deep canine puncture wounds oozed blood just below his wrist. "You found a bank statement, that along with the old man's signatures is the most important thing at this stage, we can move forward from here. The gold will not be far away, probably buried for safe keeping like our forefathers did on the goldfields."

Chang, I want you to stay here, see what you can get out of the old man on the gold stash before disposing of him." Fu grabbed a fistful of old Mac's hair lifting his head off the table while still unconscious. "Pleasure doing business with you, what's the Aussie slang again? Tough as nails, you stupid old fool." Fu laughed slamming old Mac's face back onto the wooden table with a sickening thud. "I assume his partner must be in transit if not at his residential address as you reported. It is imperative that this man is killed, there is enough tinned food for you here and Wong found a satellite phone in his search of the place so call us when the task is finished and not before. Both their bodies must never be found. Oh, and kill the dog as well if it comes back," he concluded as he once again glanced at his hand wound left as a reminder. The assassin bowed. "It will be done Fu."

The chopper landed in the exact same spot. Powering down and jumping out of his machine, the pilot looked towards the two men melting in the suits they wore as they approach him. "So where is the other bloke?" Fu answered above the noise of the blades still rotating. "He is staying on as our new caretaker." "Yeah righto, how did the old bloke with the shotgun take that news?" Fu gave the pilot a smirk. "It was hard for him to comprehend initially but eventually he conceded, loading up his belongings and leaving by vehicle a few hours ago." The chopper pilot looked slightly confused. "I didn't see any vehicle when I did a circuit of the area before landing this morning, anyway we will be cutting it fine to get back home before dark, jump in and buckle up."

Chapter 6

FIRE SHOW

Grace arrived back in Cairns, now leading the procession of police vehicles as they come to a stop outside the station. The rest of the command centre that had worked on this case stood and applauded as she led C towards the cells. She now felt some triumph for her team that had worked tirelessly by her side to get to this point, but the job was far from finished. As she slammed the cell door C pressed his face up to the bars and hissed, "You are dead". Grace acknowledged the threat replying, "So are you. The only time you will ever be outside of a prison again is in a coffin." C laughed out loud as Grace walked back down the corridor. "We will see about that," he yelled.

Grace shook off the idle threat as she approached centre command. "Right, everyone back to work, I want the hitman and this Marko located before the night is out. Give me the cop's residential address so I can check it out myself. Have we had any follow up raids on other premises since the initial sting?" The group of officers sitting behind their computers shook their heads in frustration. The coordinator who Grace had talked to numerous times earlier in the day spoke up. "We still have a few left to interview, but so far there is nothing significant to report other than a small amount of personal drugs found and drug utensils seized at some of the addresses. Basically, they are all keeping their mouths shut and feeding us crap." She took this in while grabbing her car keys. "Put an alert on the airport and other transport hubs and I want a photo of this cop on tonight's news channel, he can't have gotten too far." Leaving the building her mind was on overload trying to keep one step ahead of her fugitive.

Driving away from headquarters Grace had a nagging feeling there was something that had been overlooked. The harder she tried to concentrate on what it was the more elusive it became. Pulling into the driveway of Marko's residence she noticed a car parked further down beside the house. Drawing her firearm, Grace made her way cautiously along the side towards the vehicle. It was unlocked and the keys were in the ignition.

Opening the unlocked rear door of the house, she made her way straight to the main bedroom, checking the bedside draws. They were empty of underclothing on both sides other than a few folded handkerchiefs and some random unmatched socks. Moving from the bedroom into the bathroom the first thing Grace looked for were toothbrushes, checking the vanity thoroughly. They were also missing. At this point what had evaded her thoughts hit like a lightning bolt. She straightened, sprinting back to the police vehicle, swinging open the door as she reached for the two-way mic.

"Base this is Grace, those bikers in the cells that still need to be processed must be kept totally separated from the bloke I brought in today, it is imperative they do not collaborate. Move them into interview rooms and get them finalised as a priority, they are all in the same drug syndicate. I also want a check done if another vehicle is registered under the cop or his wife's name and run a search for any known relatives in the area who might be able to shed some light on their whereabouts."

Officers race to the main steel gate that opened into the row of cells. "That's enough talk in there, move away from each other now," yelled the first officer. C was sitting beside the steel bars in conversation with the three remaining bikies in the adjoining cell. "Half a million in cash you say to break you out of prison." He looked at his other comrades for confirmation. They all nod in unison. The heavily tattooed bikie who had taken charge of the conversation looked towards the approaching cops with little regard rubbing a hand through his goatee in thought. "So you are the hidden head honcho of our operation? I know we have a few prison officers on the tit and some members on the inside, it could still take a bit of setting up though." C nodded, "Just get it done." The conversation was cut short as the police officers unlocked the cell removing the three bikies. C smirked in satisfaction, talking under his breath as they were led away for questioning. "I will be seeing you sooner than you think cop bitch."

Tim walked through the doorway. "I was hoping I was wrong about this," he started as he gave a sideways glance at Danni to his right, sitting on the floor with her hands zip tied. "You OK?" She nodded without speaking as tears streamed down her cheeks, devastated that these two strong willed men who were closer than any two brothers she had ever met were about to clash with a high probability of inflicting serious injury on each other if not death. He took a second look in the dim light that was cast by the candles on the table. "You are hurt." Tim moved forward in anger ready to attack. John stood reaching for the trigger of the rifle that was still lying on the table with the barrel pointing directly at Danni. "I would woo up if I were you bud," John nodded towards the table, stopping Tim in his tracks. "Now let's get a few things straight here before you try anything stupid again that could cost both of you your lives. I hold all the aces here and you will do as instructed. The superficial wounds your wife received were not from me, let's just say at this point I saved her from a very awkward position at your place. Isn't that right Danni? She nodded flushing crimson in the dark as she started to feel nauseated by the ticks that were now firmly embedded, injecting their poison into her flesh. Tim looked between the pair of them confused over the last statement. "What do you want from us?"

Meg could hear the conversation clearly from her position but could not see the interior of the room. She worked her way around the railing of the old timber patio in the darkness by touch then spreading her weight on all fours to prevent any noise from the ageing timber floorboards. She slowly crawled towards a broken window with her heart beating that fast it felt like it was going to explode out of her chest. Rising first to her haunches then into a stooped position Meg peered into the room, content to at least have a visual perception of what was happening inside. John took another swig from the jar, "What do I want, you ask…I want some bush redemption that's what I want," spat John. "An eye for an eye and some good old fashion fucking respect. You wouldn't be carrying Mac's Glock by any chance partner? How about you take off that shirt, move closer into the light and turn around real slow."

Tim did as instructed. "Look John your sick mate, nobody's hurt yet, we can turn this around now and get you back to town for the best help we can find." He laughed in a bizarre and erratic way they had never witnessed before. "You have no idea about hurt, yep sick is a rosy way of putting it, how about the truth for a change, my brain is melted and fucked because you left me to die in the outback, that sounds like the guts of the story to me." It was Tim's turn to colour in the cheeks. "Mate, I thought you were dead from the gunshot wounds, remember the agreement that we made with Rick and Rob beforehand that if one or more of us were killed they would have to be left behind. So we put you in the front of that old truck to keep the dingoes and crows away till the cops arrived, there is no way I would have left you if I thought you were alive." John nodded, "Yeah, I remember that conversation. Do I look fucking dead to you?

"Rick, I saved him from death's door that day when I shot Scrubber. What did I get for that? I will tell you, two fucking bullet holes from that bitch is what I got. Then, yet again I'm left abandoned, this time in hospital facing the looming threat of being the scapegoat for every dead body on this station from the cops and looking straight down the barrel of life in prison if I did survive. Then, ditched a third time by the three of you, none of you even had the decency to turn up to my funeral. You tell me where is the fucking respect? Were you too busy stuffing your pockets full of gold with your new partner to even bother? Fuck the old partner, he's getting buried, that's the way I see it." Tim shook his head. "No bro, that's not how it was, we were told to stay away because of the high cop presence that would be turning up."

"So, let me get this straight, you three were worried about being recognised by a couple of cops, what a load of horseshit, nobody knew who was out there." Tim was about to bring up the letter found on John that implicated him, but figured nothing he could say would sway his ex-partner's psychotic mood. John threw two thick cable ties to the end of the table. "Pass these to your wife she can put them on for you, make sure they are nice and tight Danni. Then we will have a drink, it's taken a lot of time and effort for this special brew to be ready for this moment. Look I've even labelled it Tim's toad tonic."

"You have thought of everything," replied Tim sarcastically. As Danni tightened the ties around his wrists he caught a glimpse of movement from a broken window, shaking his head in astonishment. "Bloody women," he muttered.

With both now restrained John forced them to drink the toxic brew, they both gagged and choked on the rank green fluid. It was not long before the toxins entered their bloodstream and Tim's vision started to blur and his mind began to hallucinate. The prospector started to stagger slightly from side to side now seeing three of his captor. John took another slurp out of his own jar, laughing. "Works for me, how you feeling partner?" Tim slurred the words, "What about Meg?"

"That whore, she was the last straw for me after you mob… caught her fucking my insurance broker." He started that same hideous laugh slamming his jar back on the table. "Who would have thought? Anyway, he got what he deserved as did Rick. Meg gasped not believing the words that were coming out of her husband's mouth, her open hand hit the side of the building after the revelation he had killed two people in cold blood. She tried to compose herself, fighting off the urge to walk in and set the record straight over what happened on that night with Rex as it was obviously the pivotal point that had sent him down this road of death, hate and redemption. John spun to the window with the sound of the light tap on the wall, his senses extremely alert despite the large amount of potion he had consumed which seemed to react favourably with his brain condition. "Did you bring a visitor?"

The prospector tried to focus, the room was spinning slightly, he looked over at his wife who was also under its effects. "No, I came alone", he slurred stepping three paces closer to the table "So you killed Rick, what the hell for?" John turned his attention back from the window with the question, releasing the grip on the rifle to take another swig out of his jar. "It's all about respect, if someone saved my life there is no way I would leave them in the middle of nowhere for crows to feed off and shit on. Then my funeral, that was just total disrespect by the fucking three of you. I just put him where he would have been if I had not saved his life that day and fucked mine at the same time."

This was his first chance at striking since entering the building. Tim knew it was now or never, before losing further control of his speed and coordination. Timing was essential as he waited for his captor to tip his head back while swallowing the last mouthfuls of thick sediment left in the jar. The prospector lashed out kicking the end of the table with all his force. The two candles toppled off the table plunging the room into darkness as the table skidded along the timber floor slamming into John's lower thigh sending him backwards in the dark. He heard the rifle fall to the floor. Swearing under his breath, John frantically felt blindly for the weapon while hearing his partner's movement towards Danni's position. Tim touched his wife's shoulder in the darkness, and lifting her into his arms he staggered with the dead weight towards the door. Swinging the rifle as a club purely on the sound of movement it collected the escapee flush on the jaw sending them both crashing heavily to the floor.

Tim awoke as the sun rose to the buzzing sensation of a swarm of flies trying to absorb moisture from his mouth and lips. His head was throbbing hard as he twisted his neck vigorously left and right while exhaling heavily to rid himself of the pest. Bound tightly into the driver's side of the old 4x4 that they had all left John in that day of the massacre, he was now sure of his ex-partner's intent. Turning to his left Danni was secured into the passenger seat, still unconscious as each paralysis tick's abdomen had grown significantly larger overnight. Meg had hidden under the timber homestead in the dust as fleas crawled all over her from the removed station guardians. After her husband had indicated the probability of a third party near the window last night, she instantly dived off the veranda crawling on her hands and knees for cover. It did not take her long from the crude gaps in the timber flooring to work out things had not gone favourably after hearing a loud thud followed by two body's being dragged separately along the floor, down the steps and into the darkness.

Meg was unsure as to what to do from here. She was mentally torn – should she shoot the man she fell in love with many years ago and still loved to this day? Or should she just confront him face to face and hope he would listen to reason about what happened with Rex that night? Maybe he was already too far gone from this deranged vengeance stemming from the brain injury that had already accounted for the deaths of two men. Would she be next to encounter this impulsive rage if she confronted him? All these thoughts and doubts ran through her mind. Regardless, both her friends were in serious trouble and needed her help to escape. Meg made this her priority no matter what uncertain consequences might unfold. The floorboards creaked from within the homestead. She reached for the Glock loading a bullet into the chamber with a steady hand, focusing on the steps.

The footsteps come to a stop not far from where she lay under the veranda, a steady stream of urine splattered upon the bulldust disappearing instantly into the moisture-deprived ground in front of Meg. She held her position silently while her husband was stationary. Realising she would be easily visible from the distance of the old 4x4 hiding under the homestead if he looked or returned this way, Meg decided to change location. Crawling commando-style on her stomach, she lay at the corner of the building to watch him walk to the old truck. He placed a photo of Rick's bloody helmet lying on the bed on the seat for his ex-partner to view. "You are a dead man," Tim vowed, struggling at the tight restraints. John gave an insane laugh hitting the side of his head. "I already am thanks to you. Quit yapping on about piss-weak threats. Maybe I should put two bullets in you right now so you know exactly what I went through when the three of you fucked off."

Tim conceded the fact in his current position. "What about Danni? What has she done to deserve this?" John stopped in his tracks digesting the question as he started to walk away. "Yeah, you know what, you are right on that count, she is the only one that has caused me no hurt. Giving a sly smirk he turned and walked to the passenger side of the old 4x4. Drawing the razor-sharp knife from his hip John cut her binds. "There you go Danni you're free to leave." There was no movement of limbs just a light flutter of her eyelids. "Hey Tim, your wife is in no hurry to leave by the looks, it might have something to do with these little blokes." He pulled down the neckline of her tee-shirt to display the five fat paralysis ticks, teasing his ex-prospecting partner to react. "Now I don't want to state the obvious here, but I suggest you get them off her without delay." Tim went berserk rocking the entire vehicle as he tried to break free. "You gutless fuck, cut me free and we will sort this out like men." John broke into a heinous laugh. "Are you serious bud? Now why would I do something stupid like that? Yes, it would be an interesting contest to say the least, but why would I take that chance? Sometimes the tough guy doesn't get the chance to win. You sit tight and enjoy the sunshine, I'll be back before dark, I need some fresh meat seeing I have visitors to entertain tonight. That maggot crusted salted pork is starting to taste a bit rank."

John walked back towards the homestead to retrieve his rifle. Meg withdrew from the corner of the building unable to bring herself to squeeze the trigger. She highly doubted if the situation had escalated further over at the vehicle or that her bullet would have even gone close to the mark over that distance having never shot a firearm in her life. The majority of the conversation did travel on the breeze in her direction so she was able to gain the gist that he was leaving soon. She breathed a sigh of relief as he slammed the door of the old 4x4 blue dual cab and slowly drove down one of the countless faint dirt tracks. Meg ran into the homestead reaching for the first pot that entered her view, filling it with water. Half the contents spilled out onto the ground as she ran back towards the busted up old 4x4.

She tipped the small pot directly into Tim's mouth. "Have you still got your lighter?" He tried to nod in a fashion while hungrily gulping down the water. Taking a breath, he instructed, "Get them ticks off Meg. Forget about the lighter, the heat will send more poisons into her body if the tick gets stressed, just pull them out as close to the head as you can. My pocket knife is still on my belt, cut me free when you get them off her." Meg moved around to the opposite side of the vehicle taking care to get rid of the parasites off her chest, each cavity bled freely as they were removed. Happy with the result, she bent to the ground lifting the remaining portion of water towards her friend's mouth, two gun shots nearly simultaneously sounded as one punched two neat holes into the bottom of the pot spraying a mist of water all over both the women. Tim initially ducked out of instinct before seeking out any movement through the bush to give away the shooter's position. He knew it was not his ex-partner because he could still hear the vehicle travelling faintly in the distance. Startled, Meg drew the handgun in reaction firing two shots wildly towards the area that she thought the shots had originated from.

"What the bloody hell did you do that for? Now they know we have a firearm, and a complete waste of two bullets. Come around and cut me free and give me that goddamn gun." Meg went to reply in her defence as she moved around the back of the vehicle towards Tim. Another shot sounded out with dust spurting up just in front of her feet. She froze on the spot. A strong male voice yelled out from a distance beside three large ghost gums. "Drop the gun and move away from the truck or the next bullet goes between your eyes." Tim swore in frustration at still being bound to the seat. It was not hard for the prospector to work out who this man was and for what purpose he happened to be out in this isolated country. Resigned to the fact that he did not have long to live, he looked over helplessly towards his wife as she slowly started to come around. Feeling inadequate at this point after everything he had been through lately, he found he could not even protect the one person he loved most. With a burning desire just to reach out and touch her that was denied by his restraints, the only words he could muster were "I'm sorry." Tim tried to think of any other slim option left open to save the girls. None instantly came to mind.

The lanky West Australian moved from behind the large tree trunks after Meg had complied with his order, walking towards the three of them with the rifle still trained on the group. "Well, what do we have here? Been watching the place since following you in last night. From what I could work out looks like it's been a friendly little gathering of mates." He walked over picking up the Glock while not taking his eyes off them. Ejecting the magazine from the butt of the handpiece he shoved it into one of his shirt pockets then also removed the live shell from the chamber throwing the now useless handgun under the old 4x4.

Hugh, with the rifle still pointed in their direction, inspected how well the prospector was bound before he relaxed, laying the rifle up against the side of the vehicle. He then reached for his pouch of tobacco directing the conversation at Meg. "Girls shouldn't play with guns, now get into the back of the truck.

"Keeping an eye on your place in town has paid off big time for me by the looks. I was only waiting for the slippery Chinaman to turn up and settle a score with him and look who pulls in, the elusive prospector that everybody wants dead." Hugh lit the smoke taking a deep drag before turning his head towards the male captive. "Loved the fire show last night at the servo. You're a feisty little bugger aren't ya?" Tim nodded. "Only when I need to be." Hugh continued. "Nearly lost your trail a few times last night but once I found your truck it was easy following your footprints in the dust on the road. Now back to business, so you're the one that killed my brother?"

He shrugged, "I have no idea who your brother is." The hitman smiled. "If you met him and lived you would never forget about it in a hurry, he was hired by the same man that brought me over here to kill you all." The prospector looked over for the first time to engage eye contact with the hired gunman. The calm attitude he displayed screamed of professionalism, confidence and death. "Oh, that bloke, now I know who you are talking about, you just missed the man responsible, he drove that way in an old blue dual cab." Hugh laughed loudly. "Firstly, I don't miss anything," he said as he glanced at his watch. "He has got exactly one minute and eight seconds before he becomes instant ash. Secondly, I think you are a funny fella. You wouldn't be putting me on a bum steer to save your own hide by any chance?" Meg broke into a sob now wishing she had tried to confront John earlier, maybe things could have turned out different. Seconds later the sound of an explosion rolled through the surrounding hills of the station like thunder.

Danni groaned holding her head then croaked dryly, "Where am I?" Hugh moved to the back of the truck cracking the lid of a water flask on his hip passing it to Meg. "Stop blubbering and go give your friend a drink, I might be a killer but I am not an animal like that other bloke." The hitman spotted Rick's decapitated photo that had fallen to the floor. "You are fucking kidding me, so it wasn't the Chinaman who stole my mark, where did this come from?" Tim responded having no reason not to be upfront from here on in, it was do or die. "From the bloke you just blew up, and your brother was actually eaten by a large salt water croc in the river not too far from here. Let's do a deal, I have some gold bars stashed out bush, how much is he paying you per head?" The hitman smiled. "Now you have got my undivided attention, gold you say. And I probably could swallow the croc story, my brother was never one to be comfortable in the outback on his own or competent in its natural dangers. Now let's get back onto the subject of this gold and possibly cutting a deal for your life and that of the girls. Each mark was worth sixty grand and another five grand if I produced a head, so let's work out that amount times four. Two hundred and sixty grand, you got enough gold to cover that? And don't bullshit me otherwise your death will be long and slow for all of you, starting with your wife."

Tim had his doubts about the hitman's claims that John, his ex-prospecting partner, was a confirmed kill. He knew better than anybody that the bloke was a hard case and placed it as a 50 per cent chance either way. Regardless of that outcome he could see a faint light at the end of the tunnel, hoping this man was on the level. In hindsight he was now thankful Meg had not made it around to his side of the 4x4 in time to cut him free otherwise he would now be dead, that he was certain of. "Yeah, there is enough there to cover that, what about your deal with that other prick?" Hugh now lent over the old vehicle bonnet like he was about to settle in for a yarn. "Well, that dog has not paid me for taking out that cop yet, so all deals are off. He is next on my list along with his cop mate." The prospector smiled for the first time in ages not willing to pass on the information that he was now in jail. Hugh continued. "You would not believe how many targets offer far more than the standard hit price if they get the chance to talk once they are staring death in the face. It is never good for repeat business if you burn the first accepted offer – a deal is a deal in my mind and I stick to my word. But in this case, where I don't get paid for my services well, let's just say I am open to other offers and the ones that have fucked me over will pay with their life."

"I like your way of thinking, now we are cooking with gas," Tim replied. "So tell me how you work out four marks when there is only three of us?" Hugh chuckled. "You are one of a kind prospector. That would have to be the first time I have ever been hit up for a discount when a person is in your predicament, you have balls I will give you that. The fourth is for the old mate just over the hill whose ashes won't need to be spread by anyone, and from what I observed since getting here I did you lot a favour on that count. Explosives have become very expensive to buy on the black market since them radical towel heads started blowing everything up – call it increased running expenses."

He looked towards the hills as smoke started to increase, billowing high into the sky while the slight breeze began to intensify in strength, swinging erratically. "You will have to carry your woman out of here, she is in no condition, and the other one can walk. By the looks that explosion has created a bushfire and could be right up our clacker if that wind stays in this direction long enough." He cut Tim's restraints. "Don't try and fuck with me prospector or it will be the last thing you do." Believing every word, he rubbed circulation back into his hands nodding. "We are on the same page. What type of car are you driving? I need a tyre to get my truck out of this hell hole just in case that fire does come through. I make my living out of that vehicle and we will need two sets of wheels when we leave the mine site after getting your payment in the gold." Hugh took in the request reaching for the rifle. "Let's get moving I will think on it." Meg dropped to one knee and quickly reached for the empty Glock under the old 4x4 while the hitman was engrossed in cutting Tim free still in mid discussion. Shoving the pistol in the waist line of her jeans under her shirt she stood erect. Aware of the West Australian's stare, she stated "I had to have a pee."

"Right, the lot of you let's get moving now."

Old Mac finally came around, a dried pool of blood lay on the table where Fu had viciously smashed his nose into the table breaking it instantly before he left the mine site. His left eye was swollen closed with the other still slightly trickling blood from a nasty wide gash above the eyebrow partially cutting his vision as he tried to focus. The old miner lifted a broken finger to try to apply pressure to stem the flow of blood, agonising silently from the touch. Sucking up the excruciating torture he refused to show any weakness or discomfort. "My partner will kill you for this." Chang shook his head in frustration at the resilience and hard-arse attitude of this elderly captive. He had never seen such fortitude displayed at this age. He side kicked the corrugated wall in anger, dislodging two sheets that both fell to the ground outside with a clatter as they hit an outcrop of rocks, leaving a gaping hole in the wall. Resisting the urge to kill the old man before he got the answers he needed he replied, "This is the second time I have heard that. Let's see how good your partner really is if he turns up. Now, where is the gold hidden?" Mac tried to laugh out of his busted lips. "He will eat you for breakfast boy, don't worry he will turn up." Completely ignoring the gold stash question, Mac started looking for his companion within the confines of the hut. "What have you done with my dog?"

John had picked up some fresh prints of what he figured to be a small mob of pigs that had followed the dirt track he was driving on for a considerable distance before they veered off into a cattle pad that ran along the edge of a small dry creek. Bringing the dual cab to a stop he flicked off the ignition and reached for his rifle. John was thirty metres upstream, tracking the direction of his prey when the vehicle exploded. The initial concussive force propelled him to the dirt as the ground around him shook. He found it difficult to breathe from the heat of the blast instantly followed by the vacuum of oxygen, covering his head with both hands as hot shards of melted glass and metal fell back to earth starting small spot fires randomly around him in the long, brown tinder-dry grass.

He struggled to both feet searching in the long grass for where his rifle had landed with his brain and ears ringing louder than usual. Shaking his head to try to subdue the noise he could see that some of the small flames were starting to take hold quickly. By the time he located the rifle, smoke was thick in the air and the noise from the crackle of the grass burning overtook the ringing in his ears. Coughing constantly from inhaling the smoke, John knew he needed to get out of there fast or he would be caught in the bushfire and incinerated, with no significant water body left to shelter in for as far as the eye could see.

The only safe option he realised left open, was the main Hatchet River that was still many hours walk away and that was provided the fire didn't travel faster than himself and cut him off before he made it to the safety of the wide-open sandy areas in the river system itself. His eyes started to water from the smoke as he broke into a steady gait down the dry creek bed towards the river. After covering a few kilometres alternating between a jog then walking over the more difficult terrain to reduce the chances of spraining an ankle or breaking a bone, he sat under some shade breathing and sweating heavily. John looked back in the direction he had travelled and was relieved to see he was keeping abreast of the fire front. His body odour reeked of toad from the copious amount of the home-made potion he had been consuming that was now dripping freely from his entire body.

Sucking in some deep breaths, he could hear trees exploding and crashing to the ground. The roar of the fire was deafening as it consumed every living thing that could not escape its path in time. Not wanting to give up the slender lead he had achieved, John forced himself back to his feet earlier than he anticipated, realising the wind had also picked up and was blowing directly in his direction. Having lost the only drinking water in the car explosion his body was now screaming of thirst. Trying to gener-ate some saliva into his dry mouth to swallow, he vowed aloud into the desolate surrounds, "you won't beat me you bastards", as he pushed onwards testing his own willpower to the limit.

The dry creek started to widen significantly as it neared the main Hatchet River. He knew it was not far away but was now finding it difficult to place one step in front of the other. The main river's surface water had become stagnant in the past week leaving only the deeper holes. While they looked inviting, he knew from previous experience there was a high probability of at least one man-eating salt water croc in each hole at this dry time of year. John stumbled past trying to ignore what his pleading body craved. Reaching the shallow end he fired two shots into the water. Loading a fresh shell into the breach he lay it within easy reach as he quenched his thirst, not once taking his eye off the water for any sign of movement. Stripping to his waist, he soaked the ash-covered shirt, wringing the water out above his head before repeating, except this time he put it back on trying to cool his body temperature.

Now in the relative safety of the river he could slow down. Moving into the cool of the ample shade that spread along the river bank, John was smart enough to take the time out to let his mind and body recuperate before following the river system downstream towards any confrontation he would eagerly accommodate waiting for him back at home. Being the first time to properly sit down and reiterate to himself events leading into the attempt on his life, a revelation came to mind – he was now positive that Tim did not come alone as stated, and obviously the accomplice had tried to blow him into lumps of charred meat. He broke into an evil grin, and reaching for his rifle before starting off said, "Bring it on suckers, you have fucked up once again."

Tim led the silent parade carrying Danni on his back with both her arms wrapped around the top end of his chest, Hugh made sure to keep a good buffer in distance between himself and the prospector just in case he tried anything foolish. He would turn every now and again to check on the bushfire's progress as they travelled. When they were in sight of the broken-down truck Hugh raised his voice, "Where are the keys?" Tim paused and turned, wiping the sweat off his forehead with his shirt sleeve. "They're still in it, didn't plan to be this long saving my girl, anyway who would try and steal it out here with three bloody flat tyres?" The hitman shrugged at the comment. "You wouldn't have any guns stashed in there by any chance prospector?" Tim thought carefully about the blur of recent events before replying knowing full well that the hitman would check thoroughly for himself regardless of his reply. "Nah, pretty sure I only had the handgun that you got rid of."

"Fair enough, don't be offended that I doubt your word. You mob just stay put while I have a look." He walked past Meg who stood on the edge of the dirt track remaining quiet and looking solemn. "Pick up your bottom lip girl, it's been dragging in the bulldust since we left." Meg just glared at him without responding. Hugh checked out the camping gear in the back then underneath the body of the 4x4 for any concealed compartments before searching behind and under the seats in the cab, briefly opening the glove box in case there was another handgun. By this time, Tim's legs were starting to ache from standing in one spot with the extra weight of his wife. Satisfied with his search, Hugh then inspected the rim size and stud pattern. "Yeah, my spare will fit. The girls can sit in your truck while we go for a walk and get my vehicle." Hugh reached for the keys out of Tim's ignition for the pure fact that he did not trust the quiet female, flat tyres or not. Her animosity towards him was blatantly obvious which he was unable to fathom after sparing all their lives.

Tim carefully lifted Danni, who was now fully conscious, into the passenger seat before winding down the windows to let the stifling heat escape from the interior. The morning had passed and the sun was now directly overhead making its presence felt. He walked to the back of the truck rifling through his food box for as many cups as he could find while still under gun point. Filling two pannikins with water out of a plastic twenty litre container that had been sitting in the sun all day, he passed the lukewarm drinks to the girls. "Are you sure you're OK?" Looking at Danni with concern, she nodded. "My head is throbbing, I feel weak and my mouth tastes like shit." The hitman's voice cut short their conservation. "Let's get going prospector, after you change those three tyres your wife rides with me."

Not wanting to let Tim out of his sight, Hugh walked him through the bush to where he had concealed his vehicle from the road. "So, what's the story with the other one you brought out here, how does she fit into all this?" "Who Meg? She is the wife of the bloke you just took out, my ex-prospecting partner." The hitman looked confused. "Yeah right, no wonder she's pissed off then, he wasn't on my list but she was, what's the go there?" "Long story but he is supposed to be already dead and buried awhile back now." This made Hugh more confused as they approached his vehicle. "Well he's dead this time around prospector…you sit on the bull bar on my side of the vehicle." Unlocking the 4x4 wagon he exchanged the rifle for his handgun then lowered his window to train the weapon on his captive. Tim jumped up on the bull bar turning to reply to his statement, "Wouldn't be too sure on that count, he is not an easy man to kill." Hugh laughed, nobody could survive that explosion. "I don't give a rat's arse how tough they are, now hang the hell on, hate to run you over before I get my gold."

He ordered Danni to his vehicle while watching the prospector pull the two spare tyres off the back of his truck and remove the one off the hire car, he felt more at ease now having the wife within reach. Tim changed the tyres in quick time. Several times the thought crossed his mind to roll the dice and take his chances of trying to take the hitman out while he still had the wheel spanner in hand. Common sense subdued the urge, as other lives were now at stake. After throwing the flat tyres in the back, Hugh instructed, "You can lead and we will follow and do I need to point out what will happen to your wife?" Dusting himself off as he walked around to the driver's side to start the truck he replied, "Yep clear as day."

Soon as they were on the move Meg produced the empty Glock, "This any good to you?" Cracking a smile as they bumped along the track, "You bloody bet sweetheart, check the glove box I'm sure there has got to be a few bullets left rolling around in there." After pulling out the entire contents Meg announced, "There's one, that's enough to kill that bastard, and here is your pocket knife back." She passed the bullet and the knife over while Tim, steering with one hand, placed the single shot into the chamber. "Insurance is what that is. I have been watching this bloke, he knows his stuff and does not leave himself open at all. It is too risky with you girls involved. Mac will not have a problem handing over some of his share of the gold if our lives are in danger. At the end of the day it's only a rock and at least we will all still be alive. There is more to be dug up, I will just have to give him my half till we are back square...this is not Mac's problem, it's mine. But if the shit does hit the fan at least we have something to protect ourselves with even if it is only one shot."

C, restrained by handcuffs, had been denied bail and processed on initial charges with many more pending. He was now in transition from the local cells to Lotus Glen Prison via their own secure transport system. Marko's mobile phone had once again failed to respond earlier in the day when he demanded his phone call before entering the closed court. Grace watched on, standing to one side of the door of the bullet-proof unit. He recognised her and gave a smirk while he stood in line waiting to enter the vehicle. The other prisoners in the line mainly consisted of break and enter, attempted robbery with a weapon, larceny and aggravated assault causing death to name a few. These crimes had increased dramatically – not only in the North, but Australia-wide – in a short time frame and were mainly derived from the same psychotic drug C produced. Leaning his head to one side as he drew close to Grace, C stood motionless at the door briefly before stepping in. "See you soon." Grace responded swiftly accompanied by a cold stare that bore straight through him. "If I do scum, it will be through the sights of my Glock."

The prison vehicle was just short of full giving C the option of sitting alone towards the front of the bus as it swayed from side to side on its slow winding progress up the steep rainforest range. The outside humidity was high with the air conditioning struggling to keep the interior temperature cool, while it recirculated the stale body odour of its occupants much to his distaste. The duration of the trip was approximately an hour and a half to their destination of incarceration. He turned around several times over this period glancing at the other prisoners towards the rear of the vehicle. One large man also sat alone. He had Maori tribal facial tattoos, a bald head and small beady eyes that had barely wandered away from C, and he blew C a kiss on both occasions he looked in his direction. Having a long history of repeat offences, the return inmate picked C above the rest of them as different from the usual crowd. The large Maori planned to follow up on his scant foreplay that would include many pillow talk sessions with this new fish once inside.

A bead of nervous sweat broke out on C's brow as he recollected what the prospector had threatened him with that day about being gang raped on a daily basis while in prison. Refusing the urge to turn around again, he pondered if the bikie he had cut a deal with in the local cells had enough time to put anything in place before his arrival. He certainly hoped this would be the case as his mind started to run wild on the consequences if not. "Fuck that shit," he stated, shaking off the thought. Trying to erase these destructive flashes that now continuously played on his mind, his own personal dignity was now at stake. C readjusted his position on the vinyl bench seat as the vision of Tim's finger action as they passed each other on the highway stuck in his mind. "Fuck you prospector, it's not over yet by a long shot," he mumbled under his breath. With the 'old mate' behind him already blowing kisses in the first hour of this unknown journey, C's immediate concern over the salvation of his own anal virginity became paramount.

John trudged with purpose out of the river system and up the steep incline to the crest of the soft sandy bank, knowing this part of the country like the back of his hand from collecting toads during the night. He changed direction towards the homestead, his breathing became laboured, his chest heaving while his single lung struggled to expand to full capacity in the hot thin air. Taking a repetition of long deep breaths, he tried to slow his heart rate down as the heat took its toll on any prolonged physical movement by either man or animal in these peak temperatures of the day. He saw several birds drop out of the sky, having no option other than to flee from the smoke in the heat. Covered from head to toe in a sheen of sweat, he searched for some nearby shade to have a brief break before the final assault towards home. A heat storm brewed in the background as dark clouds accumulated quickly and the rumble of thunder became more prevalent. The stagnant afternoon heat suddenly changed as a cool breeze picked up and increased from the storm front that was now intensifying with lightning flashing across the sky followed closely behind by loud claps of thunder that vibrated around the ash covered hills.

Unclipping the magazine from the firearm, he welcomed the cooler change and could already smell the rain still some distance off. Counting six shells, he firmly rammed home the mag back into the rifle with the palm of his hand. Studying the movement of the storm, John guessed it would be touch and go whether he would make it home before its arrival. Having a loose plan in train he set off, unsure what to expect. His anxiety started to climb while his head throbbed and stomach cramped from the withdrawals of his homemade toxins that always managed to keep the demons contained.

Setting a cracking pace, the mentally deranged ex-prospector made short work of covering the last two kilometres with the aid of flat solid ground under foot. Immediate confirmation that the old 4x4 was empty escalated both the anger and anxiety further. His eyes glazed over and his facial expressions changed dramatically. Breaking into a heinous laugh, he yelled "run rabbits, run" at the top of his voice before becoming totally consumed by the looming thunderstorm and lightning strikes close to where he stood. Snapping his head towards the homestead, he searched for any movement for a short period – it also appeared to be devoid of any movement. Feeding a round into the rifle with rage overcoming caution, he walked down the hill with little regard to now being an open target.

Inspecting every room in the homestead, John now concentrated on the beat up old 4x4. It only just dawned on him that in all the time he had lived on the property not once had he even attempted to start it. Jumping into the driver's seat he tried the ignition. "Bloody nothing," he muttered twisting the key repeatedly. Reefing open the buckled bonnet, he lay the rifle barrel across the battery terminals. Sparks flew in all directions as they connected. Smiling at the result, he started talking to himself to solve why it would not start. "The battery has enough power, it could be just the starter motor is jammed." John slipped under the 4x4 with the rifle. Remembering to eject the live cartridge first, he spun the rifle backwards smashing the timber butt hard against the starter motor to free it up. Heavy rain drops started lifting miniature puffs of bulldust from the impact around him while he crawled back out to source a rock and a screwdriver. The rain started to pelt down as he pumped the accelerator three times then positioned the rock on the accelerator to hold the pedal at half throttle. Turning on the ignition and placing the 4x4 in neutral he slipped back under the vehicle into the mud reaching over to short the positive and negative leads on the starter motor with the screwdriver. It started to turn over. "Come on old girl, fire up," he willed to himself. It kicked twice before coughing and spluttering into life, covering the entire vehicle in a thick cloud of black diesel soot.

Spits of rain from the tail end of the storm splattered onto the dusty windscreens of the 4x4s as they turned out of the Hatchet River access track back onto the main road. Tim glanced in the side mirror to check the hitman was still following. Streaks of mud formed on the windshield impeding vision as the prospector activated the wiper blades with a continuous stream of clean water spurting from two small jets positioned on the bonnet. The late afternoon sun broke through the cloud cover, boring through the driver's side window as they travelled back towards Hugo in silence. Rounding the last corner on the outskirts of town, Tim saw a police officer dressed in a high visibility jacket directing the small amount of local traffic. The road had been reduced to one lane with two fire engines and the arson squad blocking the other, sifting through the smouldering remains of the service station. Tim stiffened at the sight of the officer as he signalled to slow down when they approached. Meg shot a quick glance at Tim. "What are we going to say?" He replied calmly while reaching for his sunglasses off the dash, "Nothing, just act normally. We need to get through this and give the hitman his gold so we don't have to keep looking over our shoulders for the rest of our lives. I just hope he does not recognise me…if anything goes wrong Danni is as good as dead."

The officer held his open palm into the air signalling the vehicle to stop. The prospector slipped the 4x4 into neutral leaving the motor idling. "Good afternoon officer, geese mate looks like a hell of a mess here, what happened?" The policeman did not answer immediately as he took a good look at both occupants then glanced over his shoulder to make sure no vehicles were approaching from the other direction. "Yes, it certainly is, has taken nearly twenty-four hours to get it under control. Not sure how it started yet, all the security cameras are melted plastic. There is a high probability it is a case of arson."

"Fair dinkum mate, hope nobody was hurt." The officer took another look at the female passenger, Meg returned a nervous smile. "One fatality that we are aware of…have you got your driver's licence on you sir."

Tim started to feel uncomfortable. "Hey honey, you want to grab my wallet out of the glove box," giving her a brief wink. Meg, with a blank expression, spent a minute fumbling through its contents. The officer stood patiently waiting then turned to see another vehicle pull up behind this one. "Shit don't tell me I left it back at the station, sorry officer I don't have it on me at the moment." Hugh, in the car behind, had time to take in the aftermath of the burnt-out servo. "I like the way your husband works, he doesn't fuck around does he?" Danni spoke for the first time since entering the car. "He is nothing like you." Hugh laughed hard in response. "That's where your wrong sweet cheeks, he is a killer exactly like me, the only difference between us is the reason why we kill."

The hitman gave a short honk on the horn not liking the extended time the prospector seemed to be taking with the cop, he touched the butt of the handgun stashed in between the seats for reassurance. "He wouldn't want to be doing anything stupid up there for your sake," he said to Danni without taking his eyes off the cop. The horn diverted the officer's attention as he finished up by stating, "I will give you a warning this time round. By law even if you hold a current open licence in the state of Queensland it must be on you at all times." Tim nodded breathing out a slow sigh of relief. "Yes officer, I will make sure of that from now on." The officer tapped the side of the door, "OK get going, I will see what this impatient driver's problem is, and be careful of roos on the road at this time of day." Tim smiled, "Thank you officer," before selecting first gear and driving away without wasting another second.

Driving up the road slowly in third gear he tried to keep the hitman's vehicle in the rear vision mirror at all times while nervously waiting for it to also move away from the police officer. Getting out of the line of sight with Hugh's still motionless vehicle, he pulled over on the side of the road for a piss stop and to wait as darkness started to fall. A set of headlights appeared over the rise as Tim stood beside the open door. The hire car pulled up alongside with Hugh instructing his passenger to lower the electric window. "You OK?" asked Tim as he touched her arm. She nodded silently. Leaning across the seat, Hugh cut in wanting to give the prospector directions on what to do from here. "We will fuel up in Bankston, then pull up somewhere off the road before midnight. I want to arrive at the gold mine in daylight hours."

Chapter 7

OLD MAC

The birds around Mac's tin shack heralded the dawn of another day, busily moving from tree to tree sounding out their own unique tune. Old Mac grimaced in pain while he slowly lifted his head from the table. Having been left overnight in the chair his old and broken bones throbbed. He was unable to open his eyes as the blood from the further beatings that night had caked dry across his eyelids overnight, welding them shut. Using his free hand that had been left unbounded after signing the documents for the Chinese, the old timer started to rub both eye sockets. Breaking the dry crusted blood he was now able to force his eyes open. He looked over to see the large frame of the Chinese killer stirring in his bed, Mac tried to assess the extent of all his injuries but eventually gave up as his whole body ached, including a chest pain that seemed to come and go. He was thankful he was numb from his arse cheeks down from lack of circulation as he looked towards the floor at both broken ankles and every toe which were a dark purple and severely swollen. The chest pain returned this time stronger than before. He grunted in pain, acknowledging the fact he was not much longer for this world.

Old Mac's chin quivered as he lowered his head back onto the table to signal defeat. The tough old miner's spirit was broken. He never thought his life journey would finish under such violent circumstances in the most tranquil place on earth. Between breaks in the bird chatter, Mac thought he could hear the very faint sound of a motor revving as it travelled along in the early morning air. Sitting up straight he tried to tune out the surrounding noises, his ears strained to confirm the slight noise. Several minutes later he heard it again, a weak smile broke across busted lips as Chang rose to his feet walking to the sink to wash his face and take a long drink from the tap.

Mac watched his enemy's movements closely to see if he could also distinguish the mechanical sound from the surrounding native bush ensemble. It was ten minutes before Chang propped at the sound of the engine. Mac was surprised at how early he picked up on it. "Yep, told you he would come, you're a dead man," he slurred through a broken jaw as the chest pains returned once again, this time with more force. Chang snarled at his prisoner's remark as he walked from the other side of the shack to stand beside him to listen more intently, unsure if he heard one or two approaching vehicles. Mac wanted to leave his own parting mark on this vicious assault and reached for the pen that was left by his Chinese extortionists. With his captor supporting his stance with one hand resting on the table within Mac's reach's and with his concentration consumed elsewhere, Mac grasped the expensive metal biro while Chang's back was turned, and in a last ditch effort stabbed it with all his remaining strength into the middle of the assassin's right hand.

The pen penetrated straight through the flesh till it hit the hard timber surface of the table driving though one of the more prominent veins that stood out on the back of his hand. Chang let out a yell in surprise and pain, instantly backhanding the old man with full force sending him and the chair flying halfway across the tin hut smashing onto the ground snapping every leg on the chair. "Well now he is here, I won't be needing you anymore." He stood above old Mac with the pen still sticking out of his hand reaching down to break his neck. "He doesn't know whe…" was as far as Mac got in reply before the brutal cracking of bones put the old miner to rest forever. A shallow raspy breath escaped from his open mouth as Mac closed his eyes for the last time.

Pulling the pen out of the wound the blood started pumping more freely. Swearing in his native language, Chang inspected the damaged vein. Being in these situations many times before he could tell by the blood loss that it was not a main artery that was hit. Holding his thumb with downward pressure on the severed vein to stem its flow, the assassin searched around the tin shack for a bandage, knowing the vein would retract and stop bleeding if he could keep continual pressure on it. Finding the fully replenished first-aid kit he patched himself up. The sounds of the vehicles had become more prevalent, and he cursed at not having brought a long-distance firearm – he originally envisaged it would only be a day job taking out both the miners at close quarters.

He had to now reassess his position. Two vehicles could mean anywhere from two opponents through to six depending on the make of the second vehicle. He already knew from the video footage at the bullion shop that the young prospector's vehicle could carry only two. The element of surprise would be lost with such a large number. He was confident but at the same time realistic of his own ability… he could comfortably take out two possibly three, but after that the remainder would have time to react, and if they were carrying long arms it would be like shooting fish in a barrel if he was stuck inside the tin shack. Chang, erring on the side of caution, decided to change tack. Remembering the gun the old miner had discharged out on the flat yesterday and finding a box of shotgun cartridges, he stepped over old Mac lying on the floor and walked outside to locate where he had dropped the ancient weapon and move to the only high ground above the shack. He moved towards a small hill that gravity fed drinking water to the hut from a natural spring that Mac had dug out and made into a dam many years ago.

Tim and Hugh had got to within three hours of the mine site before calling it quits at 11.45pm. Both girls being totally exhausted had fallen asleep hours earlier as they travelled along the smooth bitumen highway. The hitman took the precautionary measure of cable tying the prospector's wrists to the steering wheel of his 4x4 and both feet, one to the clutch the other to the brake pedal. "What you don't trust me yet?" asked Tim as the black plastic straps bit into his wrists. Without a moment's hesitation Hugh replied, "Not in my line of work, just show me the gold brother and you are all free." Hugh cut him free once more at 4.30am and they were back on the move well before daylight with Tim still driving the lead vehicle with all spotlights switched on. The area covered by the blazing light covered a considerable distance on either side of the track. Close to half an hour out from the mine site both vehicles crossed a small creek still containing small pockets of water. Nugget, recognising the sound of Tim's vehicle, limped out onto the crude dusty track on three legs standing in front of his vehicle in the predawn hours whimpering over his injury. Tim stood on the brakes hard. "That's Nugget," he stated bounding out of his truck.

The pup barked several times in the direction of home followed by a series of growls like he was trying to communicate with Tim. Picking up the pup he looked towards the steep hill as Nugget gave him a friendly lick across the face. "What's up boy, you're hurt, where's Mac? Nugget started to bark once again. Hugh walked to the front of the 4x4 with gun in hand, "What's the problem?" Tim continued to look up the hillslope with concern spreading across his face. "Something is wrong up at the mine, this is my partner's dog…looks like his leg is broken. I know for a fact he would never leave Mac's side voluntarily." The girls also joined the men, curious at why they had stopped in the middle of nowhere. "How much further to go?" Hugh asked. "About half an hour on foot if we cut straight up this hill, I think it would be safer if the girls stay down here with the vehicles, what do you reckon? The hitman moved his empty hand to his chin in thought as the first rays of sunlight appeared over the hills.   "Hmmm, I don't think so prospector, the way I see it they are my bargaining chip to keep you in line till we get that gold." Tim carried Nugget to the tray of his 4x4 letting the pup down gently in the back, annoyed at the denial of his request. "For fuck sake bud, you will get your gold, I'm telling you that something is wrong up there and I will not put the girls in anymore risk. If you make them go I'm pulling up stumps right here, you can go fuck yourself, find the gold on your own." Tim sat down on a large boulder that had been pushed to the side of the track by the bucket of the loader with both arms crossed over his chest and a look of determination plastered across his face.

Hugh's temper started to rise with the act of defiance. Did this bloke not take him seriously? His initial reaction was not to muck around with this time wasting crap and just turn around and shoot the knee cap out of the prospector's wife straight up – that would get things back on track fast. Another idea came to mind while he cocked the pistol. Lowering the hammer slowly with his thumb, Hugh stuck the firearm in his waist line and walked to the rental car. Unzipping the bag on the rear floor he pulled out a pack of zip ties some masking tape and a professionally engineered plastic explosive device. "Right the girls can stay prospector but here is how it will work, stand together and hold hands." They did as instructed, with the hitman taping one wrist to the others so they had to move as one entity, wrapping one strip of tape to cover their eyes as a blind fold. "What the hell are you doing?" questioned Tim. Hugh smiled. "You will find out soon enough, let's just say it's an adult game of hide and seek, now start walking up the track." He turned them in the right direction, "walk."

The hitman went to work setting the timer on the explosives for two hours. Opening the rental car door, he stepped up using the sideboard to reach into the middle rail of the roof rack to place the device well out of sight from ground level. Winding both front windows down an inch to allow enough ventilation for the captives, he removed the keys before leading the three back to the vehicles. Cutting the prospector free first, Hugh decided to leave his gold card blindfolded as a precaution while he dealt with the girls. "Get in," he ordered pushing each of them into the front of his car and swiftly securing their free hand with cable ties as he had done with the prospector the previous night.

Danni's wrist was secured to the steering wheel while Meg's was secured to the interior hand grip on the passenger's side. Their other hands were still bound together with tape, looking at a quick glance, like they were holding hands. Removing the keys from the other 4x4, he pulled the tape from Tim's eyes tearing out facial hair in the procedure. He shook his head watching the hitman press the central locking on the vehicle condemning his wife and friend inside. "Right, here is some incentive for ya to pull your finger out. There is a bomb set to go off in," glancing at his watch, "one hour and fifty-five minutes that I have stashed somewhere on or around both the vehicles. If I'm not back with my gold within that time frame to turn it off they will have the same fate as your mate did yesterday." The girls looked horrified at the revelation while Tim just stared at the hitman. "Let's get going then." Hugh reached for his rifle. "Lead the way."

John ran out of fuel just on dark. Grabbing the rifle and a plastic cordial bottle containing two litres of water, he set off on foot guessing it would be about a three-hour walk to the main road. After their earlier work-out that day his legs protested until the muscles warmed up and soon the footsteps became countless as the hours rolled on. Reaching the turn-off he turned towards Hugo. Half an hour down the road he heard the welcoming sound of a vehicle approaching at speed. Stepping off the road he dropped the rifle in the grass along with the drinking container so it was easier to relocate both in the darkness. Turning to face the oncoming vehicle, John started to wave as soon as the spotlights bathed the road in bright light.

The young miner had just knocked off the afternoon shift after a three-week stint out bush, overly keen to get to town to see his girl. He had opted to drive out that night straight after work instead of waiting till the morning. The dirt road held no traffic at this hour of night and he made the most of it giving the V8 a boot full of accelerator until he spotted the man waving him down from the side of the road. "What the bloody hell," exclaimed the young man as he applied the brakes, covering the stranger in dust as he ended up well past the mark before stopping. Selecting reverse, he pulled up alongside the man, turning down the stereo he wound down the window.

"What's up bloke, need a lift?"

"Yeah, my truck broke down up the road and I was wondering if you could give me a lift to Hugo… didn't think I would run across anyone on the road till morning," John replied. The young man smiled. "Yeah, hanging for a root after three weeks. Yeah, no worries bloke, jump in." John bent to pick up his water bottle and felt for the rifle. Walking around the back of the truck he loaded a round into the spout then moved up the other side to open the passenger door and pointed the rifle straight at the driver. "That root is going to have to wait for a bit longer, now get out." The young man tried to protest, "Come on dude, I only brought this rig four weeks ago." John cut him short poking the rifle barrel into his ribcage. "Get the fuck out now." The young miner obeyed, releasing his seat belt while still swearing at the loss of his prized possession. The recycled cordial bottle containing water flew out of the window skidding along the ground to end up beside his feet. The V8 roared up the road through every gear leaving the young miner kicking up bulldust on the side of the road in frustration. He passed through Hugo without incident with the police packing up many hours earlier. Crossing a small unnamed creek on the way back to town, John pulled over shining the headlights on a series of small puddles. Clawing out two handfuls of wet clay he smeared them over the number plates making them impossible to read. He hoped this would keep the cops at bay knowing for certain that once that young bloke hit Hugo it would be reported stolen. Turning off the main highway near his first destination John smiled in anticipation, driving down Tim and Danni's road under streetlights.

C hang waited patiently on the small hill for the vehicles to arrive to find out exactly how many he would be dealing with, slightly concerned at hearing the vehicles' motors die well before the shack. As the breeze had not changed since he arrived, his thoughts started to wander – had they already worked out something was amiss? He rationalised that this could not be remotely possible as they left no obvious incoming tracks after arriving by chopper. Tim made short work of scrambling up the hill, having to make impatient stops for the hitman to catch up. Above all else he was concerned about Mac's welfare. Working his way to the plateau directly behind the shack, he paused to catch a breath, listening intently for any voices or movement within Mac's home. From memory, there was an outcrop of slate beside the left hand corner of the hut. Glancing behind, he could see the hitman still some distance away struggling with the degree of the incline while stumbling over hidden obstacles lying in the tall dead grass on his climb to the top. Tim figured he had enough time to slide on his stomach to the corner of the dwelling behind the slate protrusion to suss out the situation while once again waiting for the hitman to catch up.

The West Australian, used to the dry heat from home, was struggling with the humidity of the North Queensland outback even in these cooler hours of the morning. Arriving on the plateau he wiped the sweat from his brow. Taking a couple of deep breaths he started scanning the bush landscape from the side of the hut for any human movement. Tim took charge even though Hugh had the firepower and total control over the prospector. "His quad is still parked out the front, which means he is not down the mine site and he is certainly not a bloke to sleep in. Something is fucked up in a big way," he continued as he inspected the old-fashioned nails secured to the back wall. "Do you have a heavy bladed knife so we can prize out them bottom two nails? Hugh nodded, withdrawing the blade from the leather sheath on his hip. "Yeah, but slow the fuck down will ya, I haven't come this far for you to get shot," he said with his admiration growing for this rough and ready bushman by the minute.

Painstakingly he started to pry out the nails that were embedded deep into the dry hard wood. Tim removed the multi-purpose knife from his belt selecting the pliers. He was now able to get them in behind the head of the nails, working them from side to side and up and down till they dropped on the ground. Kneeling, he was just able to get his hands underneath the sheet of corrugated iron. Leaning back he slowly started bending it upwards trying his best to avoid making any obvious noise. Flashing a thin smile from the success of his idea, he handed the knife back to Hugh. "There's some rocks for cover at the front corner, you want to keep an eye out while I check inside?" Hugh nodded, moving along the side of the hut with the rifle to intercept any intruders while Tim began crawling inside on the flat of his stomach. Breaking through to the interior he gasped at the sight of old Mac lying on the ground still bound to the broken chair with his neck twisted at an acute angle. Scrambling along the floor on hands and knees to his side, Tim tried to gently adjust his head back into a normal position, while continuously repeating the same word, "NO, NO". Fumbling for his blunt pocket knife, he cut the tape and laid his partner flat on his back while going through the motions of feeling for a pulse that he already knew would be non-existent. With misty eyes and sorrow in his heart Tim stared at the full extent of the injuries inflicted on his mate from head to toe, finding it extremely hard to come to terms with such horrific purposeful acts of mutilation. "What type of low life scum could do such a thing?" he whispered to Mac. His body was still pliable and warm telling Tim that his broken neck had occurred not that long ago. Standing, he looked around the rest of the hut. The most obvious sign of what had happened at the hut was the two sheets of iron off the front wall lying on the ground. Thinking aloud he started to move around the hut.

"Looks like you put up a hell of a fight against the mongrels, now where the hell has your shotgun gone?"

Chang sat motionless in the long grass watching the entire 180 degree elevated view in front of him. Opening the box of shotgun cartridges that lay beside him, he plucked out two shells. Having never used this type of firearm before it took him a minute to work out how to unlock the gun to replace the spent shells. He then shoved a few more in his top pocket, just in case.

Hugh had seen no obvious sign of life other than birds and retreated from his position, concerned at the time it was taking the prospector inside. "Come on prospector we haven't got all day, time is ticking away you know." Tim turned at the voice through the hole in the back wall. "Hang the fuck on," he hissed, returning his focus back to old Mac's body. "I will be back my friend, and god help them if they are still around here."

Crawling back out, Tim's grief and niggling guilt over what had transpired here today weighed heavily on his conscience. Hugh sat outside waiting, tapping the face of his watch. "We need to keep moving, the clock doesn't stop for anybody, so how far away is the gold stash from here?" Despondent, the prospector replied, "Not too far away, my partner is dead, they tortured him first." This meant nothing to Hugh as death was his livelihood, but looking at the prospector's face he could plainly see the hurt and emotion displayed. Maybe he did initially read this bloke wrong the hitman mused to himself. Did the prospector hold everyone close around him – whether friends or bloodline – in higher regard than his own safety or salvation? Answering his own question the result was a resounding yes.

Tim now became compliant with Hugh's order as the girls' lives were still dangerously at stake. He came to terms that nothing could be done to help Mac. Realising he had to now concentrate on the people close to him who were still alive, he hoped the West Australian would keep his word. Once the girls were safe he would return up the hill to search for the killer and tend to his friend's corpse. "Follow me," he stated touching the butt of Mac's Glock stuck in the small of his back under his shirt for reassurance even if it only held one bullet. Whose name was on that lump of lead yet to be fired was still unclear to him at this point of time.

Hugh left the cumbersome rifle at the hut to free up one hand to carry his spoils of the gold, reverting to his handgun. Chang propped as the two men appeared from behind the shack and started walking straight towards him. Sinking lower into the tall dead grass, he raised the double-barrel shotgun training it on the pair as they advanced up the slope. He recognised the prospector instantly from the store video but could not believe his eyes, taking a double look at the tall lanky man walking beside him. After closer scrutiny, a smile started to form across his face, praising Buddha for such luck. "Three in one day, this is going to be fun." Tim veered to the left of the waiting assassin who was still at a distance, arriving at the edge of the small dam. "Well here we are," he stated pointing at the water. Hugh smiled. "You cunning bugger, who would have thought to search in here. Looks like you are going for a swim my friend."

Tim turned to face Hugh to keep the Glock hidden from view. Pulling off his shirt, he removed the weapon in the same movement, wrapping his shirt around it, and placed the bundle on the bank of the dam. Entering the water, he slowly moved around the dam searching along the slimy plastic bottom with his feet for the gold bars. "They're in here somewhere," he stated as the water level rose to the middle of his chest in the centre of the dam. Hugh crouched on his haunches on the bank, plucked a stem of grass from a clump beside him and started to chew it in the corner of his mouth. "You want to hope so prospector."

The further he moved around the dam with no result the more concerned he became, all the while trying to keep a casual demeanour, not wanting to alert the hitman straight away to his assumption they were missing. He needed precious time to think this through. They had both counted eighty-one bars of gold that day before Mac rode up on the quad to throw them in. His mind started to race with possibilities of what could have happened after that point, coming to the realisation that they must have been stolen. But by who? Tim swallowed hard contemplating the repercussions if he did not deliver on the promise to the West Australian. Now in damage control, he glanced over towards his shirt containing the Glock and its one and only shot.

He started to move towards his shirt in a carefree motion not displaying in any way the anxiousness he was now feeling, knowing there was no choice left but to try to kill the hitman who now sat casually on the bank loosely holding the handgun. His big toe touched a solid object. "Got one," he announced. Hugh looked at his watch. "About bloody time prospector, throw it to me." Tim skidded it along the smooth bottom with his foot towards the shallows of the bank before plucking it out of the water. Throwing the gold bar, it landed beside the hitman's feet. "Now that's what I'm here for. How much is one of these worth?" Now only in water up to his knees, Tim replied "Ten ounces to a bar, so roughly about fifteen grand each." Hugh quickly did the calculations. "So you need to come up with another fifteen for me to flick the switch on the device and walk away. How many bars are in there all up?"

Tim replied instantly, "Seventeen." Hugh broke into a laugh. "Seriously prospector, why do you want to play this game with me when you are that close to the finish line, and I thought we had formed a bond of trust. The bottom could be covered in them for all I know." He walked around the side of the dam contemplating his options before stripping off the shirt, removing his hat and boots. Hugh placed the handgun down before entering the water. "You can get over that side well away from me and my gun," he ordered. Tim struggled to obey the command knowing it would not take very long for Hugh to find out there was no gold left on the bottom, and it would also push him further away from his Glock. This had now become his single focus to try to take control of this deadly situation that would shortly explode as soon as Hugh discovered the truth.

Chang had moved as close as the surrounding bush cover would allow. He could faintly hear the men talking as he sat motionless in the grass closely observing what was unfolding below, rubbing his hands together in anticipation as the first gold bar was retrieved. Watching the West Australian proceed to disarm himself and enter the water signalled the prime opportunity for him to move in on his prey. Hugh was about to repeat his order directed at the prospector as he stubbornly still had not moved when a blast from both barrels of the shot gun shattered the tranquillity. Chang waiting for the men to fall, and was dumfounded as the spray of pellets fell way short of his intended mark. He looked at the firearm in his hands confused, not realising that back at the hut he had picked up a box of bird-shot cartridges instead of the way more powerful buckshot cartridges. Mac only used the light bird shot for shooting pigeons or rabbits at close range so it did not significantly damage the flesh of his food.

Tim and Hugh ducked in reaction over the shot before locating the source, now well out in the open, and who was breaking the shotgun in half to feed the other two shells from his pocket. "What the hell, you're fuckin' joking me, it's the Chinaman," yelled Hugh as he waded out of the hip-deep water towards the bank where his gun lay. Tim, closer to the rear of the dam was out in three huge strides sprinting around the dam wall for his own Glock as the second volley of pellets harmlessly plopped into the water without any force. "Do you know this clown?" yelled Tim as Chang swore in Chinese. Now without any more ammo, Chang ran down the slope brandishing the rifle as a club. "There's your killer," the hitman yelled.

Hugh made it to his handgun just before Tim got to his. By this time Chang was in striking distance. Hugh swayed the top half of his torso back, a fraction of a second before the butt of the gun swung with brute force narrowly missing his head. The next blow was a blur as Chang, with lighting speed, kicked the wrist that was holding the pistol. Bones cracked with the impact breaking the West Australian's tight grip on his firearm and sending it flying into the dam. Chang dropped the shotgun and drove a series of punches into the chest of his adversary before he even had time to react from the kick to the wrist. Hugh was now seeing little bright lights float around in front of him as two of the well placed punches drove hard into his solar plexus nearly knocking him out. The hitman's legs started to go rubbery. He knew he was in trouble, big trouble.

Tim had witnessed what was over in seconds while he tried to get a clean shot on the Chinese killer as he delivered the punishing blows at close quarters. Squeezing the trigger on the moving target when Hugh dropped to one knee while trying to fight off from passing out, the bullet found its mark but missed hitting any vital organs, wedging in behind one of his already broken ribs. Chang yelled in pain diverting his attention away from finishing off the big mouth Aussie hitman with a kick that would have broken his neck instantly. Rising anger and adrenaline filled Tim as he visualised old Mac's tortured body that was left lying on the floor of the hut. He ran towards his partner's killer holding the empty Glock on its side tightly in his grasp. Chang did the same running towards the prospector as they clashed head on.

The Chinese assassin was nearly twice the size of Tim as the prospector leapt into the air wrapping one arm tightly around the thick neck of his adversary while pounding the side of the Glock repeatedly into the bandaged head. Blood and fragments of skin from the scalp covered the gun as Chang grunted, prying off the prospector's grip from around his neck before dipping his shoulder while pulling forward viciously on his opponent's arm. Sailing through the air, Tim landed on his back just in time to see a boot about to connect with his head. He rolled instinctively but the next one did not miss, lifting Tim off the ground as it connected with his ribcage and propelling him a good distance before hitting the ground as he continued to roll. Hugh attacked from behind smashing two heavy punches, one into each kidney, before reaching for the knife on his hip. Chang swung a roundhouse kick in retaliation, connecting flush on Hugh's jaw knocking him out cold.

Tim was now on all fours when he spotted Hugh's shirt still lying on the ground. His memory flashed back to when the hitman had disarmed Meg of the Glock back at the station before shoving the clip with the remaining bullets into his shirt pocket. He just needed to get to the shirt, praying they were still in the pocket from yesterday otherwise they both would be done like a dinner. Chang had both hands around Hugh's neck choking the life out of him when Tim threw the empty Glock over the assassin's head to land near the discarded shirt. With both hands free, Tim flicked out the small blade of his pocket knife. Chang turned at the movement to his side, first slamming Hugh's skull into the ground before bounding to his feet in one cat-like movement. Chang laughed loudly at the size of the weapon being brandished by the prospector, producing his own specially designed and weighted throwing knives from the home country. "These are weapons prospector, that thing is for cleaning under your toe nails." He laughed again, this time at his own attempt at humour.

Relishing every opportunity to display his own hand-to-hand combat skills, he threw the knives to one side, confident he had his opponent's measure. With the gold location now apparent he did not need to keep this man alive any longer. He moved forward to finish him off once and for all. With the prospector now within his strike range, he planned to use his favourite sequence of moves to destroy this man. Chang launched a frontal kick with blurring speed aimed at the chest. Tim moved backwards in response as the kick still struck home but without any force. Watching the Asian's foot movements, he pre-empted the next move, retaliating with his own lightening reflexes that also took the assassin by surprise as he went into his roundhouse kick position. The split second his back was turned in the move, Tim leapt onto his back to get the required height needed, stabbing the pocket knife to the hilt inside the assassin's ear, twisting it viciously before releasing the grip of the small handle then rolling on the ground towards Hugh's shirt in one fluid movement. He fumbled urgently feeling for the weight of the Glock clip, not taking his eyes off the

Chinamen as he dropped to one knee to pull out the pocketknife from his ear as blood flowed down the side of his face. Chang wounded, charged towards Tim yelling in Chinese. Still lying on the ground it was the best feeling the prospector felt in some time as he located the magazine. Slipping the clip back into the butt of the Glock, he fired all the remaining sixteen shots in rapid succession into the assassin at close quarters until the chamber clicked empty. Chang landed face first five foot from Tim well and truly dead after the first five lumps of lead tore through his body.

Letting out a sigh of relief he dropped the weapon and walked over to Hugh who was slowly starting to come around, the red welts clearly visible around his throat where Chang had come very close to crushing his windpipe. "I owe you one prospector," croaked Hugh as he rubbed his neck. Tim extended his hand in a genuine offer of help. The hitman accepted the hand up, groaning as he got to his feet. "Have never seen anybody fight like that bloke before, he was a straight out martial art thrashing machine." Tim smiled as the bond between the two men grew. "Yeah, he could biff on a bit that's for sure," he replied modestly knowing that Hugh was out cold for most of the confrontation. "How's our time looking?" Hugh looked at his watch. "Fuck, you got eighteen minutes to get back…there is no way you are going to make it in that time back down to the trucks." Tim started to run. "I have to try, where is it and how do I stop it?"

"It's taped to the roof rack of my car and the deactivation switch is on the side," Hugh yelled as the prospector took off through the bush.

Kicking rocks and leaping over logs, Tim's heart started to race as he made his way back down the slope. He knew the journey back would be way quicker than their ascent earlier in the day – but in less than eighteen minutes he was unsure. Without even a watch to check on his progress he knew it was going to be touch and go. Passing the hut, he dismissed the quad purely due to the time factor, and leapt off the edge going down hard as his feet skidded out from underneath him. Sharp rocks tore at his skin as he tumbled repeatedly until he was able to get his feet back underneath him. "Fuck," he yelled at himself in frustration wasting what could be precious seconds that could make all the difference when he got to the bottom. Hugh, grabbing his rifle on the way past the hut as security, followed but at nowhere near the pace of the prospector, not really sure how this tough little bushie would react towards him if he did not make it in time.

He could now see the white colour of the vehicles through the trees, expecting the explosion at any time now. Swerving around the trees and saplings, Tim muttered to himself as he drew nearer, "Eighteen minutes would have to be up by now, the bomb timer must be faulty." Now in full view of the hitman's vehicle he skidded to a halt as his mouth dropped open. Both windows of the hire car were smashed in and neither of the girls were sitting in the front. Nugget barked from the tray of the truck hearing Tim's approach, he snapped his head around looking up the track towards his own vehicle, once again his jaw dropped open this time in complete astonishment.

John started to give a series of claps. "Now, that expression on your face was well worth all the effort for me to get here. He reached for the explosive devise throwing it in the air and catching it in one hand while the other rested close to his rifle that lay on the roof. "Going off the timer you were four minutes too late, lucky I happened to be in the area, hey partner." John had taken the liberty of turning Tim's truck around so he could position it where the three of them could stand in the back tray while also keeping the cab of the truck in front of them for cover.

He had arrived well over an hour ago knowing the mine site was the most probable location after finding the house unoccupied. Smashing the side windows with a large rock to free the girls. Meg started sobbing uncontrollably in relief that her husband was still alive, tears streamed down her face as she wanted so bad just to hold him after he cut her loose. "I thought he had killed you," she stammered. Shrugging away from his wife's attempts to embrace him, her head dropped with the cold reaction. "I did not fuck anyone," Meg declared as her voice broke several times with emotion. "He tried to but I chased him out with a knife, I love you nobody else." John stood still for a moment, uncertainty and doubt over exactly what he had seen that night crossing his mind. The ringing in his head started to increase as his own emotions started to run high. He wanted so badly for her words to be true, maybe he did have it all wrong? Regardless, he knew that since that night he had gone too far and nothing he could do would ever bring back the way things were before. Meg looked into his eyes noticing the hatred and the hard eyes had vanished, replaced very briefly by the loving look she had longed to see. Danni intervened, breaking the moment, "What about the bomb?"

John snapped back to the reality of the situation, now with a reason for urgency and purpose other than just pure redemption. It took him twenty minutes to locate the device with the clean rub marks in the film of bulldust covering the vehicle's paint work from Hugh leaning over the top of his hire wagon giving away its position. Removing the device slowly he studied the design, it was quite simplistic but very effective. Depressing the button on the side, the screen went blank momentarily before reverting back to three flashing red zeros on the screen. Now neutralised, John decided to keep it in this mode just in case he wanted to reactivate the timer himself. Meg stood by his side while he started Tim's truck. "Let's just go now, you and me," Meg pleaded. John, wanting so badly to agree with his wife's proposal, knew he could not – he had killed people in this rage that had come over him and that was out of his control. He could tell by her eyes earlier that she was telling the truth about that night which had upset him immensely. If only he had knocked on his own door that night, everything could now be different. Other than the man who had made him this way, that he could never forgive. John shook his head as Meg watched his eyes change back to hard and distant, before he replied "No."

Tim was unsure exactly how to tackle this situation. "Thanks for saving the girls, what do you want from me John? Spit it out, do you want my life? Is that what you want? Well fuckin take it, just leave the girls out of it." He spread his arms wide, "Come on, don't fuck around." Tim pointed to his heart, "Right here bud." John had already reset the timer for ten seconds on the retrieved device, all he needed to do now was press the button once more to reactivate the timer. John laughed aloud. "You have it all arse about face partner, I'm not here to kill you, where would the satisfaction be in that? I want you to suffer like I have and lose everything you love like I have. This is twice I have saved your wife's life, I can guarantee you there will not be a third time. Here is your toy back, John pressed the timer as he flung it into the air falling well short of Tim as he went to ground.

Rocks and debris flew high into the air dinting numerous panels on the hire vehicle that was closest to the blast. Hugh could hear the raised voices not far in front of him just before the explosion. "Fuck a duck," he said to himself as dirt and rock came back to earth. He loaded a shell into the rifle while continuing forward to try to get a better shot at whoever the prospector was in confrontation with. Hugh swore under his breath, this time having problems holding the rifle steady without the aid of a tree or sapling with his broken wrist. Meg spotted the hitman just as he took aim, "I will always love you," she whispered close to his ear before shoving him over the side board with her shoulder, taking the bullet in the flesh of her triceps exactly where John's heart had been a fraction earlier.

Hugh swore again on hearing Meg scream out in pain as she sunk to her knees in the back of the truck, Tim sprinted towards the vehicles as John regained his feet after the surprise shove. "Forget about me," he yelled at Meg, using the trees and the vehicle as cover as he weaved making himself a difficult target for the hitman to lock on to. Bullets whistled around him tearing bark off trees as he dodged and ducked till he skidded down into a small steep gully out of sight, sprinting back towards where he had parked the stolen V8 Cruiser. Meg inspected the wound. It was not as bad as she thought even though it stung like hell.

Danni knelt by her side stating the obvious. "You've been shot, stay still." A chunk the size of a five-cent coin was missing out of the bottom of her arm that was now bleeding freely.

To give her husband more time to escape she played it to the hilt to distract both men's attention. "Help me I've been shot," she screamed, her plan worked to perfection as both men bounded into the back of the 4x4 to look at the wound. Tim looked at the hitman with a questioning expression relaying his thoughts. The West Australian replied to the silent accusation over his marksmanship, shrugging his shoulders. "He was in my sights, she must have moved in front of him." They both looked back down at Meg who started yelling, "It hurts." Hugh cast his eye over her arm. "It's only a flesh wound," he declared. They could all hear the V8 rev not far down the road as it accelerated along the track. "I will get him," vowed Hugh as he went to jump out of the back to pursue the fleeing vehicle. Tim held his arm out stopping the hitman from moving any further. "Let him go, you got Buckley's of catching him in a vehicle through the bush, that I can tell you. Meg's wound needs looking after, there are medical supplies back at the hut and Mac needs to be taken care of, and I can't leave him like that. Also, we still need to work out what the fuck has happened to all my gold."

The men lifted Meg into the front of Tim's truck while Danni and Nugget stayed in the back. Hugh walked to his hire vehicle, swearing as he brushed the broken glass off the driver's seat. The trip up the hill to the hut was a silent one as two things weighed heavy on Tim's mind; first and foremost was what to do with his friend's remains. Should he take him to town and contact the daughter? And the other was who in hell had found their gold stash? It was not till he pulled up at the front of the hut that Mac's words came back to him about changing his will before he left for town with the broken bearing. "The rock," he said aloud. Meg, applying pressure with one hand over her wound, looked at him. "What did you say?" "Never mind," he replied swinging open his door. Hugh was right behind him as he lifted Danni from the tray of the truck. "You guys stay here and patch up Meg, there is something I need to do."

Tim started to run through the bush towards the dam yelling over his shoulder back towards the hut, "I will be back soon." He walked around the lip of the dam muttering to himself, "a slab of rock on the right-hand side he said." No sooner had he spoken the words than Tim found what he was looking for. Flipping over the flat lump of slate, he saw the waterproof container full of paperwork in a hole that old Mac had described. He took a deep breath sourcing some shade to sit down and read its contents, hoping above all it would contain Mac's last wishes for a resting place. The crows and blowflies had already started to gather around the Chinese assassin's body which was in clear view of Tim as he sat down and unscrewed the plastic lid.

To my partner and friend, if you are reading this well I guess my number has come up. You my friend brought a breath of fresh air into my stale lifestyle, I have enjoyed every minute of your company, compassion and mateship. Enclosed are two packages, one for my daughter that I ask you pass on and the other to you with a list of mining leases that I have held onto including my overseas interests along with full ownership of this mine. I ask that you take care of Nugget or find a good home for him and my last request is that I be buried beside my faithful companion Jonah with my body facing to the beautiful afternoon sunsets that I enjoyed every day. My daughter will understand as I have also expressed my wishes in her letter. I am not sure by now if you have discovered that the gold is not in the dam like we agreed that day. I changed my mind when I got up there, it still felt too obvious after I threw in the first bar. If you stand at the rock you just moved and turn due east, in eighty-six paces you will see a large burnt out hollow log where I have shoved a termite mound at both ends. The gold is inside the log. Use it wisely and take care my young friend, make the most of it while youth is still on your side. Your mate Mac.

Tim slowly folded the covering letter and broke down with emotion as he unbuttoned his pocket and rolled the first smoke since before his tyres got deflated by the road spikes. He flicked the lighter then applied it to the cover letter. Flames licked up the side before he dropped the only evidence of where the gold was hidden to the ground and stamped the ash when the flame died out. Walking back to the rock for a bearing he looked directly to the east before setting off counting his steps as he went. The crows scattered as he neared the Chinaman. Drawing some saliva, he spat on the corpse, before retrieving his bloodied pocketknife lying on the ground, wiping off the blood. "It also comes in handy for cleaning out earwax, ya dumb fucking meathead. You died way too quickly for the pain you dished out arsehole, rot in hell." Tim continued counting. Thirty paces out he could see the log described in the letter. He smiled when feeling inside for the gold bars. "You cunning old bugger." With nothing to carry them in he removed his shirt. Counting out seventeen gold bars he placed fifteen in his can't tear em work shirt and knotted it and then placed the other two in his pants pockets. With the plastic capsule underarm, he started making his way back towards the hut.

All three were sitting outside on the 4x4 tray along with Nugget trying to keep cool in the occasional breeze that sprung up. Both girls had refused to stay inside with Mac's corpse still lying on the ground. Hugh had moved Tim's truck under some scant shade where he cleaned and dressed Meg's wound in silence while she openly displayed complete hatred of this man tending to her gunshot wound as he finished off bandaging it with the required amount of pressure. Hugh looked around reaching for his rifle as he could hear movement in the grass as the prospector broke into the clearing with a smile on his face. He lowered the rifle. "You look happy about something prospector." Tim slung him the shirt. "Fifteen bars as agreed." Both girls sighed loudly, it was finally all over. Hugh counted the bars and threw back the shirt. "You were good to your word as I will be to mine prospector." They shook hands as Hugh offered a slip of paper with his number on it. "Still owe you one," as he nodded in the direction of the dam. "Do you want a hand to bury the old bloke?" Tim's reaction went from one of achievement to sorrow. "No, I would rather do that by myself."

He shrugged. "Suit yourself prospector, I'm starting to like this end of the country, might even hang around for a bit…still have some loose ends to tie up. Might catch you around one day?" Tim shook his head, "don't think so bud, I have seen enough death in the last six months to last a lifetime." "Fair enough," replied the hitman as he turned around to the hire vehicle, completely ignoring both girls as he left on the track that would lead him back to civilization. With all danger now gone, Danni ran into Tim's arms. "Let's get out of here." He embraced the hug before holding her at arms-length staring his wife in the eyes. "I can't just yet, I need some time alone to bury Mac. You girls drive back to the creek out of the heat and I will walk down and meet you there when I'm done."

Tim reached for Nugget, lifting him off the tray for the first time since they had arrived just before the girls left in his truck. He barked loudly, not even waiting for a pat or rub from Tim. He scampered straight into the hut whining and licking Mac's face. It brought an instant tear to the battle-hardened prospector's eye to watch the pup continuously try to move Mac's arm with his snout for affection. "Yeah, it's really fucked up, hey mate." Nugget laid down on all haunches, pushing himself as close as possible to Mac's body while Tim searched for his new prospecting pick and the camp shovel. He nailed together a crude cross similar to that of Jonah's before the sound of the pick striking the rocky ground travelled along the ridgeline. Nugget whimpered continuously trying to dig out the loose dirt that Tim had finally built into a mound. "Here boy, it's time to let go." Tim picked him up under protest to carry him down the hill to where the girls were waiting.

The drive back into town seemed somewhat awkward. After describing the physique of the Chinese mountain he had to deal with, the rest of the trip consisted of only broken conversation, other than direct questions that were answered in single syllables. Tim put it down to both girls being completely exhausted after their ordeal. He admitted it was something a normal housewife should never have had to endure. His perception of their condition was way off the mark as John's words had burnt deep into the thoughts of both women before he scampered into the bush under sharp gun fire from Hugh. They travelled along in silence, both trying to work out how to take control of their own totally separate issues, which would come to light in the near future.

Nearing town, his main objective was to make sure the girls were safe from the dangers of his ex- prospecting partner. After that he knew the next move would be to hand himself in for questioning to the police. Tim had already started to work out his alibi that consisted of being lost out bush which wasn't too far from the truth anyway. The only concern he had with this plan was the damming evidence that Grace, the female detective, had read and no doubt copied before handing it over to Danni. This was an unknown that would play out when he handed himself in, but in his mind the detective's decision to pass that letter over instead of holding onto it for any future evidence against him spoke a thousand words. Hopefully, his assumption was right. On that thought Tim changed his mind – the police station would be his second port of call; first would be to cash in the two gold bars still in his pocket at the bullion buyers just in case Danni needed to hire a legal team if things went pear shaped when he handed himself in to the cops.

Chapter 8

GOLD STRIKE AND PRISION BLUES

C had been inducted into the prison facility and freed from his wrist and leg restraints. He noted the whispers between prison guards since exiting the prison van as he was exchanged numerous times on the way to his cell. He smirked inwardly assuming they were all in his favour after making the deal with the bikie who said he had prison officers on the inside who would look after him. It was not till the last transfer that he heard the whispered words "that's the cop killer." C immediately broke into a nervous sweat, looking around in vain for any support. A burly officer shoved him roughly in the back into his cell, "Here's home for the rest of your life." C skidded to a stop halfway down the cell that contained two bunks but came without a cell mate. C, as usual, was not able to contain his anger as he spat out, "Fuck you screw, do you know who I am?"

The large prison officer just smiled at the derogatory remark from the new fish. "Yep, I know exactly who you are. You're everybody's bitch for whichever cell I decide to open from now until my change of shift at 5am. Some lifers just a few cells down would love to get their hands on some fresh meat." He left the cell door open with the locking mechanism retracted so C could not even lock himself back in to ward off what was about to evolve. Walking back through the last gate the prison officer remotely opened three cell doors to christen this loudmouth fucker who would soon learn the respect of who was in charge on the inside.

C backed himself into a corner with his fists ready to lash out as three huge men entered his cell, their intent clearly evident by the expressions they wore. "Come on you fuckers let's tango," C yelled. The thud of fists hitting flesh was loud but very brief in the dim light that softly emanated from the yellow corridor fluro along the cell block. C was flipped over effortlessly like a pancake onto his stomach before his screams echoed through the whole B section. "Fuck you prospector," he cursed before his mouth was quickly smothered by two very large hands followed by a pillow stifling the agonising screams that continued for hours until all three inmates' sexual appetites were satisfied.

Morning did not come early enough for C as the former kingpin's high flyer lifestyle had come crashing down to earth. Being the recipient of copious amounts of sticky sperm that already had started to dry, he spun the dunny paper dispenser, gagging continuously as he frantically tried to wipe off the bodily fluid from various parts of his naked body. The thought of what had transpired in the last eight hours instantaneously brought stomach bile to his throat, spraying it into the toilet bowl. C conceded that this was, without a doubt, the lowest and most degrading point in his life.

The sound of all the cells unlocking gained C's attention while he was still on his knees, continuing to dry retch after having no fluid left in the pit of his stomach to expel. He turned to watch the line of inmates walk past towards the mess hall for breakfast. Some completely ignored his cell while others who were already privy to what went down last night smiled and slapped each other on the back, laughing at the current position he was in – on his knees with his head inches from the lip of the toilet bowl. C crawled to his clothing lying on the floor, and dressing back into the torn prison-issue uniform, he walked gingerly into the line.

This continued every night for a full week with C not even attempting to fight back after day three. There were always too many of them. Repeatedly raped and beaten, all bruises inflicted were directed at the body to avoid easy detection by the prison officers. C's fiery spirit had been subdued to the point of depression. The first and the most valuable lesson he had learnt since his very short time inside was don't fuck with the screws. Tenderly sitting down to lunch alone as usual on the seventh day, five bulky men covered in tattoos made themselves at home sitting around the table. C looked up briefly not wanting to create any more trouble than he already had on his plate. Remaining silent he returned full attention back towards the food in front of him with his head down. In between mouthfuls of stew while staring intently at this new fish, the largest man in the group growled in a deep voice, "so you're the mighty and powerful C, you look fuck all to me."

For the first time since being incarcerated a partial smile formed on his lips – he recognised the paid help had finally arrived. "About time you fucks, do you pricks know what I have suffered in this joint?" The large biker slammed his hand down on the table that made every plate jump into the air. "Listen you little arse wipe, let's get something straight, most of us won't be out of here for another nine years. The money offered to keep your arse safe and possibly get you out of here down the track has fuck all value to us on the inside, there had want to be a lot more cash waiting for us on the outside than the few crumbs being offered now." C nodded, backing off immediately. He needed to stay sweet with these blokes at all costs. "Of course boys, I hear what you're saying, there is always room for good men in my organisation that stick by my side in times of trouble."

He now perused the room with confidence. "See them fuckwits sitting four tables down on my left? I want their nuts stomped on that hard that they can never be used again." The spokesman for the group was facing C. Not wanting to alert anybody of any future intent by turning around he nodded to another member at the table who was facing in the right direction. He nodded back after locating the table of offenders in the busy mess hall that was consumed by the hungry sound of cutlery scraping on empty plates. "Done, you will be starting in the kitchen with us next week," was all that was added to the conversation as they got up from the table leaving C alone once more but in a totally different frame of mind.

Tim woke the girls out of a deep sleep as he pulled up in the darkness out the front of a motel just on the outskirts of Cairns. Paying with nearly all the remaining cash left on him, he herded them both into the self-contained room. They both flopped onto the king-size bed leaving him with the single bed. Being exhausted, it did not faze him in the least – at this point he could easily sleep on a barbed-wire fence. Grabbing his own pillow and a bowl of water, he returned to the back of the truck placing them both in the back for Nugget. "I'm knackered boy, see you in the morning."

The room was pitch black thanks to the heavy black curtains. Groaning, Tim swung his legs to the floor peeling back the curtain to be hit by the bright sunshine outside. He jotted down a quick note on the complimentary stationary for the girls before slipping out the door to cash in the gold bars.

Wong and Fu had opened the shop half an hour earlier than the usual time. Neither had heard from Chang since they left in the chopper days earlier and Fu was starting to worry that something had gone wrong. The businessman took a grip on his wild assumptions and reasoned the job had simply not been completed yet. Chang was the best assassin they had, and as close to a son as he would ever get. Chang had never failed an assignment, ever. Both stood at one of the glass displays discussing what should replace the items they had sold yesterday. The door buzzer sounded as the young prospector walked into the store. "How's it going fellas, what's the gold price like today?" Fu's eyes bulged, gripping the side of the display case for support to stop himself from falling over, while Wong with his face pale white quickly made himself scarce shuffling off into the rear office to watch proceedings from the safety of the in-store TV monitor. Tim watched the Asian move off before looking at Fu who was still trying to come to terms with how this man who now stood in his shop was still alive. "Shit going off that reaction, the price must be way lower than I thought," Tim replied with a smile. Still without an answer he studied Fu closer. "You OK there mate? Looks like you just swallowed a couple of flies, got two ten-ounce bars to sell, are you buying today?"

Fu snapped out of his initial shock realising that this outback prospector obviously had no idea that they now owned the gold mine. He briefly pondered on Chang's fate, knowing now that he had totally underestimated the ability of this seemingly harmless individual. He had already submitted all the paperwork to the mines department and knew it would only be a short time until the prospector found out the truth. While Fu was in the department he enquired on what protocol would follow and was advised the mines department would send out an approval letter to both parties acknowledging the transfer of ownership. Walking back behind the counter closer to the 357-magnum sitting on a shelf under the counter Fu replied, "Good morning sir, excuse my rudeness, you just reminded me of someone who looks a lot like you." Tim's smile returned. "Well he's a bloody lucky bugger then isn't he if he looks anything like me," he said breaking into a chuckle. "Are we doing business today or not?" Fu, now fully composed, replied quickly, "But of course my friend, come, let's weigh them ingots and get you some money."

Tim left the bullion store happy with the price, and after getting some sleep under his belt last night he could think more clearly. Parking at a phone booth he removed the waterproof container from behind the seat to locate Mac's daughter's phone number. "Well there you go, didn't even know your name was Casey until now," Tim muttered aloud. He organised a meeting at the very northern end of the park along the esplanade in two hours' time, not wanting to tell her in a crowded place or over the phone that her father had been murdered. This gave him enough time to buy some food and drop it back to the motel before the meeting.

Fu and Wong were in turmoil as soon as Tim left the building. "What do we do now, what's happened to Chang?" asked Wong nervously throwing his hands in the air. Fu, the more dominant in the partnership, replied, "Same plan as before. The prospector needs to disappear for good, nothing has changed, we just need to have protection for ourselves until that happens. Get some of them bikers over to keep watch on the building until I organise some of our own men from Sydney, and close up the shop until we get reorganised." Fu was dirty at himself after always priding himself on reading people well and couldn't believe how he had read this prospector so wrong.

Tim sat on the last bench in the park. Nugget, with his front leg now bandaged, lay obediently at his side as a constant ocean breeze blew onto his face. He could smell the salt on the wind as he looked to the south for people approaching along the pathway. Numerous joggers passed by as he vacantly gazed at the innocence of the seagulls squabbling over some bread crusts left by a young family enjoying lunch on the esplanade. It was then he noticed a middle-aged lady well dressed with long blonde hair looking around like she was lost. Figuring this was Mac's daughter he stood and gave a short wave to grab her attention. As she got closer he noticed her apprehension instantly. "Tim is it, what's happened?" she said offering her hand. He nodded looking into her questioning piercing blue eyes. "Hi Casey, well I'm not exactly sure where to start, but your father has been murdered. Let's sit, I have a lot to tell you and there is stuff that Mac wanted me to give you." Casey turned her head to conceal her emotion before staring him straight back in the eye. "I want to hear it all, everything."

The hours passed as they unintentionally held their own private wake, Mac's daughter's mood swung abruptly depending on the story that Tim was telling, from laughter to giggling to crying on his shoulder. He handed over the plastic container. "Here, you can read the contents, both yours and mine, I want all his wishes out in the open." Casey accepted the offer. Tim could tell she was astute and well educated as she flipped through Mac's sheets of paper nodding in acceptance as she read her father's wishes. Concern came across her face as she then picked up Tim's and read through it at a slower pace. "Is something wrong?" Casey looked up, "Yes, I'm afraid there are a couple of things. Firstly, this is not the Wild West Tim, you just can't bury my dad out there even though that's what he wanted. This is murder and the relevant authorities need to be notified, an autopsy will need to be done on dad's remains to find cause of death and then a death certificate must be issued before any of his estate can be distributed. On top of that I have just received by registered mail this morning a document from the mines department, some transfer papers that dad has sold the mine. Enclosed was a copy of a payment receipt for ten thousand dollars."

Tim could not believe his ears. "That's impossible this must be some kind of fraud, he would never sell the mine for a lousy ten grand. Mac would have absolutely told me if he was even thinking of selling up, there was never any secrets between us ever, he was always straight to the point." Casey agreed. "Thought it was strange, I smell a rat but on the paperwork it is definitely his signature, that I am sure of. I was going to the mines department today before you rang to try to get to the bottom of it." "Well we can fuck them up because my signature is not on there, and I owned 50 per cent of the mine before Mac even passed," Tim replied. "Does it have a name of the buyer?" "Million Bullion Buyers, have you heard of them?"

He stood bolt upright. "You bet I know who they are, I was just there earlier. I will sort this out right now." Casey grabbed his arm as he went to walk away. "Dad had told me all about you...an eye for an eye is the real man's world he used to quote to me. There is no need for any more bloodshed in your life Tim, even if you did succeed it would still not change the ownership issue…we will have to win this one in the courts." "Yeah, fair enough," Tim conceded, "but at the end of the day you did not see how much pain and torture he must have endured," he added as the huge Chinese assassin came to mind. "No doubt about it now, his death was all over signing those ownership papers, the vision of old Mac that day will stay with me for life. Come to think of it somebody else must have been there earlier because I can tell you for a fact that the Chinaman I ran across out at the mine site didn't hand in any bloody bill of sale."

Casey burst into tears. "Leave it with me, I work for a legal firm so I will get to the bottom of this I promise. The transfer papers were even signed by a justice of the peace so I can track their registered number to find out who that is. Trust the law for a change Tim, they will not get away with this." "OK, let's give it a shot and see how you go, but yeah I'm with your old man on this one, an eye for an eye, they all need to pay in blood for what they have done. So what do I do now, go dig up Mac's body and bring him all the way to town in the back of my truck? I couldn't just leave him on the floor where I found him." "No, of course not, you must contact the police and probably go out there with them being the last one to see him alive." He thought about the Chinaman's body lying out on the flat, exposed. Had there been enough time for the larger scavengers of the outback to come into play yet? Patting Nugget Tim replied, "yeah OK, I have to ring a detective that I know later today. Hey, do you like dogs?" Tim left Nugget and all the paperwork with Casey so she could take copies to mount a challenge over ownership of the mine. Resisting the urge to drive straight back to the bullion shop, he drove towards the motel to contact the female detective.

Grace was frustrated as she sat at her desk, which was covered in reports. All leads had gone cold and they were no closer to finding the identity of the hitman or the ex-cop since they had locked up the ring leader well over a week ago. Reaching for the mobile phone that rang on her hip, Grace spun her chair sideways to move clear of the desk. Standing, she quickly jotted down the address of the motel and left the office in a hurry.

Tim opened the door to Grace. The girls were awake and they all sat down at the table. Grace started by addressing them all. "Nothing said in this room today will be repeated, do you understand? You are very lucky to be alive Tim, these men you have gotten yourself involved with are playing for keeps at all costs." He nodded. "Yeah, I have noticed that."

"Listen," the detective continued, "I know you were out at Hatchet River with your prospecting partner when the blood bath occurred, but I honestly believe it was something the pair of you got dragged into. I am not out to nail you to the wall over the death of them scumbag criminals, but what I do want is the hired gun and a cop named Marko." To clear the slate, you help me and I will make any pending charges disappear."

Tim let out a sigh. "No problems, what do I have to do?"

"It will be dangerous, but I want to use you as bait to drag the hitman out of hiding. We will plaster the front page of all the major papers…you have been found alive surviving in the bush for over four months living off the land, that will make a great story and hopefully stir this hired killer into trying to come after you. We will have our best men on the job keeping you safe."

Tim smiled inwardly trying not to laugh. "Yeah, that should do the trick. Reckon that will stir up the gunman alright, count me in." "Good," replied Grace with a smile, somewhat surprised at the prospector's eager acceptance of what could put him face to face with one of the most wanted men in the state. "I will organise a reporter to do an interview with you today and get some of my men on the job – they are good, you won't even know you are being followed." For the second time in this conversation Tim had to contain his laughter. He held off reporting Mac's murder just yet, he needed some time to think this through and get the girls to a safe place first. Grace got up to leave and saw Meg's heavily bandaged arm. "What happened?"

"Dog bite," Meg answered simply.

John, unsure if they were now in pursuit or not, kept driving. He knew he was lucky to be alive after being narrowly missed by bullets under extremely accurate rifle fire. This new bloke that seemed to have suddenly sided with Tim was certainly no slouch with a rifle that was for sure. That, along with his wife's appearance and her vow of innocence, had thrown him off guard for what he had in mind. The V8 was nice to drive but was in no way set up for the bush and John decided to pull into his place hoping his 4x4 had been returned. Before abandoning the V8 across the street he checked the glovebox for any cash. As luck would have it the young owner's wallet was inside containing roughly six hundred dollars. Taking the whole wallet and locking the truck so nobody else could steal it, he entered the yard and opened the roller door of the shed. Finding the car doors locked, John reached under his 4x4 for his spare set of keys taped to the chassis. With his tucker box still full of tinned food he moved around the shed throwing in other items that might come in handy in the bush. He was not sure yet of what he was going to do but he knew staying in town was definitely not an option. John, now off the toad tonic, was acutely aware of the demon in his own head that he needed to battle. He knew that to achieve this he first had to contain the trigger points that led to the unleashing of this anger, knowing now that when it occurred he had no self-control over it. With betrayal still burning in his gut, John understood this was going to be a complex goal to accomplish which he could only do by himself in his own time.

The rhythmic crash of small crystal clear waves onto the pristine beach nearly had Marko nodding off in his collapsible deck chair. The distant sounds of children laughing and playing between the swimming flags wafted in on the sea breeze to where he and his wife had their chairs on the beach. Marko rolled onto his side on hearing the approaching footsteps in the dry sand as his wife returned from the kiosk with a newspaper along with two plastic bottles of soft drink. She tossed the paper onto his naked top half declaring, "Next time you can get off your arse and go get it yourself."

He let the comment slide, not even bothering with a reply. The ex-cop rolled over onto his back planning to spend the next hour perusing the paper as he had nothing better to do or nowhere else he needed to be – he absolutely loved this lifestyle. Marko sat upright after looking at the full colour picture on the front page with the heading, *Prospector survives four months in the wilderness living off the land*, then in smaller print on the corner of the page, full story, page three. He turned the pages quickly and read the half-page article twice before lowering the paper and thinking if this could change his position in any way. He came up blank and smirked with self-confidence, sighing out loud, "Not my bloody problem anymore." A week earlier he had read a small story on C being sent to prison to await a date for a Supreme Court trial. He picked up the paper passing it to his wife who ignored the offer as she lay down trying to work out how to send pictures on Facebook from her new prepaid mobile phone that was sent to her via snail mail from family members up North so she could keep in contact. She dearly missed all their friends and family – both over the phone and physical interaction – since fleeing the state. Marko interrupted her concentration once again shaking his head. "Unbelievable how one single prospector could bring down our whole organisation worth multi-millions a year to its knees and is still alive and breathing. He won't be for long after C and the rest of them read this."

"That's nice dear," she replied absently, pressing post to display her photos and story.

C had just entered his cell after dinner, everything had been running a lot smoother now he had backing. The three men who raped him all ended up in the prison infirmary with serious testicle injuries. Two still occupied the prison hospital beds with a third sent to Cairns for surgery to remove his manhood. Word soon got around to the rest of the inmates, who he was and what happened to the three men who had crossed his path with most now keeping a wide berth. Kitchen duty was easy work and he was never far away from his muscle. Newspapers were contraband on the inside but the front page of the paper along with the third page managed to make its way between the bars of his cell not long after he lay down on his bunk. Picking up the pieces of folded newspaper he read the contents of both pages repeatedly. He was livid. The story instantly brought out the different skin tones on his face. "Your turn's coming prospector when I get out… you, the cop bitch and fucking Marko – that turncoat piss-weak pig – will all have lead coming your way. Should have organised my own contract killer from the start instead of using that other hopeless dope from WA."

Hugh pulled in to fuel up the 4x4 while also giving the windscreen some extra attention with the servo supplied squeegee making sure to erase every single bug before returning the hire vehicle. The West Australian expected to cop some flack over its condition, but having used one of his fake driver's licences on the paperwork he was not overly worried. Being a cash deal with no credit card to charge in case of damage, the proprietor walked out anxious to inspect that his latest addition to the fleet was in the same condition as it had left the yard and the tank was full of fuel. He was speechless at the sight of both broken windows, not sure what to say just yet. He remained silent as he ran an open hand along numerous deep scrapes caused from tree branches, some down to bare metal along one side of the vehicle's paint work. Shaking his head in disbelief he ventured on, rounding the other side he groaned rubbing his hand through his hair in frustration as it was literally covered from one end to the other in various size rock dints from the explosion. The owner also picked up that the spare tyre was missing off the rear door bracket as he finished off the exterior inspection of the latest model 4x4 wagon in the series. He briefly looked inside at the interior that was full of broken glass, while bulldust covered nearly every square inch of the duco. Grey tape was still stuck to nearly every secure panel and instrument on the inside and what appeared to be minor blood stains on the driver's seat.

Stuttering he asked, "What the bloody hell happened?" The West Australian put on an innocent face, and leaning over the owner's shoulder to read the paperwork on the clipboard he held, he said, "Make sure you tick off that I filled the tank up and, as promised, not a bug on the windscreen."

"That's it, the police need to be notified over this," the owner vowed. The hitman shook his head as he removed the bag from the rear seat before lifting the handgun from his waist in full view of the owner while reading the name tag pinned to his shirt. "Now Marvin, you don't want to do anything stupid like that, do you?" Hugh then reached for his rifle breaking it down skilfully in front of Marvin before placing it inside the bag. "Surely you have insurance?" He nodded nervously "Yes." Hugh reached into his pocket throwing the keys to the owner "Thought so, I suggest you use it."

The hitman now with all his gear packed started to walk out of the yard. "Use your imagination Marvin, I'm sure you will come up with something. The last thing you want is for me to have to come back and pay you a visit." Walking a short distance into the main business hub of Cairns he froze mid-stride as a group of commuters on bench seats were reading the day's newspaper with Tim's picture plastered all over the front page. Snatching a copy off a young man dressed in a stylish business suit who stood to protest, Hugh pushed him in the chest gently back to his sitting position, "sit down shut up and show some manners boy" – he flicked to page three, quickly reading its contents before shoving the newspaper back to the owner. He spoke aloud as he continued to walk along looking for a suitable place to stay. "For fuck sake prospector what are you doing? You may as well of just painted a red target on your forehead, you silly fool."

Tim left the room as the sun was rising to grab the day's paper, keen to see what they had managed to spin together. At this early hour the streets mainly consisted of the fitness conscious as they jogged or ran past him while he walked the short distance from where he had parked along the footpath into the newsagent. It did not take him long to work out he was being followed by two plain-clothes officers unable to remain inconspicuous in the light pedestrian traffic. The third, a young female officer wearing fitness gear stretching her calf muscles on a vacant bench seat, was the most difficult to pick out. He gave her a wink as he walked back towards the 4x4 thinking aloud, "yeah, safe as houses, god help me." The unmarked car followed him three cars back as he swung back into the motel. Both girls were up and in full discussion at the table as he let himself inside. The conversation ceased immediately as he entered the room. He could feel something was just not right. Trying to lighten up the mood he placed the paper on the table, "I'm now a free man, and look they didn't even print my best side for the photo. What do you guys reckon?" he said cracking a smile.

Meg was first to reply, not even staying on the same topic. "I will read it another time Tim. I have a girlfriend picking me up shortly, I will go get this arm looked at and I think you pair need some time alone." Picking up the serious vibe in the room, Tim said, "So, what you're going home alone? What about John? He is still out there somewhere, we need to move you and Danni somewhere safe till I get this sorted." Meg's voice rose with her reply, "I am not scared of my husband." Tim looked at his wife for verbal support to his plan, none was forthcoming. A car horn sounded out the front breaking the awkward moment of silence. "That will be my lift, keep in touch you pair and keep safe." She gave them both a brief hug before slipping out of the room with nothing but the clothes she wore.

Tim turned with a worried look on his face. "I hope she will be

OK by herself, that is just plain stupid if you ask me." "Tim, you can't be everywhere and try to save everyone all the time," his wife commented. "I have been thinking, I might go and stay with my sister on the Gold Coast for a while. I just cannot cope with this anymore, it is just too much for me." Moving to her side he accepted the fact that she had been through a lot in the past week with her life being in serious danger several times. Giving her a long hug without any return affection he looked into her eyes. "That would be a good idea, you will be safe down there until I get on top of what is happening up here." "That's just the problem Tim, will it ever be over? Can our lives now ever go back to being the same?" Taken back by her defeatist thoughts, Tim burst out, "of course it will, we must believe in that or what's the use of fighting…what do you want me to do just give up and get shot?"

Danni burst into tears, "no, that's not what I want…I think I could be pregnant." "What, you sure? That's bloody great news, you have been trying for so long. How do you know?" She managed to break into a small smile over Tim's excitement as he lifted her effortlessly off the chair. "My period is late, could be from all the stress but I don't think so. I will book in to see a doctor next week when I'm at my sister's." Tim's mind was racing. "I'm going to be a dad, we need to go shopping get you some bigger clothes, and I think it's about time I get a mobile phone, and a new one for you. How long before we know if it's a boy or a girl? We need to book you a flight, and you are going to need a suitcase." Danni broke from his grasp, not displaying the same amount of excitement her husband was showing. "Slow down Tim, I'm not giving birth tomorrow. Let's just see what a doctor has to say next week and we need to go home first to get our ID, you cannot buy a phone let alone an airline ticket without it." They booked out of the motel, being followed at a distance by the unmarked police car as they headed towards the Kuranda Range.

Danni stayed in the 4x4 with the aircon running, unable to bring herself to walk inside the house with the memories of what had transpired still too fresh. Tim returned with her handbag and his wallet. "Sure you don't want to get anything from inside to take with you?" She shuddered at the thought, just wanting to get as far away from the place as possible. "No, it's OK. I will buy some new stuff when we get back to Cairns." "Fair enough, here," Tim said as he shoved a large wad of cash into her handbag after counting out a thousand dollars for himself. "That should cover you for a while." Once again, the trip contained little talk even after he tried to instigate conversation. He had let it slide on several occasions already, and after the revelation of a baby possibly on the way, supressed any further revelations from his wife's earlier conversation with Meg in the motel room. Concern started to set in as he had the feeling he was starting to lose her somehow. Tim tried once again to address any situation that could be worrying the one he loved. "What's wrong babe? I can tell something serious is on your mind, whatever it is we can work through it together if I know what it is." Danni simply replied, "I am just exhausted."

Nearing Cairns he switched over to his sub-tank as the fuel gauge registered empty. Ten kilometres down the road he watched in the mirror as the unmarked vehicle had to swerve off the highway to refuel. Smiling, he changed lanes increasing speed before turning onto the back road towards the largest shopping complex in the city where everything they needed could be purchased under the one roof, including mobile phones and an airline ticket.

Tim left the airport after wheeling in Danni's two new suitcases. Although he would miss her terribly while she was away, at the same time he also felt a weight lift off his shoulders now that he only had himself to worry about. Flipping open the new mobile phone, he scrolled through all the numbers his wife had entered from the pile of scrap pieces of paper he had stashed in his wallet. He decided to ring Casey before heading back out to the mine site to take care of the Chinaman before involving Grace in another murder.

"Hi Casey it's Tim, just checking in to see if you have found out anything." "Yes, I have tracked down the JP. He claims dad signed it in front of him in town…well, we both know that is absolute bullshit. Looks like they have influence and no shortage of money, some hot shot legal firm from Melbourne has been hired to defend the validity of the mine's sale. We are due in court seven months from today." "Righto mate. Look, I just need to shoot back out to the mine site and get rid of the bloke's body that killed your dad before I involve the police." "OK, Tim I can understand that line of thought, but I think you also need to tell them about the Million Bullion Buyers involvement in dad's murder." Tim pulled into a tyre store to get all the staked tyres plugged. Walking a short distance to a small supermarket he topped up with supplies while waiting for his vehicle. All he needed to do now was fuel up then find a bearing shop and he was back to the bush where he belonged. The bustle of the city was not for him, preferring the peace and solitude of the bush and an open fire in contrast to the lights, traffic and crowds of town life any day. Now back on the move, he tried to call one last number before the sun went down and while still in mobile service.

Hugh took a couple of days off to get his wrist plastered before starting work again. Parking down the road from Marko's residence, he walked back along the street slipping down the side of the house. He tried the doors which were now locked after the last police inspection of the house. Trying the handle on the shed door he pushed it open. Feeling for a light, the hitman looked around for anything obvious that might give him a clue as to the ex-cop's whereabouts. Other than a pile of dated motorhome magazines lying on the work bench that signalled at one stage he was interested in this type of travel, there was not much he could find that was out of the normal average Aussie male's shed. Finding a large flat screwdriver, he left the shed and prised open one of the old swollen timber windows at the rear of the house before climbing inside. Moving through the house he targeted the small room that was set out as an office, concentrating on searching for phone bills in particular. "Surname Shultz, let's see what else we can find

Marko," he said to himself as he started flicking through more paperwork. Finding what he was looking for, Hugh scanned the call list of the most recent bill to find the more frequently dialled local calls, coming up with two numbers that stood out. In his search of the office he also discovered two services conducted on a motorhome, one as recently as last month. The rego was typed at the top of the bill.

He dialled the number on his disposable mobile phone, a woman answered. "Hello Shultz residence, can I help you?" Hugh smiled, "no, but I can help you my dear. It's Jason from the Fun Fish Café, you have been randomly selected in our current promotion from the phone book to receive a family meal deal of fish and chips for free. Have you started preparing dinner for tonight?" "Have I," the woman squealed in delight, before adding "no Jason, was just starting to think along those lines of what I was doing for dinner, that's fantastic…never won anything like this before. What time will you be delivering?" "Well Mrs Shultz, I will need your address first and what time would you prefer?" She giggled excitedly into the phone running off her address. "Six-thirty would be great, my husband will be home by then."

The lanky West Australian also went through the family photo albums that were left standing upright on a polished timber shelf in the lounge room. Having never met Marko the hitman had no clue what he looked like. Towards the end of one album there was Marko and his wife standing proudly in front of what looked like a brand new motorhome with the number plate in clear view. He removed various photos from what he easily worked out were the most recent judging from the age of the people in the photos and placed them in his shirt pocket. "Got you now you worthless pile of shit, reckon after tonight's fish delivery you're done like toast." He brought an early dinner of mackerel and chips in the main street of the city. Finishing off his meal the hitman kept the white butcher's paper. Returning to his new little two-door bubble car from another hire-car company, he placed a roll of duct tape and a set of knuckle dusters inside the wrapping just in case before including an old sweat-stained shirt to fill out the size of the delivery. Lastly, he rolled up his balaclava to look like a beanie, wanting to keep his identity unknown to this family as he had no beef with them – Hugh just needed a location. Glancing at his watch Hugh, who always preferred to arrive early, liked to survey an area before committing himself finally to any job.

Mrs Shultz was taking time out on the lounge now that she didn't have to lift a finger for dinner. She flipped through the channels to find her favourite TV soapie before opening her Facebook page on her mobile phone to read her latest notifications. A sharp knock sounded on the front door just as she got comfortable. "Mrs Shultz, delivery from Fun Fish Café." Rising to her feet excitedly, she swung open the door as the balaclava-clad intruder pushed his way past her into the house before slamming the door. "Where is your husband?" Shocked she pointed towards a door. "Having a shower. What's this all about?" He pointed towards a chair with his handgun, "Sit down!" Tearing open the package he taped her to the chair before escorting her husband out dripping wet with just a towel wrapped around his waist. "What is the meaning of this, what do you want?" demanded Mr Shultz as the gunman secured him to a chair. "It's quite simple really, all I want is to know where Marko is hiding and nobody will get hurt here tonight." "The police have already asked us that question, we don't know where he is." "Yeah well, I'm not as nice as the police, and you're fucking talking shit buddy. Now I will ask one more time before things start to get real ugly for you pair." His wife's phone sounded off that a message had just been received. Turning to the sound, Mrs Shultz gasped as the gunman reached for her phone off the TV table. "Put that down, that's private property." Hugh smiled. "You just got to love Facebook, what a treasure trove of information.

"This has just saved you pair a whole lot of hurt," he added as he placed the phone in his pocket. Running a strip of tape over their mouths, Hugh pulled off his balaclava before stepping outside. Walking briskly to the little bubble car, he could hear his phone, still in the bag on the rear seat, start to ring. Not used to getting many calls other than clients he answered, "Yep." "Tim here, just thought I would give you the heads up that the cops are after you bad if you are still in the North. I would piss off real quick." The contract killer shrugged his shoulders. "So what's new, heading to a sunny beach location interstate anyway…prospector, don't tell me you rang just to let me know the obvious?" Tim replied sheepishly, "well actually, that's not the main reason. With your contacts I was wondering if you could ask around about a mob that runs Million Bullion Buyers, they were the ones that hired that bloke that nearly choked you to death. The pricks have forced my old partner to sign over his gold mine, which I half own. Now I have to face court to fight over ownership against them in seven months."

"Yeah OK prospector, let me see what I can find out."

Fu and Wong had resumed trading with a steady flow of customers after staying shut for the past two days. The business was now under tight security after the pair flew up another two of their own from Sydney. Fu was happy to see the last of the bikers he had to rush in for protection, not wanting to create any connection between them and the ice distribution that had started off somewhat confrontationally on the streets, but by all counts was now a roaring success. The two new Asian bodyguards, also solid in build, had viewed the footage and the newspaper clippings of Tim that Wong had kept. "Doesn't look much to me," one commented. Fu switched off the tape, "well, that's what we thought, but he must have taken Chang out…you both have worked with him, you know what he was capable of. Both new recruits to the North nodded having seen Chang's destructive technique on display interstate many times.

Grace got a call from the special team she had personally selected to follow Tim to try to locate the hitman. "What do you mean you lost him already, this is day one for Christ sake, find him," she yelled down the phone before slamming it down, frustrated over the report. "What a fuck up."

Tim made it onto the mine site opting to camp outside in his swag under the stars. Though tired, he was unable to sleep straight away as his mind was alive with probabilities – recent events that he could have changed and now, more importantly, the things that he needed to take control over and make happen in the future. Staring into the clear sky in the absolute silence of the bush, Tim counted the slow-moving satellites and falling stars that travelled at speed leaving a bright trail behind them before disappearing into the infinity of space. Within twenty minutes the only noise other than a few random crickets chirping in the early morning darkness was Tim's loud snoring.

Rolling out not long after daybreak, it felt kind of surreal without old Mac's early morning banter as he pottered around the open fire making a hot cuppa for them both. After four hours of broken sleep he had finally come to the decision of which method he would use to dispose of the body. His main concern about Casey's way of doing things was that he would leave himself wide open to more trouble with the police. The only witness he had to validate his story of what happened was the West Australian, and hell would freeze over before he gave a statement to the police. The girls…well the only part they could verify was where Mac lay before he buried his partner, nothing more. He did not see any use in dragging either women into this as who would believe them anyway if they told the truth? Not bothering with a morning coffee, Tim drove towards the mine site, the first thing on his plate today was to insert the new bearing on the crusher.

Twenty minutes after arriving on the mine site Tim started the loader. While the machine warmed up he looked at the piles of rock still lying over the blast site that he was unable to finish before the breakdown. Lifting the bucket off the ground he started to make a rough track through the long grass towards the dam and the assassin's remains. The noise from the approaching loader had all the wildlife around the dam scatter into the bush or the sky. Leaving the machine idling, he checked in on what stage mother nature's natural recycling process had advanced to. The stench in the air was strong –the remains were scattered over a roughly a ten-metre radius with only the blowflies and maggots unperturbed by his presence. Marking out the area he needed to cover with the loader to erase all sign of evidence, Tim got to work scrapping up thin layers of dirt along with Chang. Making a final inspection before leaving the dam he was satisfied with the result. Starting up the crusher, Tim mixed his load with another pile of rocks and started feeding bucket after bucket into the processing plant. After four hours all the free ore lying around was cleaned up, with fine fragments of human DNA now well mixed through and lying under twenty tons of crushed material. Searching through the hut, Tim located his sat phone. With the flashing screen signalling low battery, he plugged it into his 4x4 cigarette lighter as he did not expect this to be a short call before pressing in the digits of the female detective's number from his new mobile which Danni had programed yesterday.

The tall hitman was hunched over in the little bubble car as he drove straight to the airport. He was only too aware that once the Shultz family was found it would not be long before they made contact to warn Marko, and there was also the possibly they could even involve the police. Though not his preferred method of transport it would be the fastest way to locate and dispose of the target under this time-fragile situation. Throwing his bag full of gold and weapons into the boot, and knowing full well that he could not take anything with him without detection, he walked into the terminal with just the rental car keys, his wallet and the two mobile phones, and booked the next flight to Newcastle. With two hours up his sleeve till boarding, Hugh booked a hire car for when he arrived then made some calls on the prospector's behalf regarding the information that he had been given on the Asians.

It took until the third call to find an associate based in Sydney who knew the group with some relevant details he was prepared to share. "I will tell you what I know Hugh. They are bad motherfucker's brother. They bring in shitloads of ice man, and I mean fucking huge players in the powder trade. They clean the money through the bullion stores and sell it back into China. Extortion, kidnapping, the full dice man. What, did they offer you some work bro?" he asked dubiously after he had finished. Hugh listened shaking his head. "Nah mate, I had a run-in with one of them the other day. Just thought I would see what I could find out."

"Didn't think they would be hiring," his informant replied. "They never have before. Been told that they have always kept it in-house and train their own killers. How un-Australian is that shit man? These big-end boys don't give a crap about us locals. A run-in you say, well my best advice is don't fuck with this crowd buddy. If they don't already know who you are, stick your head in the sand like an ostrich brother and let them try and work out which sunburnt arsehole you are in the country. You know what I mean bro? Lay low if you value breathing air." Hugh looked at the departures screen, "thanks for the info bud, look I got to go." Hanging up the phone he stated aloud, "for fuck sake prospector, you are one big magnet for fucking trouble, that's for sure." He remembered to check if Mrs Shultz's location tracking device was activated on her phone and switched it to the off position as he stood in line before boarding the aircraft.

The hitman was livid. In the rush to get to his destination he failed to realise there was a stopover for a connecting flight to Newcastle. Having to wait for another three hours before he could board, every hour wasted could mean a tip-off to Marko that death was on its way.

Finally, on the road in another hire car, he headed north towards Port Macquarie following the GPS mounted on the dash with the exact location of the beachside motorhome and caravan park. Marko's reckless wife had taken a selfie photo in front of the welcome sign into the grounds and then forwarded it to her sister-in-law back north. Hugh, spotting a tackle and bait shop open early trying to catch some of the city's keen fishers on their way to preferred fishing spots, swung open the old timber door with ancient old brass bells attached. A salt of the earth retired old fisherman limped to the counter.

"Out to try and catch a feed of fish today young fella? What a perfect day for it, we have fresh sand and blood worms dug up by my sons last night, live yabbies in the tank over there and any other soft plastic or lure you can think of. We will certainly have your poison for the trip right here. Exactly what fish are you targeting today son and I might be able to help." Hugh cracked a smile at the old bloke's friendly sales pitch as he walked past old supermarket shelving with hand reels covered in cobwebs. "Well, what I'm chasing old mate is the heaviest hand line you have in stock, what have you got?" Loving a yarn the old fisherman continued, "Ahh, chasing the big ones by the sounds, shark, tuna, mackerel maybe?" He lent around the counter looking through the shop window to check out what size boat his customer was towing. "No, heading north for marlin," stated Hugh following the owner's gaze outside. The old bloke raised his thick grey bushy eyebrows, "must be new to this fishing game by the sounds of things, you haven't got a shit show of catching a marlin with a bloody hand line son." The hitman cut him short wanting to get back on the road. "Listen old mate, just give me the strongest nylon fishing line you have." Picking up on the tone from his testy customer the old bloke answered, "Righto then, a hundred and fifty pound is the heaviest I have. If you snag up on the bottom, there is no way in hell you will ever break it by hand. The only way to snap that sucker is to tie it off on the gunnel and use the power of the boat to break free. Do you want any hooks or lures to go with that?" Hugh declined, "just the line will do."

Driving into the picturesque coastal bay location Hugh nodded his approval. "Nice choice for a man about to meet his maker." Pulling to the side of the road well short of the administration building, the West Australian pushed in the cigarette lighter till it was glowing red hot. Having already tied one end of the thick fishing line to the car door he held it taught as the lighter melted the nylon line easily. Making two non-slip loops at each end of the line to fit his hands, the contract killer locked the car then shoved the fishing line in his pocket before moving in to make good his promise. Walking down onto the beach he bypassed the access code entry sliding gate and front security cameras. Parking himself not far from the beach entry gate, it was not long before family couples started to move in and out, mixing in with the tenants. Hugh was soon inside looking for the distinct motorhome with bold signwriting on the overhead berth that read "Out of here". After an hour of walking around the large park frustration started to set in. They were already gone.

Going against the grain of his normal professional anonymity, Hugh selected some caravans set up near the main exit road to the gated entrance that appeared to have been in the park for some time. Intruding on several families, he flashed the photo of the motorhome that he took from the Shultz album back in Cairns. Though friendly and obliging, nobody could help with his inquiries until the fourth camp. "Yeah mate, seen that rig roll out of here yesterday, about lunch time, while I was towing the tinnie back to camp after a morning fish…quite a set up that one," answered the middle-aged semi-retired resident. "Yeah right," replied Hugh with a glimmer of hope. "Do you know which site they were staying at in the park?" "Yep, right down the very end, just follow this road right round and you will see about five sites to your left, they were staying in one of them." Thanking the man, Hugh set off for the still vacant site. Asking on either side, both sets of campers confirmed to have met their previous neighbours, apparently going under the aliases of Kurt and Alicia Seyless. Portraying himself as the brother that was to meet them here to stay a few nights, the hitman displayed a look of disappointment. "They didn't say where they were going by any chance?" "No sorry mate, they didn't mention which direction they were headed." The wife, listening in on the conversation while making smoko in the kitchen of their thirty-foot motorhome injected, "didn't they say they might call in and a have look at Flathead Rocks?" "Oh yeah, that's right," replied the husband jogging his memory, "It's a shit-hot fishing spot we found years ago. Thirty-five kilometres to the north, problem is no plug-in power, no phone reception, no TV reception, no shops, with a dirt road for five kilometres. It's pretty remote." The hitman smiled inwardly. "Thanks mate, that sounds remote alright. Can you draw me a map?"

Marko with his chair in the upright position close to the pristine water's edge, tentatively held his fishing rod as the tip bent over in random attacks. Turning to his wife he said, "hey honey, you want to throw the jug on for smoko?"

Hugh wasted no time getting back to the car and following the directions he had been given. Missing the small dirt turn-off, he swore slamming on the handbrake and reversing back up the road. A sign half covered in tree branches indicated it was a no through road. "There's no escape now!" he stated aloud driving down the single vehicle track for five kilometres until it expanded into a large clearing overlooking a stunning secluded little bay. Seconds were all it took for the hitman to realise the area was empty. "Fuck!" he yelled hitting the steering wheel in anger. Reaching for Mrs Shultz's confiscated phone, Hugh turned it on planning to go through all the messages on Facebook to see if there were any clues as to where they might be travelling next. It soon became apparent that she had initiated the security pin code rendering it useless to him after turning it off just before the flight. "Bloody bitch, looks like you get to live for a while longer cop." Doing a U-turn he threw the locked mobile phone out the window. With the chance of tracking them down now unexpectedly gone cold, Hugh had no realistic option other than to return to Newcastle.

Marko's wife brought out two steaming cups of coffee. "You never told me we were hiding out from a killer as well as the police." Marko wound in his line from the crystal-clear creek to take hold of his coffee, "neither did I. Either C has this killer hunting me down for leaving him in the lurch, or he hasn't been paid for the job. No matter the reason, the result will be the same for me." She shook her head. "Lucky I got that call from your brother just before we ran out of mobile service going to that other fishing and camping spot the couple beside us at the park recommended. What the hell are we going to do now? This hole that you have dug for us is continuously getting deeper!" Marko tried to keep positive, though concerned. "Look we are a good 600km away from that area now. There is no chance in hell he could work out which way we went. We'll just have to be very careful from now on. Leave that phone of yours off until we can get another sim card, and if you had kept your trap shut in the first place of what the hell we were up to, everything would be bloody different. Now we need to play it smart. Looks like a change of scenery from the beach to the bulldust is in order. Let's keep heading west off the beaten tourist run."

Returning to the airport and now back in phone service, Hugh had devised another method of trying to locate the elusive cop. He searched on a phone app for the major players in Australian motorhome sales and servicing. Selecting the largest ones first, he started to make calls. "This is Jake Left of the Queensland crime squad, could you put me through to the owner or manager of the business thank you," he said, repeating his title. After being connected through, he further expanded on the reason of the call. "I am head of operations for Task Force Kilo. We have a motorhome that has been reported stolen in Queensland that is believed now to be travelling interstate. These persons are considered extremely dangerous and are not to be approached whatsoever.

Could you please send out a memo to all your distributors and service agents to be vigilant for this vehicle? Please do not contact your local police force over this matter. It is an out-of-state sting operation and they will have no relevant details on this investigation. You will need to contact me personally on this number, do you understand?" The manager jotted down the details. "Yes sir, I will put around a circular immediately. What is the registration number and your contact details?" The hitman smiled to himself, citing the rego off the photograph in his top pocket. After fifteen further calls he was now satisfied that nearly every service centre Australia-wide would be notified. For Hugh, it now became a waiting game.

Grace got out of the chopper in one pretty pissed-off mood, accompanied by two other officers. Tim met the small group halfway to the shack. He could tell by the annoyed expression she wore that he was about to cop it. "Where is the body, and what the hell are you doing out here?" He pointed towards the side of the hut, knowing that he had to give her some answers and quick. She turned to the other officers, "go over inside for prints while I talk with this man." Once they were out of earshot, she started. "So, you think this is a game, purposely losing the team I put on to protect you to draw out the contract killer. I thought we had a deal." Tim looked at the ground momentarily in a partial admission of guilt, as he was always a man of his word. Unbeknown to Grace, Hugh was not even in the state and the only chances of the hitman being lured out of hiding by Tim's presence would be for a beer together at a pub – not an attempt on his life! These were just some of the things that made trying to be on the level with Grace much more complicated as the whole matrix of evolving events even had Tim shaking his head in disbelief.

"Look Grace, what did you want me to do, seriously, pull onto the edge of the highway with my hazard lights on and wait until your team fuelled up so they could keep tabs on me?" She blushed slightly, never being told of the actual events that happened that day until now, other than the confirmation they had lost the bait. Not even attempting to answer that question she moved on: "So, what the hell has gone on here?" Tim weaved through the truth as he told the story while Grace jotted down notes. "You need to check out this Million Bullion Buyers mob, they are bad news. That's who had my partner killed, and they are now trying to claim ownership of the mine. You can validate this by giving my deceased partner's daughter a call, here is her number." She looked over at the recent mound of fresh piled earth. Hand-layered on top to prevent any animals trying to exhume the body were large white quartz rocks with a glint of native gold embedded. "He needs to be dug up so we can get an autopsy done." Tim nodded emotionally, realising he was going against Mac's last wishes. "I'll do it."

Back at the hut the other officers walked out as sweat dripped off their faces from working inside the confined space. After taking a multitude of photos and dusting for prints they announced: "We are done, have a total of four different sets of prints and a blood covered pen with engraved Chinese symbols down one side." By this time, Tim had finished off carefully digging around Mac's corpse. Wearing latex gloves, the four of them lifted the old timer into a body bag. The chopper pilot who had been staying at a distance moved from one tree to another seeking better shade as he waited. Now, seeing the stage they were up to, he moved forward to lend a hand carrying the deceased back to the chopper. After the cargo was loaded Tim couldn't help blurting out, "This is wrong, it's not what he wanted."

They had a few minutes alone while the others returned to get their forensic suitcases and the evidence samples they had collected. She had learnt a lot since their first meeting and could tell that he was still struggling to come to terms with the death of another person who was very close to him. "Sorry for your loss Tim, I will certainly follow up on that Chinese lead. Even though I have all the relevant information supplied – after the fact – you will still have to come in and give a formal statement. Where are the girls?" "They are safe, and to be upfront about your plan with the newspaper thing, I reckon he is no longer even in the state." "What makes you say that?" asked Grace quickly before adding, "that's why that story also went nationwide." Not wanting to elaborate any further Tim shrugged his shoulders. "Call it a hunch, I plan to stay out bush for a week at least, I have nothing to go back into town for anymore. If that upsets your plan of using me for bait, I couldn't give a rat's arse. Arrest me now." She looked him in the eye and could see he was on the point of breaking and was not about to back down on his decision. "I will see you in a week then," she replied as she joined the other officers and wasted no time in leaving the mine site.

The sound of their chopper disappeared into the distance as Tim rattled around the camp looking for a gold dish. He felt the longing to be alone and return to the basic things in life he enjoyed before all this landslide of loss, grief and pain had entered his quiet and simple world. His head was done in and he could no longer think straight, there were just too many issues to contend with. As a release valve for his own sanity, Tim decided to try to retrace his steps to retrieve his GPX 5000 metal detector and try to locate the golden gully that he was still not convinced existed, though the nugget old Mac had handed to him that day proved it was certainly worth investigating further. As an added precaution, especially since the mines location was now known to people with the motive to kill, he drove the 4x4 as far away as possible from the mine in the direction he planned to walk. He parked it close to a stand of juvenile cypress pines before making it blend into the surrounds with a camo cover. Assembling a few final things to add to the prospecting gear, he slipped in a spare lithium battery for his metal detector and the new GPS his ex-prospecting partner had bought before going rouge. Slipping on his pack, Tim reached for his back-up pick and started to descend the same incline that nearly cost him his life that day with the dingoes. Now fully fit, he regarded the dogs as just another opportunistic predator of the outback and held no malice or fear of them, reasoning that's just the way nature works, everything needs to eat.

Remembering that he crossed the creek before picking up any gold, the prospector stayed on the mine site side continuing to work his way upstream. It was tranquil and soothing to the soul as he followed along the narrow game trail, with the background sound of the crystal-clear water running its natural course around and over the rocks. Accompanied by the birdlife and insects that had become vocally active with his presence, he felt at peace for the first time in six months, albeit realising it was only a Band-Aid solution on a situation that could not be so easily fixed as just turning back to the lifestyle he loved. Tim tried to put this out of his mind for a short period as he let the passion of hunting for gold take over. Doing a series of test dishes at the mouth of numerous gullies along the way with the gold pan, he became disappointed with the results, registering only a small amount of gold in each sample and which was nowhere near payable. Pulling up for a breather and a tin of fish, he looked around while eating, trying to familiarise himself with any landmarks he could remember. A large vertical gorge towered ahead in the distance that vaguely came to mind. "Yeah, I remember the bloody shit fight getting down that gorge," he said to himself. "If this gold gully exists it must be between here and the start of them cliff faces, no further."

The next gully was the largest he had come across so far, it gouged deep through the ridgeline high above where he stood. Swinging the pick into action once more, Tim filled the dish and started to walk to the water's edge to reveal its contents. On the way with eyes to the ground as all prospectors do, he spotted a thin flake of gold the size of his small fingernail. Nearly dropping the gold dish, he broke into a laugh as he visualised another one half that size not far away from the first. Having nobody to share his find with, Tim eagerly wanted to get this dish done. Sitting in the creek like a shag on an exposed rock, he started to swirl around the gold pan reducing the contents as he went. Both hands were shaking at the early sign of fine gold already showing on the edges of the dish with a third of dirt yet to finish off. "Hell yeah, this is a real rich bitch this one, lead me to the source mum," he said, using his term for Mother Nature.

Unsure what to do next as time had now become a factor, he looked at the position of the sun to finalise a decision. Torn between going to retrieve his detector first or continue with further exploration up the gully using the gold dish, he figured he only had four hours left of daylight. Having no idea how much further upstream his detector was, Tim ventured up the gully deciding to further scope out the new find and leave at first light for his metal detector when he had more time up his sleeve. He felt light on his feet and his mind was abuzz over the euphoria of the find – he never tired of this feeling. It was something special, the sensation he was now experiencing that only other fellow gold prospectors could relate too. A series of rock crevices appeared as he rounded a bend in the gully and he paused at the natural gold traps. By eye he recovered five rough edged nuggets all around the size of a pea, with the gravel alive with hundreds of smaller flecks the size of a pin head or smaller. Holding them in his palm Tim raised his voice. "Stone the fucking crows, these nuggets haven't travelled far. I reckon the weathering and erosion in this gully has only cut through this deposit in the last hundred odd years, that's why the old timers have never picked up on it." Not much further on, he stood at the base of a dry waterfall that was a good fifteen metres in height. Turning back he looked at the amount of gravel behind him. "What the hell is under my feet after a hundred years of floods? Reckon I will be busy as a cat burying shit when I get back with my detector, this area needs a gold lease over it for bloody sure."

Placing the gold dish into his backpack, he swung the pick burying it deep into the side wall of the gully. Utilising it as an aid, he started scaling the steep-sided bank like a rat up a drainpipe. Grabbing hold of tree roots and saplings with his free hand on the way up, he scrambled to the top. Tim lifted his hat and wiped the sweat from his brow as the afternoon sun began to lose its

potency. Turning slowly, he took in the surrounding area looking for any obvious outcrops of mineral composition protruding
above the grass height. Dropping back into the gully, it was not
long before he found what he was looking for, a thick band of
iron stone that had been cut by the swift water of the gully over
a lifetime of wet seasons. "What I would give to have my metal
detector with me right now," the prospector stated while examining a mineral sample. "That's the same as what's on the ridge
back at the mine." He looked back in that direction as the concept
of what was on his mind gained more positive traction. "Nah,
couldn't be," he blurted thinking aloud. "The mine is right at the
end of this ridge line, this is the only main erosion point that cuts
through this ridge. He looked upstream, following the line of the
gorge and the creek below. "Bet my bottom dollar that this ridge
starts where we landed that day in the chopper when I got my
own pick in the friggin back."

He stood in stunned silence for a full minute over the possibility. "If I am right this gold reef runs the full length of the whole
bloody ridge and Mac had found only the tail end," he finally
pronounced breaking into a smug grin. "Like the saying goes, a
prospector's fortune can change on the turn of a shovel is bloody
spot on mate, spot on." Tim removed his backpack taking a long
drink before plotting in the location on the GPS and deciding to
stay on the ridge for the night. On further deliberation with himself he concluded it would also be quicker and easier to follow
the creek at this height instead of contending with the rigours
of ascending the wet and slippery rugged gorge below. Opting
for this new strategy, the prospector scurried around throwing
enough dead and broken branches into the barren gully as darkness started to close in. After constructing a small fire enough to
heat a tin of spaghetti for dinner, he reached for the sat phone
busting a gut to share the find with someone.

Chapter 9

WHITE LINE NORTH

Danni was just finishing off setting the table for dinner with her sister when the mobile phone rang. Picking it up she could see it was an overseas call. Placing it back on the kitchen servery bench, she let it continue to ring. Her sister threw a questioning glance her way. "Are you going to get that?" Danni shook her head emphatically. "No." "Righto little sis, about time you come clean and tell me what is happening? Danni's sister demanded. "Something is up I know, you have not been your normal self since getting down here, what the hell is going on?" Half an hour later it rang again, she flicked the phone setting to silent as they continued with their in-depth conversation while it vibrated along the table. Minutes later the house phone rang. "He is not going to give up," she said looking at Danni as she picked up the phone. "Hi Frieda, its Tim, is Danni OK? I can't seem to get her on the phone." "Oh hi Tim, no everything is fine down this way, Danni was not feeling well so she went to bed early. Could be the onset of morning sickness. Yes, I will let her know you rang, she has an appointment with a doctor in two days. Yes, call back then, that would be ideal. She will have some news either way, yep, OK I will. Take care Tim." Placing the receiver down she looked at her younger sister. "You need to work out exactly what you want to do. Tim is a good man, and please don't put me in another position where I have to lie to him again."

Wong spoke in a flurry of Chinese to his partner, throwing the official looking letter across the table towards Fu. Quickly scanning the contents, Fu's hand started to shake. Folding it slowly, he reined in his temper. "So, the prospector owns half the mine. That was unforeseen and they are now contesting the validity of our purchase. I want everybody in our whole network to be given a photo of the prospector and his car registration, he must be found. Put a $10,000 dollar reward on any information that leads to his capture. No, actually make that 20,000, that should get things happening quicker. And find out what those other pair we brought up from Sydney have been doing. Send them out in a chopper to the mine site to see if he is hiding out there. This matter is of the utmost importance, it does not matter now how many men we need to find him, just get it done." The door buzzer alerted both men to someone entering. They look at the TV monitor as Grace, dressed in casual clothing, stepped through the doorway.

"Good morning Miss, can I help you at all?" asked Fu. Grace nodded as she perused the cabinets of jewellery. "Yes, I would like to think so, some fantastic pieces you have on display." "Thank you, would you like to purchase an item?" Fu studied the customer, picking up instantly on her body language, authoritative tone and her darting looks. She was looking all over the shop instead of focusing on any one jewellery piece in particular, and this spelt out to him that she was trouble. Grace flashed her badge. "I will need you to come down to the station for questioning in relation to the murder of Malcom Randal, and I understand you have just recently purchased his share of a gold mine." Fu was taken back with the statement, trying to fathom how she acquired this information so quickly considering they had only just opened the correspondence themselves. "Yes, that is correct, we purchased what we believed to be the entire mine. Regretfully it was only 50 per cent, that would appear to be poor due diligence on our behalf. Found dead you say, that's unfortunate. Where did this transpire?" Grace had met these smooth as silk types before, and the flashes of gold teeth only added to the sinister side in her view. "At the mine site. You mention we, well I suggest your business associates in regards to this purchase also accompany us down to the station." Fu nodded slowly staring her straight back in the eye. "I will call our lawyer before we proceed any further from this point." Her thoughts instantly converted into words that just rolled off her tongue. "Got something to hide have we?" Expressing a half sly grin Fu responded, "No, not at all, actually we will be exercising our right to sue his estate over this breach of disclosure, and we have not left town to visit any mine site. Do you have an actual date and time of death?"

Grace tried to keep him talking hoping he would slip up before they engaged a lawyer. "Yes, I now have that information back at the station. What I find strange is that you purchase a gold mine sight unseen, who does that? And a pen with your company's name engraved in Chinese was located at the murder scene that you claim you have never been to." "Ah, so that's where it got to, been looking for that since the day he signed the paperwork in my office. I would never have picked the old man as a thief as well as a fraudster. It's a pity that he now cannot be charged with these offences, I detest all levels of crime in this great country no matter how small. Now if you will excuse me I will contact our lawyer interstate who will no doubt have to engage a third party that can deal with this on a local level given such short notice." Four hours later both businessmen walk out of the police station led by an associate of one of the most prominent law firms in the city. Leaving Grace inside the interview room, her elbows were propped on the table with both palms resting on her cheek bones as she looked down despondently at the coroner's report, speaking through the intercom she instructs one of her team, "Check out if their alibis are solid for the time frame in the report."

The green mountain parrots manoeuvred around the trees at speed, resembling miniature fighter jets in the early morning light, sounding out shrill tweets at each other as if they were competing in some sort of long-distance race. Tim paused briefly to watch their antics and marvel at their precision in flight. He had woken early in anticipation of what the day would hold and was now well past the straight gorge section. The creek started to take a large bend changing direction towards him, further confirming the suspicion of the sheer size of this ore body. The grass was long and time consuming to travel over slowing progress – he had hoped to cover the distance in the morning cool. Before moving on again, he plotted in a waypoint on his current position with the GPS so he could line them all up and get an overall picture at a later date. Instead of continuing on the direct path to the creek, Tim changed angle in a slightly downstream direction not wanting to miss where he had left his Minelab GPX 5000 metal detector.

All he could vaguely remember was sticking it in some tree branches. This hazy memory annoyed the crap out of him. Being the expert bushman he found it unusual being so vague over some of the simple basics of bush travel. Time, distance and landmarks. One thing he was positive of, he had stayed on the opposite side of the creek. Manoeuvring down the side of the rocky hill slope, Tim removed his boots before entering the clear cool flow of the stream. Once on the other side, he hugged the water's edge while progressing upstream. It took thirty minutes before he came into a clearing on the creek bank with a solitary tree and the remnant circle of burnt charcoal. "Thank fuck for that," he declared, relieved to be getting somewhere. He stood for a full minute taking in everything around him as the memories started to flood back, wincing at the height and angle of the bank covered with razor sharp protrusions of slate where he had come crashing down with the pick in his back. "You're shitting me, only one head gash after going down that bloody thing, that's simply pure arse getting to the bottom without ending up like a skinned mango. Now where the hell did I leave that detector?"

Taking a short time to locate the machine that previously was his only source of income before he met Mac, Tim plugged in the new battery. Wiping some dried bird shit off the rear screen he pressed the start switch. The GPX 5000 sounded out its initial warm-up procedure. "You little ripper, bloody tough these detectors, now back to that gully, bet my balls it's full of gold." Selecting a much more user friendly incline to ascend not far upstream, Tim stood on the high creek terrace beside where he had dug the hole with C as his companion. Realising he had to get over the betrayal that day and focus as a professional prospector on the huge job in front of him, he started the GPS, walking in a direct line towards the mark that was programed in yesterday at the eroded gully.

Target after target revealed itself under the detectors coil before the run of gold disappeared under the steep bank, too deep for the detector to locate. Tim had to tear himself away from his normal prospecting protocol of working a gold producing area until all targets were retrieved. Not wanting to waste time, he needed to concentrate and follow the entire strike so he could secure the whole area under lease. The deep, late shedding reef had the possibility of making the fabled Lasseter's Reef look like a piss in the ocean. He started to roughly calculate what was needed to follow through with such a huge find – the expense of pegging such a large area along with the need for a decent size dozer to push a road the entire length of the ridge to enable access for the drill rigs that would be needed to supply reef samples. The list started to become daunting when he began to add native title, environmental impact assurances, landholder compensation and geologist reports. Tim knew this side of things would be way out of his depth. He was, after all, just a prospector out in the field, not capable of supplying the required level of competency needed to get through the lease approval process. He needed people on his side that he could trust and knew how to fill out the endless piles of paperwork. One person that came straight to mind was Meg. Hours later he dropped back into the gully where he slept the previous night. The detector screamed in every direction no matter where he moved the coil. Tim needed to sit down. All prospectors dreamed of this very moment, a once in a lifetime find that would change their fortune forever.

Fumbling for the sat phone he rang Meg's home number. Since being picked up from the motel in Cairns, she had been trying to keep herself busy after finding her husband's 4x4 was missing from the shed. That, along with other outdoor equipment had been taken, leaving no message or indication of where he was going or if he would ever return. Meg longed to hold him and hear his voice. Subconsciously, she continued to listen out for the distinguishable sound of his vehicle along their street. Her days were now filled with replaying every word relevant to all events that had transpired leaving her caught in this void of loneliness and despair. Bitterness had also started to erode her line of rational thought.

On the third ring she picked up the phone. There was a brief silence before Tim's excited voice came through. "Hi Meg, its Tim, everything OK at your end?" "Yes Tim, I am safe thanks for asking, what can I help you with?" "I have just struck it rich on the gold and I need someone like you that's good with paperwork and has the smarts to run a business. You know me I'm hopeless with that kind of stuff, so what do you say mate, would you like a job? Just name your price." Meg's immediate thought was to decline but replied, "I don't know Tim, I would need some time to think it over. Can you give me a couple of days?" "Yeah, no problems mate there is a lot I need to get done before the wet season. Hey, just wondering if you have heard from Danni at all since you left the motel? She has gone to stay with her sister down south and is acting real strange lately, wouldn't even speak to me last night or return my calls…thought you might know what is going on." "No, I have not heard from her at all. Has she left for good or just a holiday?" Tim laughed. "No, she hasn't left me that I know of, think she just needed to get away from all the stress for a while. So, you haven't heard, I'm going to be a dad." "Congratulations, so when are you going down to see her?" "Mate, not sure yet. I need to tie up the gold lease first, this will be our future. I need to come to town in a couple of days, will catch up with you then for your decision."

The days slowly ticked over to months for C as he started to become agitated in how long it was taking to break out of prison and voiced as much over lunch with his bikie crew. "How much longer is this going to take? I've had a gutful of living like a fucking poxy sewer rat." They all looked towards the end of the table waiting for a response from the key man to the whole operation who slowly finished chewing his mouthful of food as he looked at every member around the table. "The hole under the fence has been done, the transport has been organised for after you get out and the delivery is due into the kitchen at 10am tomorrow, so be ready, it will be quick." C broke into a smile for the first time since his rapists got what they deserved, pushing his dinner plate away. "Shit hot, well that's my last mouthful of this fucking pig swill then, bring on the T-bone steaks."

"Right, listen up all of you, this is how it's going to work," the head biker stated.

After lockdown that night C was restless and uneasy about how the plan would unfold tomorrow. He began pacing the length of his cell trying to make time go faster. The sound of the cells automatically unlocking had C instantly on his feet after only an hour of solid sleep. Splashing some water onto his face to heighten alertness, he joined the line of inmates moving towards the mess hall. Breakfast went off without any problems and they were all given their last orders before the new stock for the kitchen arrived into the dock at the back of the kitchen. Two prison officers visually counted the number of pallets delivered then checked on the order sheets, signing off on the deliveries before moving away after the loading doors were shut securely. The bikie running the escape operation was the lead kitchen hand while also in charge of sorting and replacing incoming food items. His crew went about their job. Two hessian bags of potatoes were purposefully selected from the centre and quickly wheeled by trolley into the kitchen pantry for tonight's meal. On their return the crew all circled around the pallet of spuds. The two hessian sacks had been sown together with the centre cut out to fit a body. Velcro was also sewn inside one end so it could be closed but not visible from the outside. C moved inside the circle of men and quickly slipped into the sack and was lifted onto the pallet while all cameras were blocked by the other inmates. Other than the two fresh bags of spuds that had been removed from the centre, the rest of the pallet had been intentionally left to partially rot in the sun before being delivered to the prison. C was covered with a layer of rotten hessian sacks before the bikies commenced opening a few bags to let out the full force of stale odour. Soon, the inmates starting making a commotion that was loud enough to attract the prison officer's attention.

"What's up you blokes?" The smell hit the officer's nostrils as he drew closer. "Shit, that's rank, how the hell did they get in here?" The head biker took over as spokesman for the kitchen crew. "Well, you fellas signed off on the load. They're all fucked, every single sack, look at them." He held up a couple of squished blackened potatoes that were oozing a clear foul smelling liquid. This pallet needs to get moved the hell out of here before we have maggots through the whole fucking kitchen and mess hall, that will look really good on a health and safety report." The officer grunted reaching for his radio. "Gate one, has that fresh food services delivery truck been back through yet?" "Affirmative, a good ten minutes ago." The officer swore under his breath as he hoped to contain the incident without it having to go any further. The head bikie started to add pressure to the situation. "I want this shit out of my kitchen. Why don't you just send it over to the prison farm for them to bury as compost and re-order another load for delivery tomorrow, it can't stay here."

The officer thought this idea had merit but had to get approval from higher up the corrective services chain. He radioed in for temporary back-up for this sector while he tried to work out this problem. Administration contacted the supplier who strongly refuted his product was rotten, while the small fresh produce business unsuccessfully tried to contact its relatively new delivery driver to return and pick up the product for their own inspection. The new driver, who had been specifically inserted into the business by the bikers for this job, had dropped off the pallet at a mate's place just out of town a month earlier. It had been intentionally left in the sun, covered with shrink wrap to sweat and ferment before being swapped for the fresh pallet on the truck destined for prison delivery. No response on the truck radio or his mobile phone had the confused owner's brow break out in a sweat as the prison was his largest client.

With the outcome of a quick solution now starting to look uncertain, the officer raised the idea of the prison farm as his own. Half an hour after leaving his position, the officer returned while the inmates continued replacing the empty shelves with new stock. "Right, this pallet of crap is destined for the prison farm." He activated the roller door as the pallet was loaded onto a flat tray eight-ton prison truck used for delivering fertiliser and other supplies to the low-security prison farm. The pungent liquid started to soak through the porous hessian sacks from the rotten bags above C as the truck slowed to a crawl while the maximum-security gates swung open. The truck picked up speed, changing gears as it bounced along the single lane bitumen road travelling the short distance to the farm. C wiped the liquid from his exposed cheek with the back of his hand trying to put the stench out of his mind, savouring more the sweet smell of freedom that was now finally becoming a reality.

He could hear raised voices giving directions as the truck ground to a halt. "Stuff that bro, we're not busting our arses like pack mules carrying all them sacks from here out into the paddock to bury," stated the enormous Maori ex-biker who was also on the promised payroll for the escape. "Drop them down the bottom area near the fence and we will take care of them from there bro." The truck crunched back into gear as it moved along what C considered to be another two maybe three hundred metres. He could hear the hydraulics engage on the truck as the motor started to rev, tilting the tray until the angle came to the point that his pallet skidded off the back onto the bare earth causing C to let out an unintentional grunt. Hearing the truck move away he breathed a sigh of relief. Opening the Velcro end of the sack with an arm now free, the escapee tried to move the hessian bag above him inconspicuously, not sure if anybody was watching. C had been advised while eating in the mess hall the day before that there was hired help at this end to finish the job. The two men that were selected were guaranteed to keep their mouths shut at a price. They were proud of their efforts, digging a shallow tunnel intermittently over the past couple of months without detection. Using their hoes originally supplied for chipping out weeds in the low-security area of the prison, they added the excess soil from the tunnel to the dirt rills that grew fresh produce for the kitchen. Removing every second timber slat from under their bed mattresses, they covered the escape hole by lightly shovelling a layer of dirt to conceal their efforts.

The huge Maori walked over to the rejected pallet that was placed five metres from the tunnel entrance. Removing the top layer, he effortlessly dragged the extra-long sack to the ground before hoisting two bags, one over each shoulder. He looked around for anyone close by before speaking towards the ground. "You must be a high flier with lots of bucks bro. Stay flat on the ground. Right in front of you are some timber slats just under the soil, replace them once you're in the hole. The height of the pile of spuds will hide what you are doing, nobody can see from the building. Wait until I draw the attention of this mob up here before exiting the other side, then bolt for it across the road real fast bro. Move out of sight from the road and head west, your ride will be waiting five hundred metres down."

C did not respond and did what was instructed, while the Maori dropped the sacks in the middle of the paddock before turning towards the rest of the inmates looking on from a distance. "This isn't a spectator sport you clowns, pull your thumbs out of your arse and go get some tools to start burying these spuds." Returning to the pallet, the enormous inmate covered the exposed timber bed slats using his extra-large boot to inconspicuously move around the loose dirt. Content that his involvement in the escape had gone without a hitch, the inmate with only six months left to serve sat on top of the hessian sacks secure in the thought that he would now have a lump sum of cash to start up a lawn mowing business when he got out. He watched the rest of them begin to randomly filter back out of the building complex after being issued their digging tools by the two prison officers who supervised the entire farm. The unchallenged self-appointed foreman of the population in the low-security facility barked out another order. "Some of you jokers can come down and give me a hand to move these bags of crap." First to reach him was the accomplice, answering his questioning expression before he had time to speak. "Yep, job's done bro."

The fugitive jogged along keeping a conservative distance between himself and the road unable to wipe the smile of success off his face. He figured he had at least a good four hours' head start before the screws would work out he was missing from maximum security. The biker in the adjacent police cells in Cairns beside C who took up the challenge of springing this high-profile drug manufacturer out of prison had been waiting for close to half an hour before hearing his human cash card come crashing through the bush towards the bike. "Oi, over here." C pulled up puffing slightly, the biker screwed up his face as he passed the prisoner a helmet and a set of overalls. "Fuck me dead, smells like you have been rolling in dog shit, did you even have a shower while inside? Strip off and throw these on before you get on my bike," he ordered.

C broke into a rare snigger as he tore off the prison issue uniform. "Fuck ya, it is good to be out of that joint. Did you find out where the cop bitch lives? What about a handgun? Has anyone found out where that prospector is?" The biker fired up his hog. "Get on. Yeah, have a piece on me just to make sure you have the half million buried like you said. If not, well yeah, you will be seeing it up real close that I can guarantee. To do with the prospector nup, not a clue, but the cop yep, found out where she bunks down, piece of piss. That's your business not mine. I want no part in that shit just my half million bucks. A lot of people need paying off for getting you out of here, what you do with that information after that money is in my hand is not my problem." They slowly weaved around shrubs and saplings while they talked. On reaching the bitumen road the final comment was, "where are we going?" C lent forward, "chill buddy, the money is like I said back then, head towards Bakers Town." The biker nodded. "That far, righto, hang the hell on." With rumours of cameras even being located on all side roads surrounding the prison facility the biker had cautiously taped his registration plates. The bike roared down the side road onto the main highway.

C enjoyed the ride on the big bore Harley as it rumbled through the small towns with pedestrians turning their heads to look as they passed through. On the open highway, its throaty exhaust roared as the biker rolled on the throttle along the straight sections of road. C, not suitably dressed for a high-speed ride, had to endure the wind factor tearing at his loose-fitting overalls that flapped uncontrollably. That, along with frequent bugs hitting his exposed face because of the open helmet, raised a colourful and continuous vocal volley of swear words from the escapee with every impact. An hour out from their destination the alarm was triggered back at the prison of the missing inmate. After an extensive search of the facility the police were notified.

Grace had run up against what seemed like a ghost trying to locate the hitman. Turning her attention to more recent events, the acute detective had been around long enough to smell that the Chinese bullion buyers were also into a lot more than met the eye with word filtering back to her from the street that it was an Asian invasion within the drug world. Grace took the call as she walked towards her car knocking off early for the day. Her temper flared. "You are kidding. Escaped! How the hell is that even possible in a maximum-security prison for fuck sake?" Recalling the prisoner's vow as she walked out of the cells that day, the detective subconsciously touched her firearm for reassurance as her mind whirled into action.

"Right I want plane, train and bus terminals covered, also a road block to the north before his residence. Contact Bakers Town for that job, it will be quicker and more effective if he is heading in that direction. Also, place a car out front of that biker's clubhouse, and a news bulletin, both radio and television, needs to be compiled immediately. Notify all stations between here and Brownsville with his mug shot. Does anyone know how long since the escape? I will head to the prison to see what information they have. There could be a small chance he's on foot but in my line off thinking he would have needed help, you just don't walk out of maximum. So my initial assumption is if he has gone into that much detail to escape you could nearly bet that transportation would have also been organised."

The fully grown eastern grey buck kangaroo stood upright on its powerful rear legs to its full height after resting during the hottest period of the day under a shady gum tree. Scratching his chest, the dominant male looked around for the rest of his mob now that the afternoon sun had started to lose its potency. He bounded off towards the sweet green shoots of grass that run along the edge of the highway. With his mob following, they all spread out to graze.

The Bakers Town officers wasted no time in setting up the road block as instructed, consisting of two patrol cars and four officers to enable quick searches of vehicles approaching from the south. C, accustomed to travel by air, started to become concerned at the time factor knowing that the alarm would have well and truly been raised by now on his disappearance from within the prison walls. The uncertainty was how long it would take them to conduct a full search before they contacted the cops. He tapped the biker on the shoulder who cocked his head to the side and slowed to a speed that he could hear what his pillion passenger had to say. "Can this bucket of bolts go any faster?" C yelled at the biker's helmet. "I'm not here for a fucking scenic tour, the pigs will be up our arse at this rate." The biker laughed. "Hang on money man", as he opened the throttle to full nearly jerking his passenger straight off the back of the bike with the force of acceleration. C ducked his head and torso in behind the large body mass of the bikie trying to reduce the wind factor as their speed hit over 180km per hour as they followed the white line north.

The large buck roo pricked his ears at the advancing rumbling noise. Indecisively, he tried to escape the oncoming threat by blindly attempting to bound across the road. The motorbike, now doing nearly twice the speed limit, had no time to react or swerve as the 85kg roo slammed into the Harley. It was like hitting a brick wall at speed, demolishing the front wheel and buckling the forks like cooked spaghetti with the force. Both occupants were instantly catapulted from their sitting position straight over the handlebars. C's one good eye opened wide as he sailed through the air. "Fuck my luck," was all he managed to get out, futilely holding both palms out in front of him preparing for the impact that would take both men's lives instantly. The motorbike began to cartwheel down the bitumen gouging chunks out of the road as it went, parts flying in all directions until the twisted wreck finally came to rest fifty metres away from the broken skinless corpses left in the middle of the highway.

The ageing station owner had spent nearly a full day in town at the cattle sales yard. The old flat-bed truck, now empty, rattled along the road towards home as the sun started to wither. Content with the prices received for his premium condition heifers, the cattleman was buoyant – a good year was ahead with plentiful rain falling on the property. In a good mood after years of crippling drought, he turned up his favourite country and western singer on the ancient cassette player singing word for word loudly. He lent forward in the seat trying to figure out what was lying all over the road at a distance in front of him. Slowing initially, he slammed on the brakes as the carnage that lay across the road became evident. "Struth, what the hell?" Shaking his head, he spritely swung out of the truck for a man of his age. Not bothering to check for a pulse, the cattleman could easily tell both men were dead. Swearing under his breath that the two-way in the truck was on the blink, he realised this day would now become longer with no other option than to travel past his station turn-off and continue towards Bakers Town to report the fatality. Three kilometres up the road the flashing blue and red lights of the road block pulled his truck over. "We need to search your vehicle for any stowaways. Where have you come from sir?" the officer asked. "There's nobody with me son, but I reckon a few of you blokes need to head back down the road a bit, I found two men dead splattered all over the asphalt from a motorbike accident with a roo by the looks. Here's my station number if you need to get in contact. Like I said, I did not see what happened but there is a dead roo just hit by the looks of things not far from the bodies, makes it not hard to figure out what's happened."

Grace had not long entered the prison when she received the call. "Your joking me, killed by a roo, are they absolutely certain it is him?" The female in charge of communications and operations replied, "Grace, they have confirmed him from the mug shot that I have sent to everyone as you requested. I don't think there could be any doubt, he sure was one ugly son of a bitch." She nodded in agreement visualising his distorted facial features. "Fair enough, give me a call when they are two hours out from the morgue, I need to see this for myself." The detective had mixed emotions over the astounding news, feeling somewhat robbed that this man would now never rot in jail for the rest of his life as she had envisaged. But at the same time relieved that this murderous drug king had met his own fate so quickly without another death by his hand or instruction. She turned to the warden that stood not far from her side. "You can call off the search parties warden, the body of the escapee has been located, identified and now on the way back to Cairns in a meat wagon after a collision with a kangaroo of all things. I have no further need to follow up with any interviews regarding this matter, and I expect you also have a pile of paper-work to complete over such an incident." He nodded vowing a full internal investigation would continue until they had all answers on how the escape was successfully orchestrated.

Tim entered the city after the week away as promised to Grace, deciding to book a room instead of returning to his house, assuming it was now also being watched. A chopper had been flying around the mine site for hours on end while he was still working further upstream trying to configure the shape and size of the gold leases he needed to apply for, figuring it must be someone else after his hide – that now seemed to be a regular occurrence. After paying for the room, Tim sat on the bed and dialled his wife's number. Danni reached for the phone finding it difficult to put her thoughts into words. "Hi babe, thought you weren't going to pick up there for a second, how did the scan go?" "It went well, we have a baby on the way. I have made the decision to stay down here for good. It has just become too dan-gerous to live up that way and now there is the baby's safety to think about as well." Tim was stunned to the point of finding it difficult to reply. "Don't you think that should be a decision we make together and try and work through this?" "There is nothing left to discuss, Tim, I am putting myself and our child's life first. Had it not been for John I would already be dead. Look, I have to go, when I get my due dates I will text them through, that should give you enough time to decide if you want to live down here with us or not." Incredulous, he went to respond but the line went dead. Redialling his wife's number numerous times was futile. Letting the phone slip from his hand, the bone-weary prospector laid back on the bed for an hour with the emotions of confusion, rejection and guilt running high.

He tried to turn these negative thoughts around, having never been one to give in or lay down over anything that life's journey had thrown his way. It was just not part of his upbringing. "Where's that bloody phone, got six months to turn this around and make it right before the birth." Hugh was first on his list. "Bloody phones!" he though aloud as he dialled in the number. "Hey bud, I've had a gutful of these fuckers out to kill me every time I turn around. My wife has left me and is even too scared to come back home. You interested in a full-time bodyguard job, what do you reckon mate?" Hugh laughed. "I like you prospector, reckon you're a tuff little nut buddy, but from what I'm hearing about these Chinese you have upset, I don't think your job description of full-time would be for too long. We are talking about a branch of the most powerful crime syndicate in the world, you don't do things in halves do you prospector. It would be pure suicide to take on such a job." Tim, left out on a limb, let rip. "Well thanks a lot, looks like you're full of piss and wind buddy, you seem to have a very short memory of who saved your bacon out bush." Pissed off, he hung up before receiving a reply. Dialling Meg's number, he took a deep breath to settle his anger before speaking. "Hey Meg, any thoughts on the job, I need to know today, my marriage is on the rocks if I can't pull this off within six months." She cut short an in-depth conversation with a New Guinea national as she stood beside his collection of native hand-made highland ornaments at the local markets to take the call. "You know what, I've had a change of heart on the whole idea, it just might be what I need to take my mind off things. Count me in Tim, when do I start?" Tim smiled with a renewed vigour. "Knew

I could count on you Meg, this means a lot to me. I will be around tomorrow to fill you in on what needs to be done."

Next was Grace to provide a statement on Mac's death. Arriving at the police station, he felt uneasy walking towards the entrance. The female detective was notified by the front desk of his arrival and walked out to greet this bushman that looked totally out of his depth inside the precinct. Dressed in khaki from head to toe and wearing his wide brim bush hat she smiled at the lost expression on his face. "Come with me Tim," leading him into an empty interview room. "Before we start with your statement just thought you might be interested that Chris the chopper pilot escaped prison." Tim's eyes hardened and his stomach flipped as he sat down. "You're fucking joking, how can that be possible?" Grace smiled. "That's basically what I said, but you wouldn't believe what happened then." They were like chalk and cheese in their backgrounds and professions, yet they had somehow managed to form a relationship that worked for both of them. She filled Tim in on the events.

The unusual sound of laughter drifting from the interview room made passing officers pause, curious as to what was transpiring behind the closed door. Tim shook his head continuing to chuckle randomly. "You have just made my day, sounds like he is now well and truly ROOted." Emphasising the first three letters, he sniggered at his own quick-witted humour before adding, "He escapes maximum security prison and ends up accidently getting taken out by our Aussie icon. What a crack up." Grace settled down the mood by changing the subject. "OK back to business, we have had the Asian gold buyers in and they both have rock solid alibis for the day of Mac's murder according with the time of death in the coroner's report. I am looking further into other activities that I cannot elaborate on, but they have now become people of interest. "Right, you ready to give a statement on what happened that day?" Grace continued as she opened her laptop. "Yep let's start, I've got to see Mac's daughter about this court case over the ownership of the mine yet." Two hours later Tim walked out of the station with a sense of achievement for the day, happy in the fact that C would not be hiring any more guns to send his way. Voicing his thoughts aloud as he opened the door of his 4x4, "that's one less to worry about."

Getting late into the afternoon he decided to defer contacting Casey until the morning. His head was done in with the day's events and he wanted a clear fresh mind to absorb all the information Casey had no doubt gathered since their last meeting. Foremost on his mind was a big feed cooked by someone other than himself over an open fire along with an ice-cold rum. He headed towards the Cairns Esplanade figuring he earned a few hours of R&R. Wiping his plate clean with bread rolls, the bushman watched the tourists walk past hand in hand, smiling, laughing and just enjoying the balmy clear North Queensland night. Loneliness started to set in as his wife's ultimatum kept playing on his mind. He ordered another rum from the waiter who arrived to clear his empty plates.

Looking around the open restaurant while he waited for the beverage, Tim got the sudden feeling he was being watched. Sculling the rum in three mouthfuls, he opted to get a taxi instead of using his own vehicle. Paying the bill, he mingled with the tourists moving along the pavement towards the nearest taxi rank. Giving random directions to the taxi driver, he watched behind as the bright yellow bubble car followed – at an inconspicuous distance – their every move. The silhouette of a single occupant became briefly illuminated under the street lights. "Fuck you're good," Tim voiced aloud as he watched the bubble car manoeuvre in behind other traffic. The Indian taxi driver half turned his head towards the back seat and, in a heavy accent, replied, "Thank you sir, I hope my driving skills have impressed you enough tonight for a tip on your departure from the vehicle." The bushman smiled. "Wasn't talking to you Apu…look just drop me off at this corner, I will take it from here." Swinging expertly into a tight parking space he replied while punching in the total price of the fare, "I would like a dollar for every time a passenger has called me that name since that cartoon TV show started. That will be eighteen dollars. "Only mucking around buddy, here's a hundred, keep the change." Cutting through a mall that led back onto the Esplanade, he walked briskly past many open style market stalls that were vibrant with tourists for this hour of night. Exiting back onto the footpath he dived into the first vacant taxi giving his motel's address, confident it would take whoever was following him a good fifteen minutes to get around the block with the volume of traffic on the streets.

Six months flew by as Tim and Meg buried themselves into the work of successfully getting the gold leases granted, while at the same time creating a close working relationship. During this period he received a handful of text messages from Danni advising him of gender and scan results as the pregnancy got closer to full term. Replying to the messages, he gave her updates on the project and assured her there had been no further events of violence and it was now safe for her to return. All his replies went unanswered as did the phone calls. This frustrated the hell out of him as never had they been apart for so long without verbal contact, nor had he ever witnessed her so determined and unwavering in her resolve. Taking a break from his work schedule that now had the drilling rig onsite ready to start after having to get the access road widened by a bulldozer over almost its entire length, Tim took Casey to the mine site to bury Mac's ashes back beside his faithful companion Jonah. After completing this sombre task and placing s small engraved brass plaque describing Mac as the founder of the mine and the date of his murder, they returned to Cairns.

Tim enjoyed Casey's company though he felt awkward and hopeless when she broke into tears saying goodbye to her father, reigniting his own emotions. Dropping Casey back to her front door she thanked him before asking: "Tim do you have any clothes other than khaki?" "Of course, I do," he answered slightly indignantly. "Got camo as well, why?" She laughed. "Well, we have that court hearing tomorrow at 9am, I suggest you buy something that will be more in line with the occasion. I will see you there in the morning." Before he could ask advice on what to wear she bounded up the driveway. Looking down to self-assess his attire, he asked himself, "what's wrong with khaki?"

The owners of Million Bullion Buyers had been at their premises early going through last minute details before they fronted court. Today was the day that they would finally be able to dispose of this thorn in their side for good. They were amazed and frustrated how so many dangerous and resourceful men within their organisation had not been able to successfully locate this single prospector and cash in on his hide to date. "That prospector is to be dead before the sun sets," the owners stated to their new hired hitmen who now numbered four. "Today he is given to you on a platter, do not fail us." Two left with the proprietors in Wong's Mercedes that was left parked down the side alley of the building out of sight, while the other assassins followed close behind in their own vehicle armed with a multitude of weapons specifically designed to kill.

Selecting a car park in the large area set aside to alleviate parking congestion adjacent to the courthouse, Tim made his way towards the entrance. Directly out front he spotted Casey mingling with her colleagues who were representing them today. "Didn't even recognise you in that suit," Casey commented smiling. The hair rose on the back of his neck as he went to reply detecting two large Asian men lurking in the background of the small group. They stood out like dingoes in a hen house. The bushman's earlier perception that this would be the ideal time for his adversaries to strike was now a reality, trouble was brewing. They turned their attention towards Tim. He grabbed her arm, "let's go."

He led her the remaining twenty metres to safety inside the front door of the courthouse, where two armed security officers supervised people emptying their pockets before walking through the metal detecting unit. Looking over his shoulder as they joined the queue, he relocated the two men who had split up but had kept their distance. He felt uneasy, it was like they were being herded inside. The two assassins remained outside the front door which also indicated to Tim that they both must be packing weapons. A new message vibrated on his phone. Still waiting in line to pass through security he glanced at the message that read, "Love the suit prospector." A thin smile formed on his lips as he tapped Casey on the shoulder who was in front of him. "Where did you park?" "Over at the big car park to the side of the building, why?" "Good, after the hearing, no matter which way it goes, stay close." "Why, what's going on…and that was simply rude earlier, I was about to introduce you to our legal team."

"Forget about that, let's just try and get out of here alive," Tim whispered as they entered the court room. Wong and Fu were already seated at the front of the room and turned to give the prospector a venomous stare. The glare was returned. "Fucking dead shits," he said just loud enough for Casey to hear. "We have got this, believe me," she said patting his shoulder. Tim focused on another pair of Asian henchmen who sat towards the back of the room close enough to control the exit. "Yeah righto." Everybody stood as the judge entered, and the rest of Casey's firm that were in conversation at the front of the building scrambled down the aisle towards their seat.

The judge sat down directing his attention towards the paperwork submitted by both parties. The room remained silent as he flicked over the pages clearing his throat. "Interesting case this one. Firstly, how can the deceased sell the mine to a third party after already gifting half its ownership to his co- worker? Another point that concerns me deeply is the second document, the hand-written last will and testament produced here today dated well before this bill of sale, which clearly states that on death his mining partner will receive full ownership of the mine and all other mining tenements abroad. I raise doubt over the validity of this sales contract. Is the JP who witnessed and signed off on this contract present here today?"

"Yes your honour, we subpoenaed that witness and would like to call him to take the stand."

Fu and Wong shifted in their seats nervously as the JP, now perspiring heavily, took the stand swearing the oath. Casey's legal team attacked relentlessly, eventually summing up his testimony an hour later. "So, you claim to have been present and witnessed the deceased sign this document at the bullion shop when in fact he had not left his gold lease in fifteen years – he had no mode of transport to even get to town. Then you claim he produced a current driver's licence for ID when in fact the last licence the deceased acquired was the old original paper edition back in the eighties. So, sir I put it to you that you have never met the deceased and have just purposely committed the crime of perjury."

The judge intervened hitting his gavel on the wooden base. "This case is shaping up more like a criminal case than a civil one. I will intervene at this point and refer this case to criminal court with it already evident in my view that fraud and perjury have been committed with possibly other charges to be laid. On the civil side of this matter, I favour the plaintiff's full ownership of the mine on the provision he returns the ten thousand dollars to the defence. All court costs are to be submitted and paid by the defence, this court is now adjourned."

Fu and Wong gave their lawyers a scathing look before being the first to rise and start moving towards the rear doors with Fu's hands still shaking in anger. Casey jumped up and gave Tim a hug in celebration. "See, justice has prevailed, isn't that a better result than having to resort to violence?" Tim was happy with the ruling but carefully watched the pair of businessmen who gave a slight nod towards the muscle now standing at the exit. Fu whispered as he walked past, "when they get outside this building kill them both." Tim grabbed her hand, "stay with me," he said as he led her into the courthouse common area, scanning the ceiling for cameras while also watching the back of Fu and Wong exit the courthouse. He moved towards a series of snack and drink vending machines. "Aren't we leaving?" asked Casey. The two assassins walked past slowly, sitting down on some seats towards the entrance to wait. "Nah, feeling a bit hungry and thirsty, how about you?" "You're not skimping out of shouting me lunch for today's outcome?" Tim cut her short, "yeah, that will come later, let's just hang here for a bit, reckon you could do with a chocolate fix."

Fu spoke to the pair who had been lounging around outside all morning and they fell in beside the fuming businessmen making their way towards their vehicle. "Start up the car, then I want to watch these two die in air-conditioned comfort. When that is done, I want our lawyers followed to where they live and both their hands cut off for taking our money for fuck all."

The first shot drove into the chest of Wong. Not even having the chance to react, his heart exploded as he fell chin first in mid-stride onto the concrete footpath. Hugh, concealed on a building roof top across the street, ejected the spent cartridge with a fluid rapid motion that had another fresh shell in the breach of his silenced high powered rifle. Moving the barrel slightly he sent the next bread and butter shot at Fu. The assassin's reaction speed surprised the WA hitman. In that split second recognising the threat, he shoved Fu to the ground with the bullet already in flight, smashing into his elbow instead of the heart shot that was intended for his boss. A shattered elbow joint and torn muscle were all that remained of his lower arm as it sprayed blood over the concrete pathway. Hugh swore, with the next shot putting the assassin out of his pain.

Pedestrians started to yell and scream as hysteria took hold in the crowd with many rushing towards the front entrance of the courthouse for safety. In response, the security officers left their post with guns in hands closely followed by the two unarmed assassins assigned to stay with the prospector as they fought against the mass of people running inside to escape the gunmen. With civilians scattering in all directions, Hugh's precious time to complete a quick clean kill between his first shot and the public's reaction had lapsed.

In the stampede Fu had picked himself up and now was crouched beside the passenger's side door of his Mercedes out of sight of the hitman. Frantically he looked around for his driver who had also reduced his exposure to the shooter by crouching beside a coffee stand that had been abandoned while trying to pinpoint the origin of the shots. Yelling in Chinese, Fu ordered him to throw over the keys. Tim moved towards the vacant seats while he polished off the packet of potato chips from the vending machine as people started to pour into the building. "Just wait," he firmly instructed Casey who was bewildered by his cool manner, until it dawned on her, "You knew this was going to happen."

A swarm of blue uniforms wearing bulletproof vests spilled out onto the footpath and spread out from police headquarters which was beside the courthouse. Tim rose to his feet placing the empty chip packet in a bin close by before replying, "two can play for keeps. Right, let's get moving." Hugh was acutely aware he was running out of time. Every second from now reduced his chances of a clean escape even though everything was in place to abseil straight down the back of the building and a short distance into the next street which was full of tourists unaware of what was transpiring just around the corner. Holding his nerve, Hugh noticed the lights briefly activate to unlock the Mercedes, concentrating the rifle on the vehicle he waited for the driver to appear behind the wheel. Fu started the car that immediately aroused a response from police officers as they moved in from all directions to attempt stopping the car. Hugh swore aloud as it hindered his shot at Fu and became agitated, having no option other than to watch the Mercedes swing out onto the road. One officer, unable to get out of the way in time, was run over. Fu sped down the road under heavy fire from the relatively short-range accuracy of the service revolvers.

Fu smiled as he straightened up behind the wheel, now out of effective range of their side arms. He felt the sting on the side of his face as the front windscreen shattered from the high-powered projectile exiting the interior. Swerving all over the road as Fu steered with one hand while touching where his ear had been split seconds before, the smile suddenly vanished as the next bullet nearly simultaneously behind the first penetrated though the back of his skull. The interior of the Mercedes became splattered in blood and bone fragments before careering into a parked car on the side of the road.

Hugh pulled a black motorbike bandanna from his pocket and left it at the scene to induce self-destruction between the two rival drug gangs before commando crawling backwards from the edge. He was down the side of the building and had walked around another set of building apartments out of sight by the time his sniper position had been compromised. Tearing off his overalls to reveal a colourful Hawaiian shirt and matching board shorts, the hitman shoved the discarded item of clothing and his gloves into the soft sports bag that already contained the still hot barrel of his partially broken down weapon. Within a minute, he was mingling in with the holiday maker's enroute to one of the island ferries that was due to depart in fifteen minutes.

Another to escape at the height of the courthouse melee were the two unarmed assassins who drifted off while all the attention was aimed at the speeding Mercedes. The armed driver who threw the keys to Fu was swarmed by police as he tried to make a run for it. Tim and Casey managed to manoeuvre around the side of the building toward their cars. Tim's phone alerted him to another message. "Hope holiday pay and super are included in that full-time position." He smiled, relieved that all threats were now accounted for. His phone rang moments after the message as they arrived at Casey's car who was still in shock over all the bodies and bloodshed. Without even looking at the number he answered, "I will even throw in free life insurance bud, thanks for saving my arse." "Not sure who you think you have on the line Tim but it is Danni's sister Frieda, she has been rushed to hospital, apparently the baby is huge and its heart rate has dropped to a dangerous level. If you want to be involved in this birth I suggest you get on the next plane." Casey wound down her window and went to speak just as Tim hung up. "I will have to take a raincheck on that lunch…I'm going to be a dad. My son is on his way. I will bring my wife and the new edition to the family around to meet you when we get back and we will all do dinner or something."

Running to his vehicle before she could reply, he called Meg's number on speed dial. "Meg can you book me on the next flight to the Gold Coast…also if you can check out a motel close to the hospital for me and book a taxi from the airport to the hospital, I don't have time to wait around for a cab, I'm on the way to the airport now." Five hours later Tim rushed into the maternity section waiting area with a bunch of flowers in one hand. Danni's sister stood as he entered the room and after a brief hug he asked, "how is my girl going?" The sister shrugged, "haven't had any news yet." Twenty minutes passed before two security staff entered the waiting area, followed minutes later by a middle-aged, short thickset matron who walked towards them. "Danni has had a difficult birth, the baby boy is now doing fine weighing in at a whopping twelve and a half pounds," the matron informed them in a rough gravelly voice. She has made it emphatically clear that she wants no visitors at this point in time, the bleeding was significant. I suggest you give her a day or so to recover." Tim nodded. "Can I at least see my son before I leave?" The matron raised an eyebrow looking at the sister for confirmation. "Ah, so you're the husband. OK, I will organise the midwife to bring him out for you shortly."

Tim nervously paced the room, both his palms became sweaty as he subconsciously rubbed them up and down the sides of the suit he wore to court that morning. A young midwife brought out the baby wrapped tightly in a small blanket and looked around the room. Tim was glowing as he moved forward holding out his hands. The young nurse looked surprised, before instructing him how to hold the child as she passed over the baby. "Hello son, come say g'day to dad." He looked down at the little bundle in his arms. A confused expression crossed his face as he looked again, this time for a longer period in silence. With arms outstretched he gently passed the baby back to the nurse. "There must be some mistake, this child is not mine, it is Asian." "I can assure you this is your wife's child, I delivered this baby and he has not left my sight since birth."

Danni's sister moved in closer for a look, fearing the worst. "I want to see my wife," demanded Tim. The two security officers moved forward to block the doorway as the nurse hurried off with the child. He looked at both men sizing up the threat as anger and frustration started to build. Having not seen his wife in so long, he needed answers and these pair didn't have a shit-show of stopping him. "Move out of my way," the prospector instructed in a tone barely above a whisper. The matron returned just in time to defuse the escalating situation. "Listen son, these men are just doing their job as instructed, you will have plenty of time to be reunited with your wife. She could be in for close to a week yet. The most important thing at this point is your wife's health and wellbeing, wouldn't you agree? I think you will find it more frustrating if you are banned totally from the hospital for making a scene here tonight. I suggest you return in two days' time and not before."

Tim settled down to listen to reason. Turning, he looked straight at Danni's sister. "What do you know about this?" She flushed bright red, unable to hide the reaction under his clear questioning stare. Being put on the spot, she was incapable of responding in words and started gesturing with her hands. Tim felt anger starting to rise again feeling betrayed as her reactions added further weight to the nurse's words about the baby. "I thought higher of you until tonight." Tim didn't even give her time to respond. Throwing the flowers in her direction, he turned his back and started to walk out. "Forget it, I will find out for myself in two days' time."

The bushman walked onto the city street, bracing against the night cool of the south-east corner of the state. Deep in thought he just started to walk, having no relevance in direction or location. His mind was in a tangled mess trying to comprehend what the hell was going on. He ignored the phone in his suit pocket that continued to ring as he walked towards the sound of the waves crashing onto the beach. He felt lost, not in location but within himself.

Meg gave up calling to try to report the first day's drilling results from the new leases which were stunning. The contractor was ecstatic saying he had never seen samples so rich with thick bands of gold clearly visible to the naked eye in the majority of initial test holes that Tim had selectively chosen weeks earlier to try to establish the extent of the ore body. It had now finally come to fruition, the rich gold reef ran for kilometres.

Locating the motel just as the sun started to rise he booked in. Feeling mentally drained he headed straight for a shower with his body screaming for sleep. It took the two full days for the North Queenslander to contain his emotions as his mind ran rampant with speculation and assumptions. Wrapped in only a towel he answered the door, accepting the return of his suit from the dry cleaners along with a room-service breakfast that he tried to force down after days of no food. Exiting the elevator on the maternity level with no flowers in hand this time around, he approached the service desk announcing who he was and politely asking for directions to the room Danni was in. "Excuse me for a minute sir," responded the nurse as she picked up the phone and pressed an extension number. The matron he had run across the other night appeared. He rolled his eyes, "not again." She ignored the comment. "Your wife checked herself and the child out early this morning, strongly against our advice I can assure you. The baby is fine but Danni is still weak from the loss of blood." The matron passed an envelope towards him as he stood motionless. "She left this for you."

In a robot-like movement, he reached out tearing open the envelope not even blinking as he read its short content. *Tim, I was praying the baby would be yours so I could try and move forward and put that dark day I was raped by an Asian monster out of my mind. This violence that you have brought into our lives I cannot and will not live with any further. Every time I look at my son I'm afraid it will remind me of that day. I now have my own mental scars to contend with. I wish you all the best. Goodbye Tim.* He screwed up the note and dropped it to the floor. Without a word he left the building.

The jumbo touched down in mainland China four days after the courthouse drama with the two remaining assassins, who had been summoned home, on board. After bypassing customs completely, the men were escorted immediately to a waiting vehicle and were driven in silence to a gathering of the four men that led the world-wide underground empire. Concerned over the recent news filtering in from their operations in the northern part of Australia, the four businessmen wanted to hear first-hand the events that led to the deaths of their two best operatives abroad, and then consider the most effective way to counter-strike. After an hour of deliberation, they were still unable to identify the perpetrator of the killings. Unsure whether it was retribution from the remaining small gang in competition to their drug distribution, or this stand-alone prospector that the pair of assassins described as impossible to kill. "You disappoint us with such foolish words that this lone westerner's ability is above that of our own people. Sounds to me like you men have become soft in the western ways. You will both be replaced and sent back to training to harden up. Firstly, we will strengthen our position in the north and crush the opposition, then in time we will send over a small hand-picked group to dispel this myth of a single man."

EIGHT MONTHS LATER

The final geological reports, including various drill sample values, had leaked out to some of Australia's most influential miners who all showed interest in purchasing the leases. At first Tim had scoffed at the idea, but after listening to Meg's advice pointing out rough estimates on costings to get into the first stage of production soon pulled the prospector into reality. The only other option was to become deep in debt with the banks which he flat out refused to consider. Tim now found himself sitting around a corporate table with Meg on one side and Hugh on the other as lawyers thrashed out a few finer adjustments after working on the deal for a month. "Right Tim, I think we have this in order now for both parties to sign. First, you get to retain the small original lease shown in Appendix A as Mac's lease. If at any point it comes onto the market for sale the company that is present here today has first option to purchase. You agree to sell 100 per cent of the other leases for 1.8 billion with a royalty agreement of one per cent of net profit per annum. You must surrender all copies of drilling reports to the company and sign a non-disclosure agreement stating that no information you have acquired since pegging these leases is to be passed on to any third party. Do you agree to these terms in this contract?" Tim looked at Meg for confirmation. "You happy with that?" Smiling, she nodded. "That sounds close to the figures we discussed Tim." Picking up the pen he paused halfway through. "Hang on a minute." Everyone in the room went silent and the smiles all round changed to concern. He looked around the room at every member before breaking into a grin. "Only messing with ya fellas, it's a deal."

The handshakes and hugs flowed as did the champagne. Meg as usual, kept her distance from Hugh openly ignoring his existence ever since Tim had hired the hitman. The hatred stemmed right back to their first meeting out at the Hatchet River when he was trying to kill her husband. Meg had not seen or heard from John since he stated those words that day, "Forget about me." After shaking the CEO's and other company director's hands, Tim searched for one person through the swelling crowd. Meg was in mid conversation with one of the lawyers when she was picked up and swirled around in circles by an ecstatic Tim. "Have I got a surprise for you, brought it today pending the sale," he enthused passing her a set of keys. Dumbfounded, she looked at the keys in her hand. "They look like house keys." "Close," he excitedly whispered in her ear, "a penthouse apartment on the Cairns Esplanade, three bedrooms, it's awesome. I think it is time for both of us to seriously look at moving on. Hugh hasn't been able to pick up any leads on Danni's whereabouts after eight months. Sell up the house full of memories Meg, do you really want to grow old and lonely waiting in vain for something that is never going to eventuate. He is damaged not to mention dangerous and will never be coming back." Her smiling and happy outlook changed slightly with those last words. "I don't know what to say Tim." "How about thanks boss," he replied with a beaming smile. "Let's leave and I will show you around."

The dull morning light was enough to wake John. He had been making a meagre existence over nearly a year with his metal detector. He came into Hugo once a month – except during the wet season – to trade his small amount of gold and buy the bare essentials to live, other than meat which he sourced himself. The initial months had passed without incident which surprised him after spending a lot of time preparing for, and expecting a confrontation with the hitman at any time. He had come to terms with his condition from the brain injuries. These days he was on the toad tonic wagon. Though it had relieved the relentless head pain in the beginning, he now realised the side effects led to toxic thoughts and hallucinations. John had now devised ways to keep the anger contained, but admitted this was yet to be put to the test in the real world. His heart ached every day after hearing the truth from Meg first-hand. That was his sole reason for staying focused. It played on his mind daily whether she had moved on like he told her to. Now he was ready to find out. John looked around to what he called home, unsure at this point if he would ever be back.

Swallowing hard he turned into his old street to see a 'Sold' real estate sign standing in their front yard. Leaving the cruiser idling out front of the house, he lay his head on the steering wheel unsure what to do next. John's old neighbour, who never missed a trick over anything that happened along the whole street walked out with his wheelie bin for garbage collection. Recognising the vehicle, he walked over and tapped on the window. John lifted his head. "Haven't seen you around for long while, figured you must have shot through for good." Not bothering to answer the statement John asked, "How long ago did she leave?" "You only missed her by days. Sad to see that, a woman left to fend for herself. That was until that other bloke that you used to leave with at all hours of the morning for days on end started to turn up regularly." John's head started to throb and pulsating veins began to protrude from under the skin exposing themselves across his forehead. He glared back at his old neighbour who took a step back with the change in his facial disposition. "Is that a fact, did Meg mention where she was moving to?" The old man could sense the information he had just given had not been very well received, "It was a Cairns removalist truck, that's all I know."

Sitting at a coffee shop one street back from the Esplanade, Meg passed Tim and Hugh their itinerary for their tour of Mac's mining tenements abroad that Tim had been gifted in the will. Connecting flights, car hire, accommodation was all included along with company credit cards. Hugh's phone rang while they were all still seated. "It's Mick from Perth. Listen mate this is the number that we were emailed to report a stolen motorhome from Queensland, it has just come in for a service. What would you like us to do?" Hugh smirked in satisfaction after nearly giving up on any result after such a long period. "Thank you for the call Mick, do not confront the pair they are considered dangerous. Can you try and stall them for long as possible? Even if you need to advise the couple there is a problem with the vehicle and you need to order in parts. Book them into a complimentary motel for the night and text me the details. I will have the department cover the costs. It is imperative that this motorhome does not leave your workshop until I arrive, do you understand?" Mick on the other end of the line looked at the couple fussing around with cameras before they embarked on a local tourist venture. "Righto… fair dinkum, I would never have picked it." He looked at the other pair's inquisitive looks after he hung up. Ignoring Meg, he addressed Tim. "There's something I need to deal with back over in WA, I will meet you at the airport in Sydney. Where are we off to first, Columbia?"

After being given the green light, that the motorhome was ready to go Marko and his wife reversed out of the service centre, she held a handful of pamphlets highlighting local attractions, but her husband had another idea in mind. After spending months touring the inland routes, he was keen to wet a fishing line and relax along one of the stunning secluded beaches. An hour north of the city he found a spot to his liking. Positioning the motorhome as close to the beach as possible he extended the electric awning to take full advantage of the ocean view. Marko wasted no time in setting up his lounge chair and fishing rod close to the crashing surf. Turning to face his luxury unit on wheels, he said, "Hey honey, a cold beer would be nice. It can't be too far away from lunch time either, how about knocking us up a few sangas while you're at it." Slipping on her favourite CD, she started to bop around to the rhythm of the music while making lunch. She paused briefly to adjust the surround-sound speakers incorporating the external weatherproof set that were mounted on the side of the motorhome.

Hearing the squelch of dry sand underfoot he held out his free hand without looking backwards. "Thanks honey, reckon I might land a good one shortly, been awhile since we had a feed of fish." Marko's outstretched hand was filled with sand. "What the bloody hell woman," he blurted as he turned spotting the black leather gloves of Hugh. "A fool is a man who does not take a threat seriously from a killer for hire. How long did you think you could hide?" "Shit!" was the only word that came to mind as Marko scrambled to reach for the bait knife in the plastic bucket beside his chair.

Stepping out of the motorhome with a plate of sandwiches and a cold beer in hand, she frowned as she noticed Marko's chair was empty. Slightly confused where he could have gone, she looked up and down the deserted beach. The incoming tide slewed the banana lounge on its side while erasing all signs of a struggle as the water receded leaving not a footprint before the next wave crashed onto the shore creeping further up than the last. It was then she noticed her husband's body rolling over and over in the white water. Screaming, she dropped what was in her hands running to the water's edge. With the closest help more than ten kilometres away, she struggled to drag his dead weight from the ocean alone.

Meg moved through the crowd in the busy markets to the stall she had now frequented over many months. The New Guinea national nodded as soon as he recognised her while she perused the artefacts waiting for the other customer to be served before her. "Miss Meg before you ask, yes it has finally arrived." He produced a small clear bottle of liquid from under the counter. "It took my brother a bit longer because you increased the original order." She held the small bottle in her hand to scrutinise its contents. "Doesn't look like much to me, so this little bottle is enough to kill two men." "Oh yes Meg, it is very powerful. Made from special plants that are only found in certain areas in the highlands a day's walk from our village. When combined the extract is very deadly. It is tasteless and odourless, only five drops is required per victim. It paralyses the heart from beating and toxicology reports will reveal no traces of the poison if given slowly at a dose of one drop at a time. You are a very dangerous woman Miss Meg." She smiled placing the bottle carefully in her handbag. "Only to those who have destroyed my life."

Tim rang Meg as they entered the departure lounge at Sydney airport. "Just thought I would check in before we boarded our 18-hour flight." "No, everything is fine up here nothing I can't handle," Meg said. "I have been thinking when you get back from overseas why don't you come over to the apartment and I will cook you dinner." "Sounds good to me Meg, I will look forward to it." "Oh by the way, invite Hugh over too, it's about time we buried the hatchet." Tim hung up looking over at Hugh smiling. "Meg has just invited you over to dinner. See, I told you she would get over that dislike thing, it was just a matter of time."